WILLOW Springs

PRAISE FOR
WILLOW SPRINGS

"A grand, sweeping adventure that brings the old west to life, with characters whose share of problems continue to get in the way of their happiness. Steele manages to make her characters—even those who are secondary—feel alive and current. Crissa's growth and maturity from her childhood in Sweden, to her tragic time in Boston, her heartbreaking crossing with a group of Mormon pioneers, and finally her life that she builds in Utah will have you crossing your fingers for her deserved happiness."

—CINDY C BENNETT, author of *Rapunzel Untangled*

"*Willow Springs* is a charming historical romance with all the right ingredients. An intriguing plot, endearing characters, and impeccable pacing all blend together to make a great story. Crissa, a Swedish immigrant who escapes a troubled past to make a new life in Willow Springs, is a heroine to root for. The romance unfolds with perfect timing and tension, and the ending is very satisfying. Recommended to anyone who loves a good historical romance!"

—SARAH BEARD, author of *Porcelain Keys*

"*Willow Springs* is a story about romance in the 19th century West, but it is much more than that. Crissa is a wholesome Swedish immigrant, who attracts all kinds of men, including a ruffian and the son of the town's wealthiest man, but she is also a woman running from a complicated past. Carolyn Steele has written a first novel with a series of twists and turns and surprises worthy of an established author. This book will win her a following among readers looking for an uplifting tale with depth."

—MARILYN McKINNON, retired editorial writer for the *Salt Lake Tribune*, *Deseret News*, and *Standard-Examiner*

"Carolyn Steele delivers a gripping historical romance, rich with suspense and unforgettable characters. Her heroine's dauntless spirit had me rooting for her from the start. With an inventive plot that unfolds in high-stakes twists and unexpected turns, *Willow Springs* is one exciting read."

—DIANA J. OAKS, author of
One Thread Pulled: The Dance with Mr. Darcy

CAROLYN STEELE

SWEETWATER
BOOKS

AN IMPRINT OF CEDAR FORT, INC.
SPRINGVILLE, UTAH

ISBN 13: 978-1-4621-1457-3

Published by Sweetwater Books, an imprint of Cedar Fort, Inc.
2373 W. 700 S., Springville, UT 84663
Distributed by Cedar Fort, Inc., www.cedarfort.com

LIBRARY OF CONGRESS CATALOGING-IN-PUBLICATION DATA

Steele, Carolyn, 1958- author.
Willow Springs / Carolyn Steele.
     pages cm
Summary: Crissa Engleson, a Swedish emigrant running from a cruel past but unaware that she is being pursued by a relentless bounty hunter, finds a new life in Willow Springs, a small mining community in Utah.
ISBN 978-1-4621-1457-3 (pbk. : alk. paper)
1. Women immigrants--Fiction. 2. Swedes--Utah--Fiction. 3. Mormons--Fiction. 4. Utah, setting. I. Title.
PS3619.T4334W55 2014
813'.6--dc23

                              2014006098

Cover design by Kristen Reeves
Cover design © 2014 by Lyle Mortimer
Edited and typeset by Melissa J. Caldwell

Printed in the United States of America

10 9 8 7 6 5 4 3 2 1

Dedicated to my Swedish grandmother and gold-mining grandfather,
to my dear mother and father, and to my sweet husband,
who so kindly indulges my many late nights of writing.

With gratitude to my children,
my friends in the Tuesday Night Enclave editing group,
and to my new friends at Cedar Fort for making this book possible.

CHAPTER 1

Would you look'a there," Myrtle Thompson said, nodding toward the door as a young man raced past on horseback.

"That's not!" Ethel gasped.

"Oh, yes, it is," Agnes chimed in. "That's the Bateman boy." Agnes clucked her tongue. "And with his wife still in confinement."

"He's up to no good, I tell you," Doris said. "It's shameful."

Ruth and Mary bobbed their heads in agreement. "Indeed. Shameful."

Cringing at the cackles coming from the dining room, Crissa peered through the kitchen doors to where the six Thompson sisters dominated the near corner of the room. That table was their table— on the last Thursday of every month, anyway. There wasn't anything special about this table except that it sat in the corner between the kitchen and the stairway and had a direct view to the front door on the opposite wall. Any comings and goings, and eatings for that matter, were thoroughly scrutinized by the ladies of this table. The unused bar was also within their line of sight, and gentlemen of proper upbringing made sure not to duck behind the bar to refill their flasks if "the sisters" were present.

"Wicked gossips," Marida whispered. Her simple English was laced with a thick Italian accent. "They usually gone by now. Must be waiting for miners come in."

For Crissa's two weeks in Willow Springs, Henders Inn had been mostly quiet, save for the few bachelor shopkeepers who took their meals there. The stagecoach had come in earlier in the evening, depositing four guests for an overnight stay. In the middle of Crissa trying to situate the travelers, the Thompson sisters had arrived for their monthly gossip fest—and to give Crissa a collective looking over. The potatoes weren't quite as fluffy as usual, it seemed. The corn bread was too gritty, the meat loaf drier than they had remembered it—even the green beans were stringy until Molly informed the sisters that Marida had done all of the cooking, same as usual.

It didn't seem to matter that Crissa smiled extra friendly or spoke extra politely. She was met with frowns and turned-up noses from "the sisters' table."

"Don'a you worry," Marida tried to reassure Crissa. "They see you not after their husbands, they like you fine."

Husbands. Crissa had to suppress a shudder at the thought. *If I had wanted a husband, I would have stayed in Boston.* The last thing she wanted was to get involved with any of the men in the town. Indeed, Crissa considered Willow Springs to be the nearest thing to her idea of purgatory. It was dry and desolate—nothing like the bustling city of Boston or the rich farmland of Uppsala. She certainly did not plan to stay here long.

"Miners?" Crissa asked. "Why will the miners be coming?"

"Is payday. They come for dinner on way to Ely." Marida gave Crissa an exaggerated wink. "Are sporting women in Ely."

"How many will be coming?" The thought of more strange faces to watch made Crissa edgy.

"Depends on if miners more hungry or more . . ." Marida winked again.

Gasping at Marida's boldness, Crissa turned back to study the guests in the dining room. "We do not have many tables left tonight."

"No worry," Marida informed her. "When miners come, many these people will leave."

"Why? Do they not like the miners?"

Laying her finger alongside her nose, Marida gave Crissa a

sidelong glance. "Today payday at mine. You watch out for them. They no gentlemen."

"But, Marida, surely—"

"You listen. You watch out."

★ ★ ★

Smiling uneasily, Crissa wound her way through the crowded dining room to the center table, balancing an enormous round tray laden with plates and mugs. Hard liquor was no longer served at Henders Inn, not since Hank Henderson died, but that only meant many of the miners would get thoroughly soused before they came in for dinner. It was no small feat for an attractive woman to negotiate her way untarnished past countless filthy, grabbing hands, leering grins, and ribald comments.

Payday came only once a month for miners at the Gold Hill camp. For a day or two afterward, the few shopkeepers in Willow Springs eagerly jostled for their business. The women at Henders, however, were not as eager to have their inn overrun by a bunch of men looking for a good time.

A group of men were laughing raucously, and as Crissa approached, a renewed wave of jeers erupted. Edging between their chairs, she grimaced inwardly each time she bumped one of their shoulders or elbows. "There you go, gentlemen. Enjoy your supper." Crissa tried to make as little conversation as possible while doling out the steaming platters.

"Supper?" Garth Wight bellowed, shoving his platter of pot roast and mashed potatoes away from him. "You call this pig swill supper?"

Crissa stood her ground, glaring. "Is there something that does not please you, Mr. Wight?"

"You bet there is," he said, locking a massive arm around her delicate waist. "Got a wild hankering for a juicy bit of rump roast." He pulled her in snugly. "What d'ya say?" Appreciative guffaws burst from the three other men at the table.

Crissa struggled, unable to loose herself, keenly aware of the gawking eyes focused on her throughout the room.

"Calm down there, darlin'." Garth smirked, turning her from side to side to get a better look at her. He turned to his friends, who were grinning at Crissa. "Too much fight fills a woman with gristle. Ain't that right, fellas?"

Frantic, Crissa flipped the searing plate of food onto Garth's chest. Springing to his feet and spewing filth as easily as spittle, he brushed hot potatoes and gravy off his scalded chest. As Crissa turned to flee, Garth grabbed her by the wrist, twisting her arm behind her, and drew her body close to his.

Crissa fought back the retching sensation welling up from her stomach while Garth pinned her to him. She tilted her head back to glare at him. His clear amber eyes, hooded with heavy brown brows, sent a streak of fear from her throat to her knees. "Are threats the only way you can woo a woman? You *träsk hund*."

Tangling his fingers in the tousle of curls on top of her head, Garth pulled Crissa's head back even farther until she feared her neck would snap. "Don't get uppity with me, Crissa Engleson. You're a foreigner here, and you'll never be anything better. You're not likely to get a better offer, and you know it."

His breath stank of stale whiskey. The putrid odor brought a flash of confused remembrance to her mind, breaking through her fright. She was a little girl in Sweden, sitting at the table in her family's small cottage. The rickety door slammed open, and her father stood in the doorway, framed by the darkness. Crissa cried out in alarm as he crossed the room and jerked her mother from the chair beside the fire. He was yelling and laughing, dragging her mother behind the curtain to their bedchamber. Crissa couldn't remember the words her father spoke, only his smell. Liquor and vomit and urine.

"No!" Crissa spit in Garth's face. With all her might, she stomped on his foot. As he loosened his grip, she struck the heel of her hand into the bridge of his crooked nose, heaving herself away from him. Garth rubbed his brow with the back of his hand, laughing heartily. Crissa stumbled against the next table and fled back to the kitchen.

Her first instinct was to pack her few belongings and leave on the next stagecoach. *I will not go through this again*, she told herself.

4

But where can I go with no money? She was lucky to have found this position, and she knew that she might not find another job so easily. *At least I am not married to him*, she thought. *I'll just stay well away from him.* Recalling the blow she had landed on his nose, she almost laughed out loud. *Maybe it is he who should be afraid of me!*

★ ★ ★

Clouds of pale dust billowed behind Drake Adams as he raced into town. Tired and hot after the four-hour ride, he envisioned a clean bath, a hot meal, and a soft bed. Of the three weeks he'd been away, only three or four hours had been spent riding each day, but with all his aching bones he felt as though he'd spent the entire three weeks in the saddle.

He trotted up to the livery, where the next rider was waiting to take his saddlebags and resume the ride toward San Francisco. Willow Springs, Utah, was only one stop on the Pony Express route, but it was the stop Drake called home. Eschewing his father's ranch and mines outside of town, he now kept a room above the livery.

"There ya go, Duncan," he said to the young rider. With one fluid movement, Drake swung the *mochila* off his mount and settled the mailbag behind the waiting horse. "Keep an eye out for rustlers this side of Carson." Drake slapped the rump of the mustang, and Duncan lit off on his stretch of the route. Drake and the livery hand turned their backs on the receding plume of dust, leading the tired horse into the stable.

"I still get a kick out of that fancy saddlebag ya'll use," Victor Danello said, laughing. Very little of his Italian accent punctuated his new cowboy twang.

"The *mochila?*" Drake asked, referring to the specially designed mailbag. "As funny lookin' as it is, it sure makes the ride easier. Without it, I don't know if we'd ever switch horses on time."

The *mochila* was a leather rectangle thrown over a stripped-down saddle. Cutouts in the leather fit around the pommel and cantle of the saddle. Mail *cantinas* were sewn to each of the four corners and secured with padlocks. Because it was held in place only by the rider's weight, it could be pulled off one saddle and onto the next in well under the two minutes allotted in a Pony Express rider's schedule for changing mounts.

"Well," Vic said, "whatever you call it, watchin' you boys throw it from one horse t'other makes bein' a livery hand not so bad work."

"I'm glad you're so easy to entertain, my friend. Say, you have supper already?"

"Not yet. Let me put your tack away 'fore we go." Hanging the harness on a nail, Vic smiled and then nudged Drake in the ribs with his elbow. "Molly's got a new gal."

"That so?" Drake propped a dusty boot on the side of the stall, absently stroking his exhausted bay. "Anything to look at?"

"Boy howdy. Real cute little filly. Came from Sweden a while back. Been livin' in Springville with her folks 'til she came out here."

Drake rubbed a callused hand across the back of his neck. "Pretty thing, huh? Speak any English?"

"Yeah, talks pretty good. Sounds kind'a like a schoolmarm."

"Anyone taken up with her yet?"

"Naw." Vic shook his head. "Keeps to herself mostly. Garth Wight's been eyein' her, though."

"She eyein' Garth?"

Vic chuckled. "Not to hear my Marida tell it."

Drake flashed a white-toothed grin. "You still sweet on Molly's cook?"

"Yeah, guess I'm stuck."

Drake laughed and clapped him on the back.

★ ★ ★

"That snake," Marida said from behind the swinging doors. "I'll take care him if he bellows again." Marida's black eyes blazed as she gestured wringing Garth's neck in her hands.

"No, Marida," Crissa said, regaining her composure. "I cannot let Garth think he has gotten the best of me. I will take care of him myself."

They peeked out of the kitchen doors at Garth and his loud friends, surveying the damage. Unfortunately, aside from food smeared across his chest, her sharp blow hadn't seemed to hurt him at all. Already tongues were wagging at the corner table. Snatches of mean-spirited conversation floated back to the kitchen from voices not meant to be discreet.

"*Vad nu.*" Crissa groaned, placing icy hands to her flushing cheeks. "The Thompson sisters. I will be a *skratting lager.*"

"Eh?"

Crissa impatiently fumbled for the words. "A laughingstock, Marida. I can never show a public face again."

"Oh, Crissa, don'a be silly. Old women have their fun and then forget all about this. You no need worry."

As they watched, a tall man with thick black hair climbed up onto the porch outside, peering into the dim dining hall. Dressed in denims, chaps and a limp white shirt that pulled slightly across his broad chest, he looked hot and tired. A slight breeze whisked at his back, ruffling his wavy hair. Vic Danello joined him, and together they entered the dining room.

Crissa studied the stranger with great interest as he strode through the room to a table on the far side. A smile turned up the corner of her lips while she tried to make her voice sound casual. "Who's the stranger with Vic, Marida?"

Marida gave her a sidelong glance that turned into a broad grin. "Drake Adams. He's Pony Express rider."

"A rider?" Crissa feigned indifference.

"And the son of Warren Adams."

"Oh," Crissa said, crestfallen. Surely no son of Warren Adams would pass the time of day with an immigrant. Crissa turned to look out the door again. "Well, he is a customer," she said, cinching the ties of her apron. She smoothed her upswept hair, leaving a few blonde tendrils to curl about her shoulders. "And I am here to serve customers." She smiled, shrugged pertly, and marched back into the dining room.

Crissa was heading across the room, carefully avoiding Garth and his friends, when Molly Henderson, the owner of the inn, lowered herself into a chair between Drake and Vic. While she was never a small woman, the effects of two children and years of serving Willow Springs's heartiest meals had made themselves evident in her robust figure. Though Widow Henderson was only ten or twelve years her senior, Crissa saw Molly as a second mother. Wedged between the table and an inadequate chair, Molly trained her friendly attention on Drake.

Not wanting to interrupt, Crissa stood in front of the big mahogany bar with her back to the room and watched the reflections of the two in the large gilt mirror hanging above the bar. Obviously Drake and Molly had been friends for a long time. Straining to hear snatches of their conversation, Crissa polished the gleaming bar with swift circular strokes.

Molly's reflection motioned Crissa to the table. She spun around, embarrassed at being caught spying on Molly and her friends. Trying not to seem too eager, too forward, Crissa crossed the room to the table.

"Drake Adams, I'd like you to meet my new girl, Crissa Engleson."

Unnerved by his deep-set, blue eyes framed by thick black lashes, Crissa struggled to find something intelligent to say. All thoughts fled from her mind while she studied his sun-bronzed skin, so different from the weathered faces of the men she had known in Sweden. He smiled openly, warmly—not the brazen leer she had come to expect from most American men. Realizing he was studying her as well, she felt a flush erupt on her cheeks, and she dropped her head timidly.

★ ★ ★

Drake was captivated by her eyes—the color of cornflowers with flecks of gray—mesmerized by the way the window's reflected light danced off them, making them twinkle when she looked directly at him. A smile slowly played on his lips as he studied how her mouth naturally turned up at the corners, punctuated by dimples.

Standing, Drake lifted Crissa's hand gently in his. "Pleased to meet you, Miss Engleson."

"I am pleased also—I mean—to meet you," Crissa stammered. Her hand lingered in his until Molly diplomatically cleared her throat. "May I b-bring you some handsome?" Crissa gasped, realizing what she had said, and clamped her hands over her mouth.

Drake's grin lit his entire face. "Not just now, but I would like some supper. Any meat loaf tonight, Miss Molly?"

Molly couldn't resist joining the fun. "Always meat loaf for you, handsome."

"Fine. I'll have a helping of that." He winked at Molly. "Two helpings, and milk and coffee. Oh, and some of Miss Molly's fancy spice cake, if there is any."

Crissa smiled at his not-so-small order, trying to regain some semblance of dignity. "And you?" she said, turning to Vic. "I am sure I can find something left in the kitchen."

"Meat loaf will be fine for me, ma'am. One helping's enough, though."

"Meat loaf it is." She smiled back at Drake. "Will there be anything else?"

Drake grinned in return. "I'll let you know." He loved how her smile came easily, how her voice flowed soft and gentle. It was comforting—the way his mother's voice had been. He tilted back on his chair, long legs extended before him with ankles crossed, his fingers laced behind his head. She seemed innocent, unassuming—not at all like the other girls in Willow Springs who boldly threw their attentions at him. This one was as refreshing as she was beautiful. A sigh escaped his pursed lips in a soft, slow whistle while he watched Crissa glide away.

Molly sat back with her arms folded across her ample bosom, her thumb and forefinger cupping her chin. "Well, I'll be."

As Crissa passed Garth's table on the way back to the kitchen, a new round of jeers and crude remarks broke out.

"Those vermin aren't usually your customers, are they, Molly?" Drake asked.

"Most of them only show up on paydays, but Garth's been hoverin' 'round here ever since Crissa came on. He can't seem to get it through his thick skull she's not on the menu. He got ahold of her earlier, pawin' her like a piece o' meat. She's a feisty one, though. Took him down a peg or two right quick. Thumped him solid right between his eyes."

"Wish it had been my fist, Molly. I'd turn his face to horse dung."

"All right, Drake. Take it easy. I've seen you two going at it since you were boys. I don't want no trouble in my place. I can't afford to clean up after you, and I'm not in the mood to play nurse if you get whupped."

When the kitchen doors swung shut, Garth's crude remarks about Crissa began anew.

Drake stood up and walked to Garth's table, planting one hand firmly on Garth's shoulder. "Now, is that any way to talk about a lady?" Drake's quiet voice rolled like distant thunder.

"Git your hand off'a me, Adams." Garth turned slowly, eyeing Drake darkly. His stubbled face spread in a leer. "She got yer fire lit already, huh? Well, once me an' my boys have our fill—"

The words had barely passed his lips when Drake grabbed him by the collar and spun him back against the table, scattering chairs and dishes in his wake. Though Garth was at least twenty pounds heavier, Drake stood a good six inches taller. His body was lean and taut, ready to unleash pent-up energy. "Time somebody taught you a lesson."

"You ain't man enough to teach nobody nothin'."

"No one's teachin' anyone anything in here!" Molly bellowed, shoving the two men apart with such force that each man stumbled to keep his footing. "Garth, take your stinkin' boys and get outta my place. And don't you come back 'til you can keep a civil tongue in your mouth—and your hands off'a my girls." Molly stood with her hands on her hips, ready to attack again.

Garth stalked to the doorway, his face red and his amber eyes glowing with anger. "Cain't hide behind Widow Henderson's apron forever, you yella jackal." With that, he stormed out, leaving the café doors swinging wildly.

★ ★ ★

Crissa returned from the kitchen a few minutes later with a serving tray piled high with plates of food, loaves of bread, and drinks. "I saw what you did for me," she said timidly, carefully unloading her tray. She raised her head, looking into Drake's azure eyes. "I appreciate you standing up for me like that. Do not worry about Garth, though. I can take care of him."

"I can take care of him a lot better."

"Oh, he is just a lot of talk."

"I'm not too sure, Miss Crissa," Drake said with a genuine note of concern in his voice. "I'm not too sure."

CHAPTER 2

You can handle all that?" Marida fussed, checking the pantry for anything she might have forgotten.

"Marida, do not worry so. I am only going to the store. Mr. Potter can give me a hand if I cannot carry it all." Despite the row the night before, Crissa saw no reason she shouldn't do the shopping as usual. "Did Molly write down more lye?" she asked, peering at the list Molly had scribbled for Marida.

"She's asking me?" Marida raised her eyes to the heavens.

"You really should learn to read and write in English, Marida," Crissa chided. "I could try to teach you."

"For what I need to learn writing? I marry my Victor, and he take care of writing things. I make good cook and make good wife. What more I need make good at?"

"Marida, you are impossible," Crissa said, laughing, "and I love you dearly."

As Crissa crossed the empty dining hall, two young children intercepted her, their bare feet slapping the wood plank floor as they ran.

"Crissa! Crissa!" Will grabbed her hand, trying to pull her along with him. "Momma said we could go to the stream before dinner. Please come with us."

"We're huntin' for gold, Crissa!" Amy chimed in. "We need your help!"

"Oh, *min älsklings*, I would love to come," Crissa crooned, hugging Will's little red head to her skirt, "but I cannot just now. I have to do the shopping."

"You can shop later! Please come and play with us."

Crissa struggled against the urge to do just that. Molly's children had instantly filled a vacant place in her heart, and she yearned to spend every free moment with them. "Sweet Amy," she said, stroking Amy's blonde braids, "if I go with you now, what would Marida cook for dinner? Your mother would lose all of her guests, and the inn would close down. We could not have that now, could we?"

"Oh, Crissa, you're essaggerating." Seven-year-old Will thought he was too grown up to use simple words.

"Yes, I am exaggerating, Will," Crissa said, chuckling, "but I do need to do the shopping now. I will come look for you if I get back before dinnertime. How is that?"

"Okay," Amy said with a pout, "but it won't be any fun without you."

"Well, then, you will just have to find a way to make it fun on your own. Now scoot." With that, Crissa ushered the children outside toward the stream while she turned the other way toward Potter's General Mercantile.

The warm May sun cheered Crissa as she strolled toward Potter's. She reveled in the warmth, letting it flow through her body. "Good morning, Mrs. Stanford, Mrs. Blanding." Crissa smiled and nodded her head as she passed two ladies on the boardwalk.

"Hmmph," was their reply.

Crissa slowed a step, trying to figure out why they had answered so. They were usually so friendly, and they had been among the first to extend a welcoming hand when Crissa came to town. And, fortunately, they had not been privy to the scene between her and Garth last night. She turned to the sound of a buckboard rumbling past her with a load of furniture piled in the back. The newlywed Taylors were carting their furnishings to the ranch they had just rented outside of town. She waved her greeting, but when Buck Taylor raised his hand in return, his new bride jerked it back down.

I wonder what's gotten into Annabelle, Crissa mused. At fifteen, Annabelle was six years Crissa's junior, and Buck was not much older than his bride. She watched the buckboard rattle off into the distance and turn the corner that led out of town.

Crissa let out a little sigh and turned her attention to the open doorway at her side. Potter's General Mercantile was one of her favorite places in Willow Springs. Although it wasn't as large as some of the stores in Salt Lake City, Potter's had an amazing array of wares that Crissa loved to browse through.

"*God morgon*, Mr. Potter," Crissa said, laying her list on the counter with a longing look at the glass jars of candies that lined the counter just out of children's reach.

"Good morning, Miss Engleson," he replied. Mr. Potter was an elderly gentleman about sixty years old. His wife, Hulda, had been a neighbor of Crissa's family in Uppsala, Sweden, before she immigrated to America. Crissa's family immigrated several years later and made their home in Springville, Utah. What a wonderful surprise it had been to learn that their friend Hulda had married and settled so close by.

"Will Mrs. Potter be helping with the decorations for the dance tomorrow?"

"I'm afraid not, Crissa. She put a little too much effort into hoeing the garden yesterday, and now her lumbago is acting up. I think she'd best be taking it easy for a couple of days."

"I am sorry to hear that. Please give her my best and tell her that if I may be of any service, to just let me know."

"I'll do that, Crissa, I'll do that. Now, surely you didn't come in here to chat with an old man. What can I do for you today?"

"Just a few things for the inn, if you please." Crissa slid the shopping list toward him.

"I'll get right to it, dear. You look around a while. I got a new shipment of calico in the corner and some buttons to match."

"Thank you," she said, already moving past the double aisle of dry goods toward the small alcove of fabric and millinery.

Crissa fingered a light pink floral, dreaming of the flowing dress she could make with it. A square neck with darts in the bodice would be just the thing to catch the eye of a certain Pony Express rider. Her thoughts returned to meeting Drake last night. She could almost feel his warm hand cupping hers, sending a shiver of excitement surging through her body. She remembered his full, smooth lips smiling at her from beneath his thick black mustache. And his eyes, the deep warm blue of a Swedish sky during the days of the midnight sun. She pressed the soft fabric to her cheek.

"Of course, no good could come of it."

Soft voices filtered from behind a pyramid of flour sacks, interrupting Crissa's reverie.

"Bad enough he married Hulda with his wife still warm in her grave, now she's brought her foreigner friend to stir up trouble."

Crissa strained to hear better, trying to identify the female voices.

"Woman like that's got no business in a decent town like Willow Springs."

"Can't understand Widow Henderson hiring her in the first place. Next she'll be turning her inn into a dance hall, that's what."

"What's wrong with the woman anyway? I'd like to know. Pretty thing like that ought to be married up proper, not left loose to roam the country flaunting herself."

"Can't say as I blame Garth myself, watching her prance around with her big bosom like a no-account trollop. She was just asking for trouble."

The forgotten fabric dropped from her hands when Crissa realized these two women were talking about her. Her face flushed scarlet as she tried to think how to declare her innocence.

"I heard she practically threw herself at Drake Adams. Can you imagine! No-good foreigner, working just to earn her keep, making designs on Warren Adams's boy."

"Well, 'course she's eyeing Drake, Myrtle. She wants something to show for her efforts. The cheap little hussy."

"Well, good morning, ladies." Mr. Potter's cheerful greeting interrupted their tirade. "I'll be right with you." He rounded the corner of the alcove where Crissa stood by the fabric. "Here you are, my dear. Can I cut you some fabric today? Why, Crissa, what's the matter?"

Crissa stood staring at him, her stomach twisted in a knot and her throat constricted with the threat of tears. "N-nothing, Mr. Potter." She took the two large bundles from his outstretched hands. "Th-thank you." Crissa kept her eyes downcast, sidling past two women whom she had supposed were her friends.

Crissa whirled out of the mercantile doors and right into the arms of one of Garth's friends. "Whoa, there, little darlin'. Where you runnin' in such a hurry?" His arms tightened around her, pulling her uncomfortably close.

"Let go of me," she snapped, trying to push him away from her. Her packages fell to the ground as she struggled to get away.

"Well, you came to me, now, didn't you, sweetheart?"

"Get your hands off her, Wakelin." Mr. Potter stood in the doorway gripping a broom handle across his body, ready to attack.

"Relax, old man. I'm just helping the lady to her feet," Wakelin replied, releasing his hold on Crissa.

"Now get off my porch."

"Thank you once more, Mr. Potter," Crissa said meekly. Then she hurried back to the inn, Wakelin's loud guffaws echoing in her ears.

★ ★ ★

Marida cautiously stuck her head in the kitchen door at the sound of supplies being slammed on the pantry shelves. "Got bee in your bustle, eh?" she teased. "Thought band of Indians came to call."

"Oh, Marida," Crissa huffed. "Do not tease me today."

"Crissa? Something has happened?"

"It is nothing."

"Is more than nothing. Is written all over you. Come, tell Marida before Molly sees what mess you've made in her kitchen."

As the two women straightened the kitchen, Crissa related the events at the mercantile. "I have tried so hard to be like other American women—to fit in. I even went to school with American children to learn my English without an accent." Tears cascaded down her cheeks while she told how the women had implied she was a hussy out to seduce Drake.

"Perhaps they were right," Crissa finally said. "I should not have come here without my family, and I do find Drake quite handsome. Maybe it is my fault. Maybe I did cause Garth to think I would enjoy his attentions."

"Don't be goose. Of course you not do anything to encourage Garth. He's just hot-blood who thinks he can have his way with any woman he wants. That's no way to treat woman. And for being here alone, why, so am I. Your family needs you be here. They depend on your pay. If you weren't here at Henders Inn, you be somewhere else with same sorrows. You're desirable woman, Crissa Engleson, and where there is desirable woman, there is trouble also."

"I do not want to bring trouble to Molly. She has had trouble enough already."

Marida motioned Crissa to sit down, then set a pot of coffee and two cups between them. As Marida poured the steaming coffee, Crissa brushed away a speck of flour dust left from this morning's baking. Marida sprinkled a spoonful of cocoa powder in each cup, stirring until it dissolved. "You're good kind of trouble, Crissa. Keeps Molly's mind off her own problems." She pushed one cup toward Crissa before popping a small lump of sugar in her mouth, letting it dissolve while she sipped her coffee.

"Now, about Drake. There are unspoken rules in small town like this. Rule number one: foreigners stay with own kind or labor man. We don't marry men American girls want. Drake's father is most important man in this town. He owns biggest mines, and he hires most men. Without him this town be *finito*. When he dies, it will be Drake step into his shoes."

"But Drake does not even work the mine."

"Drake rides with Pony Express, making believe he doesn't want father's name, but he still his father's son. Time will come when he will live in big Adams house, and he will take proper wife with him. He makes lovey eyes at you now, but he never marry you. Best take your head out of clouds, Crissa. There are plenty men in Willow Springs for you choose from. You will find man to marry."

Crissa sat transfixed, listening to Marida's speech, and carefully dusted a few grains of cocoa off the table. A look of determination gleamed in her eyes, and she clenched her jaw. She spoke in a calm, measured voice. "Marida, except for your Vic of course, the laboring men I have seen in Willow Springs seem to be no better than Garth. If I cannot marry a man I can love and admire, then I will marry no man at all."

"I pray you find him, Crissa. I pray for you."

★ ★ ★

"Will, Amy, are you still here?" Crissa called, crossing the patch of scrub and brambles that bordered the creek. "Amy, Will!" she called louder. "Where are you?"

"Here, Crissa! We're over here," the children's voices chimed in unison. "Come see what we've found!"

Found! Crissa's heart began to flutter with excitement. Could the children have actually found gold? She quickened her pace, scanning the winding creek for signs of them.

"Quietly." The whispered baritone command was so close to her side that Crissa jumped at the sound. There, in the shade of a lonely cottonwood, Will, Amy, and Drake huddled over their find. "Look, Crissa, kittens!" Will beamed, tugging her down to see the worn-out box sheltered among the tree's tangled roots.

"Brand-new baby kittens!" Amy bubbled with excitement.

"So I see," Crissa said, kneeling and scooping Amy into her lap. She watched the fluffy kittens tumble over each other. "They are precious."

Drake knelt on one knee and watched the children swarm over Crissa, who showed the expected enthusiasm for their find. A smile curled the corners of his mouth when she looked up to catch him staring. "Miss Engleson." He tipped his bare head in greeting.

"Mr. Adams. What brings you here?"

"He was helping us pan for gold, Crissa," Will piped up. "He knows all about gold. He's the best gold finder in the world!"

"Oh, he is, is he?"

"Well, maybe not the world," Drake said, grinning. "We haven't been too lucky so far."

"Drake says gold likes to hide under tree stumps," Amy said. "We were looking for it here when we found the kittens."

"Under trees? Mr. Adams, really."

"Really, Crissa." Will came to Drake's defense. "That's how he found the strike out by Ely."

"The Ely strike?" Crissa was dubious. The Ely strike was the biggest find in the area since Gold Hill. That strike was the talk of the territory—even as far away as Springville. "If you made the discovery, why is the claim in your father's name?"

"The Adams name," Drake corrected her quietly.

"Tell her, Drake! Tell her how you found it!"

"I doubt Miss Engleson would find the story as interesting as you do, Will."

"You have my attention, Mr. Adams." Crissa smiled, settling herself in for the tale.

He eased himself into a sitting position, folding his long legs in front of him. His eyes drifted to a spot on the horizon while he absently scraped trenches in the sandy earth with a twig.

"Several years ago, Garth Wight and I were riding back from Ely when a rattler spooked Garth's horse and he was thrown."

"Garth?" Crissa could not suppress her surprise that Drake had been riding with Garth.

"Garth had had some trouble with the law in Nevada, Miss Engleson, and since he was the foreman of our biggest mine, my father sent me to fetch him. Anyway, he was feeling the effects of a mighty good hangover when his horse bolted. Garth's leg was broke so bad the bones stuck out. I didn't think he could make the ride back, so I talked him into waiting while I fetched help. I cleared a patch in the shade of a cottonwood like this one for him to rest. When I pulled some brush out from around the tree, I uprooted a couple of gold nuggets the size of my knuckle here."

Drake paused, caressing his knuckle as though it truly were a nugget. He turned his gaze on Crissa. "Something gets into you when you strike gold, Crissa. Makes a man hungry—greedy. I pocketed those nuggets and never told Garth about 'em. I rode to the ranch at top speed to get help. I told my folks about the accident and about the find. Pa sent me and Oliver—that's my brother—back to Garth while he rode the rest of the way to town to get Doc. When Doc was on his way out to us, Pa got over to the land office and filed the claim."

"Oh, but that was just luck!"

"Lucky for us, but when news came in about the size of the strike, Garth took the notion that half the claim belonged to him."

"Did you give it to him?"

Drake's stare went back to the horizon. "Garth had no right to it. I found it; my father claimed it. That's all there is to it. You gotta understand Garth, Miss Crissa. Time was when he was a pretty decent sort of fellow. He's always been a hard worker. My father wouldn't have made him foreman otherwise. He was a good friend of Hank Henderson, Molly's husband. Garth would come into town at the end of his shift to help Hank fix up the inn. It's not much to look at, but he built his ma's house from logs he cut and planed himself. And he dug the irrigation ditch clear out to Rachel Hampton's house without any help. I can't really say why Garth and I have never gotten on. But even back then, something about him just rubbed me the wrong way."

Crissa shook her head. "That does not sound much like the Garth I met last night."

Drake pondered a blade of grass before twisting it into a knot. "Garth's mother and Hank died within a few months of each other a couple of years ago. Garth started drinking after that. Started drinking a lot. And getting in fights with anyone who crossed him. Then after the gold claim—well, he's just not the same man anymore. He drinks almost constantly now. If he's not at work, he's usually in jail."

"Jail? But why?"

Drake leaned forward. "You've got to understand just how dangerous Garth has become, Crissa. He looks for trouble. Figures someone owes him something, and he's out to collect." Drake's voice trailed off, leaving a half dozen thoughts unspoken.

Crissa watched Drake leaning over his crossed ankles, his face so close she ached to reach out and touch it. She followed his gaze toward the afternoon's setting sun, wishing they could sit here to watch the sun set. Instead, there were hungry customers waiting for her at the busy inn.

"It is time we got back to help with dinner, children."

"Dinner already?"

"Yes, *min kära*, already." She stood up, brushing the sand from her skirt, then turned to Drake. "Will you be eating at the inn tonight?"

"No, I have . . . other plans."

She forced a light smile, trying not to let her disappointment show. "Amy, Will, it is time to go."

"But, I, uh—" Drake jumped up, startling the kittens. "I wonder if, uh . . ." He looked off to the horizon, his hands jammed in his pockets. "That is to say . . . "

"Yes, Mr. Adams?"

"What I mean to say, is—" He folded his arms in front of his chest. "Well, I have some business to see to tomorrow. I've staked a claim of my own about an hour's ride north of here. I'm going to homestead the site, so I need to set out some markers. I've invited Vic and Marida to come along and make a picnic of it. Would you like to join us?"

"Tomorrow?" Crissa chewed on her lower lip, remembering Marida's words of caution. "I am afraid not, Mr. Adams. I promised Molly I would help decorate for the dance."

"If we leave right after breakfast, we can be back in plenty of time to decorate."

At the sight of his smile, Crissa's will dissolved along with her misgivings. "All right then, Mr. Adams," she said lightly, trying not to let her smile eat up her entire face, "a picnic it is."

He took her hand in his, stroking the length of her slender fingers. "One more thing, Miss Crissa."

"Yes?" His touch sent shivers of excitement through her body, and the word barely escaped her constricting throat.

"My father is Mr. Adams. My name is Drake."

She scarcely nodded, not wanting to break the spell he held over her. "Drake."

Hearing her whisper his name, he stood a little taller and brushed his lips against her soft knuckles.

"Can we bring them home with us?"

"What?" Crissa whirled around to the forgotten children, color rushing hotly to her cheeks.

Will was crouching over the kittens. "Can we bring them home with us?"

"No," Drake said, interceding, "their mother will take care of them." He motioned over to a tiger-striped cat watching them from the edge of a stand of brush. "Why don't we come visit them tomorrow morning?"

Will and Amy were delighted with the invitation. They grasped Crissa's hands, tugging her back to the inn.

CHAPTER 3

Fumes From the lye soap stung Crissa's nose and brought tears to her eyes as she scrubbed the dining room floor. With guests sleeping soundly upstairs, Marida kneading bread in the kitchen, and Molly out back tending the chickens, Crissa was left alone in the cool morning to do her share of the chores—and mull over her newest acquaintance. Feeling happier than she could ever remember, snatches of a folk tune she had learned as a child escaped her lips.

"Inte sticka snö, inte aisa vind, inte hungrig varg; kæn stjäla en fröjd jag känna idag. En fröjd min äkta kärlek medföras."

Crissa reflected on the words of the song, drawing parallels with her own life. Not stinging snow, not icy wind, not hungry wolves . . . Almost involuntarily, memories of her childhood came to her: bitter cold winters when there was never enough to eat, the passage to America on a rat-infested ship, and a man's face, twisted in anger— the wolf in her nightmares. The dining room seemed to close in around her, the fumes from the lye became suffocating, and the moist morning air filled her lungs with the dank humidity of a ship's hull. Threads of a familiar panic tangled with each breath. Frantically bounding for the heavy oak door, she pushed it open and gratefully sucked the crisp air in cleansing gulps. She squeezed her eyes shut against the memories while her heartbeat returned to normal.

Standing in the peaceful morning, thoughts of her life outside Willow Springs were easily pushed to a far corner of her mind. Crissa took one more deep, refreshing breath and returned to her half-scrubbed floor. Almost involuntarily, her thoughts returned to her Swedish tune . . . *Can steal the joy I feel today, the joy my true love brings.*

Could this be happening? Could she really be going on a picnic with Drake Adams? She sat motionless on her knees, hands planted firmly on the forgotten scrub brush while she dreamed.

"Heavens, girl!"

Crissa jumped at Marida's booming voice.

"You plan sitting there like lump while customers walk over your backside?"

"I am sorry, Marida," Crissa stammered, the faraway look still obvious in her eyes. "I was just thinking . . ."

"I know you just thinking. You been just thinking since you got back from the crick yesterday. Lordy, girl, is just picnic. Remember what I say? Drake not marry foreign girl like you, no matter what you wan' believe." Marida shook her head and laughed. "You see my lips move, but you not hear words I say. We have hungry guests be coming down soon. Don'a you think we should serve breakfast 'fore you start make wedding dress?"

"Oh, Marida," Crissa sighed, hooking her elbow through her friend's. "This is too good to be true. Can this really be happening?"

"What is happening, you silly thing, is that folks be wanting breakfast, and you standing there mooning. Picnic hasn't happened yet, and won't if we don'a get breakfast over with."

"Yes, Marida," Crissa said with mock submission and a genuine smile. "Breakfast is served."

★ ★ ★

Try as he might, Drake had a hard time looking at Crissa without his heartbeat quickening. The way her curls glowed in the sun reminded him of sunlight dancing off of ripples in a stream. She even smelled fresh like sunlight—it reminded him of the lavender water his mother sprinkled on sheets before she hung them to dry.

And those lips—how the corners always turned up in a perpetual smile—and how her dimples deepened when she pronounced the D in his name . . . her countenance was as cheerful as sunshine. Of course, Drake hadn't exactly simplified the matter when he sat squarely in the middle of the buckboard seat, leaving barely enough room for Crissa to sit beside him. Each time the buggy hit a rut or a rock, Crissa bumped against him in a way that left Drake nearly breathless.

Enveloped by the pungent smell of sagebrush, Crissa, Drake, Marida, and Vic made their way on an overgrown trail up Overland Canyon northwest toward the foothills. The buckboard rocked to and fro, keeping time to their conversation.

"When I was a small girl in Sweden," Crissa mused, "I would gather buttercups like these and weave them into a wreath for my hair."

Drake looked across the meadow, imagining the beautiful, fair-haired girl running through the buttercups and forget-me-nots, blonde hair flowing behind her, arms spread to embrace the wind. An unaccustomed warmth spread through his chest as he considered what his and Crissa's children might look like. *Drake! Get a hold of yourself!* he thought. He tried to concentrate on the conversation around him, but his mind strayed again—lying with Crissa in the sweet, wild grass, a ring of blossoms crowning her silky hair, glorious . . .

"Glorious?" Crissa asked. "What is glorious, Drake?"

"Glorious?" He realized he must have spoken the word aloud.

"Yes, Drake," Vic teased. "Just what is so glorious?"

"Um, uh . . ." In a panic, he looked at Vic for support. He received only an amused stare in return. He felt the color rising in his cheeks and briefly considered jumping from the wagon. "The, uh—" He swept his hand in an arc in front of him. "The meadow. I was just thinking how glorious the meadow is this time of year."

"Right," Vic said, playing along. "Glorious."

Drake guided the horses off the path, following the bend of the foothills. He steered into a small copse of willows and pulled up beside a rocky stream fed by a gently bubbling spring. It was these springs, hidden among the foothills of the Deep Creek Mountains that gave Willow Springs its name. The sage along the banks of the stream was sprinkled with yellow blossoms and surrounded by willows and cottonwood trees.

"How is it you pick only prettiest sights for to claim, Drake?" Marida had jumped off the buckboard even before it was completely stopped.

"This," Crissa added, letting Drake help her down, "is truly glorious."

Drake paused with his hands encircling Crissa's waist. "I'm very glad you think so."

"So, Mr. 'I'm-a-no-gold-miner'"—Marida's bold voice jolted them both back to earth—"how you find this place?"

"I staked this land a few months ago. Figured I'd try my hand at ranching."

"Fixin' on settling down, are you?" Vic could no longer hide his smirk. "Looking to get hitched?"

Drake glared at Vic, contemplating pulling his friend's tongue out. "The telegraph is almost done. There won't be a need for the Pony Express once the line goes from coast to coast. Time to find a new line of work."

"So how did you decide there was gold here?" Crissa seemed as curious about this story as she had been about the Ely story from yesterday.

"Well, as I said, I was looking for a nice place for a ranch. I set camp here the evening I decided to homestead it. I scooped some water from the stream for coffee, and darned if that water didn't glitter."

"Luck once again?" Crissa asked, gazing at him steadily.

"Luck once again."

Though nothing remained to be said, the two stood locked in a visual embrace, neither one able to turn away.

"So," Marida broke in again, "you gonna do work, or what? We don'a got all day, y'know. Be off with ya."

"My Marida," Vic said, giving Marida a swat on the behind, "such a pushy filly."

Drake winked at Crissa. "We won't be long."

★ ★ ★

With the men gone to set stakes to mark this side of the ranch, Crissa snapped a meticulously pieced quilt in the air before letting it settle on the ground. Then she and Marida began laying out the picnic fare.

"I wonder what it would be like to be married to a man who is as kind as Drake," Crissa said, more to herself than Marida.

"I don'a have to wonder. I know. Cooking, cleaning. Cleaning, cooking. Then, when you too tired to stand up anymore, man comes in and demands husbandly rights. I think man gets best of that bargain."

"Surely it is not all work. You love Vic, Marida. What does it feel like to be in love with a man? To be with a man who really loves you?"

Marida paused with a crock of pickled beets in one hand, a plate of carrot and turnip sticks in the other. "My momma told me once, there no greater pain. God made pain to bear children, and God made pain to bear husband." She smiled and winked at Crissa. "When I with Vic, though, I not feel pain. My chest feels like will burst with love. I don'a think my momma try find pleasure in loving. She too busy finding pain."

Crissa's thoughts drifted back to another time, another pain, sending a shudder through her. Willow Springs and Drake seemed like a fairy tale in comparison. "When I look at Drake, my heart starts to pound, and I cannot seem to breathe properly."

Marida put her arm around Crissa's shoulders. "Don'a fall for Drake, Crissa. You just get hurt. Many girls make lovey eyes at Drake, but he not marry them. Don'a be like them. Don'a let him break your heart too."

"Marida!" Crissa could not contain the fear in her voice. "You do not think Drake would do that! I think I am falling in love with him." She chewed her lower lip thoughtfully. "I hope you are wrong about him, Marida." But she knew there was more than a grain of truth to what Marida said.

★ ★ ★

"My," Vic said, sitting back to massage his belly. "Feels like I've eaten a horse!"

Marida slapped his slightly rounded stomach as if she were thumping a watermelon. "With all you ate, would be faster to cook you horse."

"A man needs hearty vittles to pound stakes all day. What's for dessert?"

"Dessert! You get so fat you don'a bend over pick stakes up!"

"Here, Vic," Crissa said, interceding, "let me get you some pie. Would you like apple or currant?"

"See there, Marida? You should take some lessons from Crissa. She knows how to treat a man. Slab of each, if you don't mind, ma'am." He smiled at Crissa with mock adoration.

"Humph." Marida gave his shoulder a shove. "You be laid out on slab if you don'a watch out."

Crissa handed Vic his heaping plate. "How about you, Drake? Are you ready for dessert?"

"Apple, please."

Crissa served Drake, then Marida, before taking a dainty slice of currant pie for herself. The pie disappeared from the four plates nearly as fast as the dinner had.

Drake stretched his arms behind his head, stifling a satisfied yawn. "Vic, why don't you take Marida down and show her the pond?"

"Tryin' to get rid of us, eh? Come on, Marida. Help me walk some of this dinner off." The two were on their feet instantly, laughing and pulling each other in the direction of the pond.

Crissa fumbled to make small talk—the weather, Marida and Vic, Henders Inn, the weather . . .

"Has your family lived in Willow Springs for very long?" she finally asked. From the look on his face, Crissa decided she had definitely stumbled upon the wrong topic for small talk.

"My family doesn't live in Willow Springs." Drake seemed reluctant to talk about it, but he sketched a brief biography nonetheless. "My father lives in Gold Hill. More accurately, my father *is* Gold Hill. His mines cover nearly the entire mountain. If a man in these parts makes a living by some means other than ranching, he more than likely works for my father."

"Your father sounds like a successful man."

"My father is a man of great power and influence. Any accomplishment has been at the hands of his employees."

"Why do you not work with him?"

"I don't want to become like him. Crissa," Drake said, squeezing her hand slightly, "you can't understand my father without knowing more of my family history, and I'm afraid I've bored you enough already."

Several moments of uncomfortable silence passed between them, interrupted only by the hum of bees and the faint lullaby of the stream in the distance.

"So, what do you think of my little piece of heaven?" Drake laid his empty plate down and stretched his legs out in front of him, reclining on one elbow.

"This must be the most beautiful site near Willow Springs." Crissa spoke lightly, scraping the remains of their picnic off the plates and stacking them in a bushel basket, leaving only jars and empty pie tins scattered on the quilt. "This is where you will build your home?"

"Well, not here, exactly. Upstream a bit. Would you like me to show you?" Drake jumped to his feet without waiting for an answer and grabbed Crissa's hand to carry her along with him. His long-legged stride caused her to almost run to keep up with him as they passed through the trees clustered between the meadow and the stream.

Coming into a clearing, Crissa gasped and clasped her hands together in delight. The stream wound its way along the edge of the trees, tumbling over small stones with a delicate gurgle. Beyond the stream was a flat, grassy meadow, in the center of which stones and branches had been placed to indicate the parameters of a building. The gentle hills of the Deep Creek range played backdrop to this serene sight.

"Oh, Drake. It is beautiful. It takes the breath from me."

"I was hoping you would like it." He placed an arm about her waist and twirled her across the narrow stream. "Come, let me show you."

Drake paced his way through each soon-to-be room of his soon-to-be house, describing in full detail how the rooms would be situated. "If I work quickly, I can get the main floor finished and roofed before the weather turns bad. Then next year I can add the second floor with more rooms."

"It will be such a large house!" Crissa was dismayed by his plans of grandeur. She had seen only a few houses with more than one floor since coming west, and only the wealthiest families owned these.

Drake smiled at her evident approval. "As we outgrow this house, I can add wings to accommodate a large family."

"Any woman would be proud to live in such a grand home."

Drake turned to her, studied her face, and gently stroked a golden curl from her brow. Taking her hand, he towed her to what would one day be the back door. He stood behind her, turning her to face the yard.

"Imagine standing here," he said softly, almost reverently, "in the kitchen, watching the sun rise over the willows on a quiet spring morning. Chickens scratching in their yard over there, a couple of Holsteins in the barn, maybe a few pigs in a pen behind the barn."

As he spoke so close behind her, his breath tickled her ear with little puffs. His breath was sweetly scented, like cedar. She had never known a man whose breath was so fresh. Feeling safe here with him, Crissa tried to memorize the way it felt to have him so close—the way he smelled, the way his chest rose with each breath, the way he held her shoulders while explaining his plans. His hands were firm but not rough, and she memorized this too.

Crissa smiled at the images he conjured. She could picture herself in a crisp gingham apron kneading bread, scrambling eggs, pouring coffee, and shooing three or four children out from under her feet.

Drake showed her how, by placing the kitchen in this quadrant, water from the stream would be mere steps from the back door. He pointed out the kitchen garden, located close to the stream so that irrigation channels could take care of watering the crops. With a self-conscious grin, he even pointed out where he would plant an oak tree to hang a swing for the children he hoped for.

Crissa exclaimed with delight over each new detail he revealed. She reveled in his plans as though they were meant to include her. Listening to him, she imagined they would be together forever. Yet she had only known him for three days. He had chosen this land before he had met her. Before she had even come to Willow Springs. Drake had certainly never said anything about including her in this dream. Was there another woman Drake was planning this "piece of heaven" for?

A wispy cloud skittered in front of the sun, sending a shadow across both the meadow and Crissa's hopes. Marida's warning words came back to her: "He could not marry you."

Of course there is someone else, she told herself. Could Drake have brought her here to gloat? To show this little foreigner what she could never have? Crissa felt all her hopes disappear while Drake sat against a rock, immersed in his world.

Putting on a mantle of primness, Crissa interrupted Drake's gleeful prattle. "It is time we returned to the picnic. Vic and Marida will wonder what has become of us."

Drake looked at her curiously. "Are you all right?"

Belying the tightness in her chest and the cloud of depression that had settled over her, Crissa answered, "Yes, I am fine, but I do not want them to worry about us."

★ ★ ★

"I wonder where Vic and Marida have gone." Crissa picked a cold chicken leg out of the basket, scanning the distance. The two of them were nowhere in sight when Drake and Crissa returned to the abandoned picnic still spread on the quilt.

"I'm sure they'll be back soon," Drake said. Sensing Crissa's unease. He wasn't sure if she was embarrassed at being left alone unchaperoned for so long or if he had done something to offend her. He wasn't about to add to her discomfort by guessing what Vic and Marida were most likely doing.

He studied her long fingers gently placing strips of chicken between her pearly teeth. How could her every move leave him breathless? *Exquisite.* It was the perfect word—the only word—to describe Crissa.

Trying to relieve some of the tension he felt sitting so close to her, he reclined back on one elbow. Rather than gaining any relief, however, Drake found himself staring at her generous curves. The faint, clean scent of lye soap, combined with the heady fragrance of lavender water, conquered the restraint he had struggled to maintain.

"Oh, Crissa." Drake's voice was soft, almost pleading.

As Crissa turned with questioning eyes, Drake's hand cradled her neck, gently pulling her face down to meet his. As his lips brushed hers, a shiver shook her body, and she drew back in shock.

"Drake . . ." She could barely speak through her trembling lips. "Please, I . . . do not."

Her tears forbade further explanation. Crissa ran, stumbling, toward the wagon, trying to conceal them. No matter what her responsive body told him, Drake knew she wouldn't throw herself at him like so many others had done. How could he care for her so much after knowing her for such a short time? Crissa stared toward the trees as if willing Marida and Vic to return and take her back to the safety of the inn.

Drake sat up and ran shaking hands through his hair. Her words were seared in his mind. *Do not what? Do not want me? Do not care for me?* Their brief encounter had filled him with the need to have her, to build a life with her. Why had she run? Couldn't she sense how he felt about her? Surely she was the woman he had dreamed of when he planned a ranch here, the woman he would spend nights with in front of a warm fire, the woman who would sing to his children. He realized then that had scared her off. Crissa was the kind of woman who would be his bride before he took her as his lover.

★ ★ ★

The rustle of grass and the giggle of young love signaled the return of Marida and Vic from their disappearance in the trees.

32

"You remember." Marida laughed, giving Victor a shove. "First ring on finger, then roll in hay."

"I didn't see no hay back there."

"Well, it's time we were heading back," Drake said, shaking crumbs from the quilt they had been sitting on. "Give me a hand loading this stuff, will ya?"

Marida pulled Crissa aside. "You all right?"

"Yes, I am fine."

"You look like you been rolling in hay too!"

Crissa turned away without answering, partly to hide the flush burning her face and partly to hide the tears still wet on her lashes.

CHAPTER 4

Kerosene lamps lent a golden glow to the large hall
of the church house. Blue-and-yellow bunting bedecked the rafters, and streamers cascaded down to encircle the crude bandstand.
Widow Henderson let the piano from the inn be brought over
for the spring social, and now it took center stage as Matt Parker
pounded out rollicking tunes. A couple of men joined in with
fiddles, and before long a guitar and an accordion rounded out the
makeshift band.

The spring social was the official start of "courtin' season" in
Willow Springs. The young ladies of the area dressed in their finest
new frocks to encourage the advances of handsome young men
ready to shake off the memories of a cold and lonely winter. Com-
petition was keen for males and females alike, and the merrymaking
would go on for as long as the band (and the smuggled-in spirits)
could hold out.

Crissa caught her breath as she entered the hall. "Buffalo gals,
won't you come out tonight," sang the band. Joyful voices rose to
the rafters as the dancers swirled through the room. Never had she
seen so many people moving together in such a way. Keenly aware
of the eyes on her as she stepped from the doorway, Crissa nervously smoothed her peach calico skirt and tried to blend in with
the woodwork.

"Ma'am?"

She jumped at the voice behind her.

The speaker's boyish face showed dimples when he smiled, and he had a fresh shaving nick in the side of his jaw. "Would you care to dance?"

"I . . . I do not know how." Crissa's stammer made her blush like a schoolgirl.

"Well, I'd shore be pleased to teach ya." Without waiting for another excuse, the young man took her hand and led her to the middle of the floor. He placed one of her hands on his shoulder and cradled the other hand gently in his. With a hand on her waist, he guided her carefully around the floor.

"My name's John Flannery."

"I am pleased to meet you, Mr. Flannery." Crissa knew she would never remember his name. "I am Crissa Engleson."

"I know, ma'am. I was waitin' for you to get here. I wanted the first dance."

"Now that you've had it, mind if I cut in?"

Without taking his eyes off Crissa, John tried to discourage the interloper. "Ah, Ned, we just got started."

"Well, there's a line formin' for this little lady."

With a halfhearted smile and a nod of his head, John handed Crissa over to the other man. "Thanks for the dance, ma'am."

"Hope you don't mind my cutting in like that," the newcomer said. "I just didn't want to be left out."

Crissa turned her attention to the new dancer, trying to adjust her steps to his.

"Ned Peterson, at your service."

A steady succession of eager faces accompanied by forgotten names twirled her around the dance floor. Each time a conversation began with one man, another would cut in. Each time one tune ended, another began with scarcely a missed beat.

Crissa was trying doggedly to learn a polka step when the door of the church opened and Drake stepped through with a woman on his arm. Dressed in lemon yellow satin with dark brown hair falling in ringlets about her shoulders, she was the most beautiful woman

Crissa had ever seen. *The kind of woman Drake would be expected to marry*, Crissa thought bitterly.

Watching him, Crissa forgot about dancing, missed a step, and twisted her ankle painfully. Begging her leave, she sought the refuge of a nearby bench, only to be deluged with offers of punch and cookies.

Crissa felt Drake's gaze on her as the crush of young suitors pressed in around her. He did not speak to her, but his eyes were hooded—brooding, almost. Was he angry that she had not let him kiss her earlier? Angry enough to escort another woman mere hours after he had picnicked with her? And if he was so angry, why did he linger right in front of her instead of leading his lady friend to the other side of the room? What was this game he played?

"Drake, darling," his satin-clad partner whined, hugging his arm to her boldly exposed bosom, "have you forgotten who you came with?" Her voice dripped with feigned sweetness as she demanded his attention.

This is the kind of woman your family wants you to marry? Crissa watched Drake's jaw clench and his chest rise and fall with a silent sigh.

"Of course not, Suzanna. I . . ." Avoiding Crissa's gaze, he led his date onto the dance floor.

"Crissa, come with me." Marida's urgent summons sliced through the crowd of voices jostling for Crissa's attention. "S'cuse me, boys. Crissa, come on!" She reached through the mass of bodies and pulled Crissa, limping, toward the door.

They were outside, seated on a bench before Crissa could draw a breath to protest. "Marida! What ever is wrong?"

"Wrong? Not wrong. Only right! Vic asked me marry him!" Marida thrust her left hand in front of Crissa's face, displaying a band of braided grass with a wilting buttercup woven into the top. "He wanted world know I was his as soon as I say yes. Is so romantic, no?"

"Dear Marida," Crissa said, hugging her friend tightly and mimicking her accent, "is so romantic, yes! I am so happy for you. Have you set a date for the wedding?"

"Not yet, but we want be married soon! We want for you and Drake to come."

Crissa drew a painful breath. "Of course I will be there. Of course I will."

After listening to Marida chatter about her proposal for what seemed like an eternity, Crissa could contain the inevitable question no longer. "Marida, did you notice Drake tonight?"

"You say, did I notice Drake, but you mean, did I notice woman with him."

Crissa studied her best friend a few moments before breaking into a huge grin. "All right then, did you notice the woman with him?"

"Of course I notice! Everyone notice Suzanna Hampton. She thinks she's prettiest girl in territory. Most of men think so too. Remember I told you Drake only marry certain kind of girl? Well, she very much that kind of girl. Their parents been planning wedding since forever."

Crissa struggled to control her emotions as Marida explained the way some marriages were planned, regardless of the bride and groom's wishes. "But if he knew he must marry this girl, why did he invite me on the picnic? And"—Crissa said, swiping at her escaping tears—"why did he try to kiss me?"

"Because some men think is best to taste as many sweets as they can before they get married!" Marida chuckled at the analogy she had made, though Crissa frowned at the thought connected with Drake. "I think that why he rides Pony Express. He knows one day he take over mines, he marry Suzanna, he have family take care of. He wants freedom now, before it too late."

"Marida!" The call cut their conversation short.

"That's Vic. I must go. You be all right, no?"

"Of course," Crissa said, trying to muster a smile. "I will come in a minute or two."

A heavy darkness enveloped Crissa as she sat alone, trying to sort her thoughts. Strains of music from inside carried her daydreams, interrupted now and then by a chirp of a cricket, a burst of laughter ringing through the night, or secret whispers from lovers escaping the crowd. Thoughts of what might have been for Drake and her gave way to thoughts of what would be for Drake and Suzanna. Though the spring night air was growing chilly, the knot in her throat made it impossible for Crissa to rejoin the gaiety inside. She wrapped her arms around herself, trying to generate some comfort. *Oh, Drake,* she thought. *Why did I fall in love with you?*

Large, masculine hands gripped her shoulders firmly. "Waiting for me, darling?"

Crissa's heart leaped, thinking it was Drake, then leaped again when she realized the voice was not his. She spun around and found herself in the arms of Garth Wight.

"Let me go!" she cried, trying to push him away.

"But we ain't had our dance."

His breath reeked of whiskey. From his slurred speech and the way he leaned against her, Crissa realized Garth was several drinks beyond drunk.

"Let me go!" A huge paw clamped roughly over her mouth, stifling her scream for help. Garth dragged her around the corner of the church into a stand of trees and brush. With her backed against a tree, he covered Crissa's face and neck with wet kisses. As his lips found hers, she bit him savagely.

Oblivious to his grunts and his hand tearing at her hair, Crissa clenched her teeth until she tasted his blood in her mouth. She shoved him away and ran for the safety of the church, her screams bursting out between ragged breaths. At the edge of the trees, he lunged for her. Her face slammed to the ground, and she felt her skin ripping as her cheek scraped against a jagged rock. She fought against the dizzying darkness threatening to overcome her.

Like a cat after a mouse, Garth pounced on Crissa. He leered at her through bloodshot eyes, his lips curled back over yellow teeth. Closing her eyes against the pain, Garth's face was replaced by another. In Crissa's mind, it was another time, another place, another man's drunken advances that came back to haunt her.

"Time to dance, sweet Crissa."

As she gritted her teeth against the inevitable, Garth's body was torn from her as though by a tornado. She opened her eyes in time to see Drake hurl Garth against a tree.

"Dance with this, you son of a—" One punch, fired by years of hate, was all that was needed to render Garth unconscious.

★ ★ ★

Shards of sunlight found their way through Crissa's drawn draperies. Squinting against the intrusion, Crissa tried to roll over. A plaintive cry escaped her lips as pain shot throughout her body.

"Easy there, Miss Engleson. Don't try to move just yet." Drake hovered over her, his unshaven face drawn in concern.

"What . . . ?" Crissa tried to focus on consciousness. She lifted her head until an eruption of pain forced her back to the comfort of her pillow. "What are you doing here?"

"Well, I thought someone should . . . be here . . . in case you needed anything."

It was obvious that Drake was uncomfortable. As the cobwebs cleared from her head, it also became clear why. Drake was in her room, and she was in bed—dressed only in her chemise! Crissa gasped and burrowed deeper under the blanket covering her, pulling it up tight under her chin. He tried his best to suppress a smile. Crissa felt a flush rise in her cheeks and tried to disguise it with indignation.

"That does not explain why . . ." Her voice trailed off as the memory of the previous night forced its way into her consciousness. She groaned when she realized what Drake had witnessed. "Have you been here all night?"

"All night long, honey." Molly thrust her head through the doorway. "Planted himself in that chair as soon as Doc Robbins left and wouldn't budge. Couldn't have chased him away with a shotgun. How you feeling this morning?"

"Doc Robbins was here?"

"'Course he was, sweetie. You were pretty torn up when Drake carried you in last night. Doc patched up your cheek but said that, aside from some nasty scrapes and bruises, you'd be fine in a day or two. Don't you remember, child?"

Crissa shook her head. "I just remember Drake . . . and Garth." She pressed her lips together against the nausea in her stomach and turned her head away.

As Molly laid Crissa's breakfast out on the side table, Crissa couldn't help but steal glances at Drake. Snatches of his all-night vigil began to piece together in her memory—images of him leaping to her bedside each time she stirred, stroking her forehead until she slept peacefully again, pulling the covers back up each time she furtively kicked them off. When their eyes locked on each other, Crissa ached for him to lay down beside her and cradle her in his arms—to make time stand still so she would never fully remember what she had been through.

"Drake!" He jumped at Molly's command. "I said, why don't you go get cleaned up and have Marida rustle you up some breakfast?"

"Uh, yeah . . . sure." He looked at Crissa, seemingly not wanting to go but without a reason to stay. "You, uh . . . take care of yourself."

Crissa gave Molly a questioning look at Drake's awkward retreat, then remembered her own less-than-modest condition.

"Molly! I am . . . I have no . . ." She lowered her voice to a whisper and uncovered her bare shoulders. "Did Drake . . . ?"

"Goodness no, child!" Molly let out a hearty laugh. "Drake carried you home, and I put you to bed. He was out there pacing the hallway like an expectant father. He was so worried that, well, I didn't see no harm letting him sit with you awhile. I never dreamed he'd stay all night!"

Molly helped Crissa thread her bruised arms through her cotton wrapper, then sat down beside her and folded her into a warm embrace. "Drake told me what happened, honey. I been thinking. Maybe it would be best if you went away for a while."

"Went away!" Crissa's voice was choked with tears. "Why must I go away? I did not—"

"There now. I know you didn't do anything to cause this, but I'm worried about you. When the rest of the men at the dance heard what happened, they came after Garth with a rope. The sheriff has him in jail 'til he sobers up, but he won't be there for long. I wouldn't put it past him to come after you again. Drake won't be around, what with his Express rides and all. I just thought, maybe, if you went away for a bit, things would simmer down after a spell. I don't want to lose you, baby, and I sure don't want no bunch of vigilantes hanging around trying to protect you. Go visit your folks for a couple of months. Give things a chance to settle down."

Crissa recognized the frown of concern etched on Molly's kind face. There were so many reasons for her to stay here: Molly, who needed her help; Amy and Will; Marida's wedding. But the one reason to leave overshadowed all else.

★ ★ ★

The rising sun was burning the last of the prairie grass's dew as the stagehand tossed Crissa's satchel up to the driver on top of the stagecoach. A solemn group gathered to see Crissa on her way to Springville. Marida promised to postpone her wedding, and Molly gave her assurance that she would manage just fine until Crissa returned. Little Amy clung to Crissa's skirt, sobbing her grief, and Will stood before her, stiff and somber, clenching his teeth to keep his bottom lip from quivering. Will's dad had been killed when Indians ambushed the stagecoach he was driving between Blackrock and Dugway stations, and Will was sure that once Crissa got on that stage, something terrible would happen.

Crissa peered down the quiet street, hoping against hope that Drake might come see her off. Aside from Mr. Potter sweeping his porch, the street was deserted. Thrusting aside her guilt at not telling her friends where she was really headed, she boarded the stage. In her pocket she clutched the transfer ticket to Salt Lake City.

CHAPTER 5

The Overland Stage station in Salt Lake City teemed with people. Because this was a central stop to the smaller stage routes crisscrossing the West, the Salt Lake station was almost always bustling. Stagehands rushed about loading or unloading baggage; teamsters bellowed at their animals; passengers stumbled over each other, trying to keep track of their stages, baggage, and children; and babies screamed with hunger, fright, and sheer exhaustion.

A robust gentleman stood on the boardwalk, issuing orders to a variety of women and children clustered about him. His knee-length, black, wool coat added to his somber air of importance.

"President Young! President Young!" Another man, also dressed in a black coat, rushed through the crowd. As the two men huddled together, their words were drowned out by the crescendo of onlookers' shouts as the two o'clock stage approached. Gingerly stepping off the stage, Crissa straightened her aching back as best she could. Placing the heels of her hands in the center of her lower back, she stretched luxuriously, unconscious of the admiring stares her profile was attracting. "Give yer a hand, miss?"

"Excuse me?" Crissa turned to stare into the face of a middle-aged man, not much taller than her five-foot frame. Except for a sagging potbelly, he was scrawny to the point of being sickly looking.

"A hand with yer baggage, darlin'."

"I'll be takin' that, thank you." Another man's thick Irish brogue broke into the conversation.

Crissa spun to face the man who had rescued her. "Charlie!" She flung her arms around him in joyous abandon. "Charlie Callahan! What a joy to see you! How did you know to meet my stage?"

With a few grumbled words about cursed Irishmen, the straggly man sauntered off.

"Well, now, I didn't exactly plan on meetin' ya, dear. I'd be doin' some business at the stockyard when I sees the prettiest colleen I ever laid eyes on steppin' off'a the stage. I says to meself, 'Charlie,' I says, 'only one lady as pretty as that. It must be Crissa Engleson.' So's I come to have a look, and here we are!"

"Charlie," Crissa said, threading her arm through his extended elbow, "I am so lucky to have such a dear, dear friend."

Charlie smiled down at her with adoration, politely ignoring the purple bruise staining her cheek and brow. "Now then, which way will ye be headin'?"

"I have come to visit the Bjorksons. Is that out of your way?"

"Out o' me way! Why, with you on me arm, China wouldn't be out o' the way! The ol' buck an' Betsy are just down the way." The two friends threaded their way through the crowded station to Charlie's waiting buckboard and mare. They rode north, past the stock- and lumberyards and the few merchant shops that formed the westernmost side of the city's commerce district.

"Well, Charlie, tell me how you have been since I left. Are you and Margaret still enjoying married life?"

"Aye, that we are, that we are. In fact, I have a little piece o' news to share." Charlie looked at Crissa, his eyes twinkling and a mischievous grin appearing on his lips.

"Well?"

"Mrs. Callahan, she has a wee one a-bakin' in the oven."

"A wee one in the oven?" Crissa puzzled. "Charlie, whatever are you—? A wee one! A baby!" She hugged him with delight, nearly knocking them both off the rickety seat. "What a wonderful surprise! Oh, my."

Charlie was chuckling so hard he too had a hard time keeping his balance. "There now, Crissa. You're about to knock the whole rig for a spin."

Crissa sat back with her hands clasped in front of her. "Please give Margaret my fondest congratulations. I hope I may visit her while I am in Salt Lake."

"Well," Charlie began on a more somber note, "Maggie doesn't go out much right now. The sickness has her down most mornings, and I won't let her ride in the buggy 'til the little tyke's a bit bigger in her belly. I saw too many problems on the crossin' to take a chance with me own child. I'm sure you'd be more than welcome if you dropped by the house, though."

"Of course, Charlie. I will visit as soon as I get settled in at the Bjorksons'." Crissa's thoughts went back to her own journey from Boston to Salt Lake. The wagons were reserved for only those who were too old or sick to walk, and even then the ride was so bumpy that the walk would have been preferable. The toll was high on young and old alike. But so many babies. So many babies. Crissa's moist eyes wandered to the jagged purple peaks of the Wasatch mountains in the east—soldiers, high on horseback, cloaked with snow on their shoulders that formed a formidable barrier to the Rockies and vast plains beyond.

"Crissa?" Charlie called her gently from her reverie. "I didn't mean to upset you, darlin'."

She braved a smile. "No, of course not. I really am very happy for you. I just—sometimes I cannot help remembering."

"He was a part of you, and you'll always be remembering. But someday, darlin' "—Charlie patted Crissa's hand—"you'll have another wee one to care for, and a large part of the hurt will heal."

Dear Charlie. Always there when I need you. Without you, my family may never have found the way to Salt Lake. Without you—but then she stopped. Some memories were best forgotten.

"Well," Crissa said, trying to chase the huskiness from her voice, "we are almost to Swede-town. It will be nice to see the Bjorksons again."

Charlie turned the buckboard westward into a section of houses clustered closer together. The narrow, dusty roads ran in front of adobe huts that soon gave way to small wooden houses. Here and there a picket fence encircled a house, and, even more infrequently, a variety of early flowers brightened the simple yards with bursts of spring color.

"I see the snow is nearly gone from the Oquirrhs." Crissa gazed at the western mountains. "Has the planting begun?"

"Not yet. Soon, though. Last year about this time, the Oquirrhs were just as green as they could be. 'Tweren't more'n a patch o' snow on 'em. Planting was about done when the worst spring storm ya ever seen come by. May sixteenth, it was. Got snow nearly to me knees. Well, you can imagine what it did to the tender seedlings beginning to sprout. Figure this year folks'll be a little wary 'fore planting their crops."

After passing a couple of blocks, Charlie turned the horse north, then east. In the distance, the pastures and orchards were laid out in a verdant patchwork rising among the foothills of the regal Wasatch range. They rounded a corner northward, and a smile spread across Crissa's face as she beheld the familiar street lined with white clap-board houses, picket fences, transplanted cottonwoods, and fruit trees with fading blossoms. Children ran between the houses, laughing and yelling in a game of hide-and-seek.

This was her beloved Swede-town, the gathering place of most of the Swedes who had settled in Salt Lake. Crissa and Charlie passed two walkways and pulled up at the third. Before ascending half the distance to the front door, she was nearly bowled over by three squealing youngsters.

"Crissa! Crissa! Mama, come see! Crissa's here!"

Crissa had barely extricated herself from the children when she was caught in the embrace of a woman nearly twice her size. "*Cristalina! Min* Cristalina! *Min alskling! Be det verkligen du?*"

"*Dyr Signe, jag æm här. Var god, vara inte skrika.*"

In her excitement to see her family, Crissa nearly failed to notice Charlie standing awkwardly behind them.

"Oh, Charlie." Crissa turned around to face her escort. "Please forgive our bad manners."

Smiling, Signe Bjorkson turned her attention to the Irishman. "What a present you have brought me today, Charlie."

"The pleasure be all mine indeed, Miz Bjorkson. All mine, indeed."

"Crissa, let's get you in the house. Lars will be home shortly. Charlie, would you care to join us for an evening meal?"

"Ah, thank ye, ma'am, but I best be on me way. Me missus like to be in a stew herself, with me gone so long. Crissa, it's indeed a pleasure to feast me eyes upon ye once more."

"Thank you again for your help, Charlie."

"I'll say good day to ye, then." With a tip of his cap and a nod of his head, Charlie Callahan was whistling his way off down the street.

★ ★ ★

An antelope roast, rubbed with sage and simmered for hours in a dutch oven, served as the main course for the evening meal. Mashed potatoes and honeyed carrots sat on the back of the oven to keep warm while Signe fried sliced apples and dusted them with raw sugar and cinnamon. Fresh apples were indeed a treat at this time of year. One of the neighbors had discovered that if you filled a keg of water with fresh apples in the fall, sealed the keg, then sank it in the millpond, the apples would stay fresh and crisp through the next spring.

Gathered around the dinner table that night, Crissa found it next to impossible to carry on a continuous conversation with anyone.

"It is not fair, Momma!" Six-year-old Aigner was beside himself that his little brother had gained one of the two prized seats on either side of Crissa and that his sister was smugly sitting in the other. "Tell David he has to sit by you. He's the baby!"

"Aigner! You will stop that now!" Signe was out of patience. "I will not have you carry on like that in this house."

The sullen Aigner shot his mother a dark glance before plopping down in the chair opposite Crissa. Five-year-old Britta didn't help the matter when she stuck her tongue out at the already seething Aigner. Fortunately, Aigner didn't see the offending gesture until David, still considered the baby, although nearly three, joined in with a food-covered tongue of his own.

"Momma!"

"Aigner!"

"But, Momma. David!"

"Britta!"

"But, Momma!"

"That is enough!" The bellowing voice of their father put an immediate end to the fracas. Lars stood at the head of the table, waving a potato-laden spoon at the malcontents. In a soft, even tone, he put an end to the bickering. "That will do."

An incessant game of showing off dominated the evening's conversation, ranging from who was doing the best in school to who could hop the longest on one foot. Eager children clamored over who would stand next to Crissa to wash the dishes (even though Signe protested that her guest would not be allowed to do dishes in her home). In the end, an exasperated Crissa set Britta to wash, David to rinse, and Aigner to dry and put away the dishes while she hovered behind them, giving the proper attention and words of encouragement where needed.

The kitchen sparkled, the freshly milked cow lowed contentedly out back, and three high-spirited children were finally asleep before Crissa had the chance to sit down quietly with Lars and Signe Bjorkson.

"Well, Cristalina," Signe began, "you certainly have a way of bringing excitement to our household unexpectedly."

"Oh, leave her be, Mother," Lars chided. "How are your folks, Crissa?"

Crissa turned a sad smile his direction. "To be honest, I have not had a letter from them since I left here. I wrote to let them know I had arrived in Willow Springs safely, but I sent the letter by stage. The Pony Express requires a return address on each letter, but I did not know if, perhaps, someone would trace the letter and find out where I was. I instructed my parents to send any letters here first, so you could forward them to me. I hope you do not mind."

"Mind! Why, Crissa, that seems the only prudent thing to do, considering the bounty on you and all."

"Have the bounty hunters made it this far west yet?"

"I have not seen any posters, but I still would not take any chances."

Crissa cupped her chin in her hands, shaking her head woefully. "I do not know how I got put in such an *oreda*."

"Well, Cristalina." Signe took Crissa's face in her hand, turning it so the oil lamp illuminated the bruised cheek. "It looks as if you have found yourself in another mess."

Crissa pulled her head away, turning her cheek back to the shadows. "Oh, that," she said lightly. "It is nothing to worry about."

"Of course we worry. You are like our own child. Now tell us how this happened." Obediently, Crissa gave a brief sketch of her painful memories of Willow Springs. Signe was shocked, and Lars was outraged. "How dare he lay a finger on our Crissa!" he stormed. "I will leave first thing tomorrow to put the fear of God in Mr. Wight!"

"Lars, please," Crissa said. "You must not do that! I have promised Molly that I will return to help with the inn. I will stay here for a few weeks. By then Garth and everyone else in Willow Springs will have forgotten all about it. If you go there now, I will never be able to return. Please do not add to my shame."

"There now, Cristalina. Of course Lars will not go. He's a fool who speaks nonsense in his anger. He won't go if I have to tie him to his chair myself." Signe scooted her rocking chair closer to Crissa and laid her hand on Crissa's shoulder. "Now, tell us about this man you are sweet on. Drake is his name?"

"Drake!" Crissa cheeks flushed in embarrassment.

"See there, Lars. Our Cristalina glows."

"No! I do not—"

Lars gave a hearty chuckle. "Our little Cristalina. Breaking hearts from Boston to Willow Springs. Now, gone from us for not even a month and again in love, leaving an entire town in an uproar!"

"Again?" Crissa bristled.

"Lars! You leave her alone now!"

Crissa's indignation quickly turned to meekness. "If this is love, it is certainly the first time I have felt this way."

"*Min* Cristalina, it is a delight to have you back." Through hugs and tears and laughter, their conversation lasted long into the night until Crissa felt safe, once again in the care of her second family.

CHAPTER 6

"*God morgon,* Cristalina." Signe turned from frying biscuits in bacon grease to greet her sleepy guest.

"*God morgon,*" Crissa replied through a muffled yawn. "Are you up early, or did I sleep late?"

"Oh, a little of each. If I do not get the family up early on Sunday, we are never ready for church on time."

"Sunday already? I cannot believe I have been here almost a week." Crissa paused to stretch once more. "What time is your church?"

"Nine o'clock. Would you like to come with us today? President Young is dedicating our new meetinghouse."

"A new meetinghouse? I thought all of the Mormons met at the Assembly Hall for your meetings."

"We did, but the Saints' numbers have grown so quickly, we have had to build a new meetinghouse. The Twentieth Ward will meet there. We had a barn raising—well, I guess it would be called a church raising—last Saturday. The brethren worked all day, and then we had a big picnic afterwards. The sisters have been working hard all week to get the inside finished in time for the meeting today." Signe lifted the biscuits out and cracked a dozen eggs into the pan, added milk, and began whipping them with a fork. "It should be a very nice meeting. Would you like to come hear the prophet?"

Crissa smiled at her friend's obvious devotion. "It will get pretty lonely here without all of you." Though not a member of Signe's church, Crissa appreciated Signe's efforts to include her.

Crissa dressed in a soft brown calico and plaited her golden hair into two braids, pinning them along her nape, back and forth, from ear to ear. The Bjorkson family was waiting in the buggy when she shyly emerged from the house.

"Crissa, you look lovely," Signe called out. Lars helped Crissa into the buggy.

"Not too lovely, I hope."

Lars squeezed her hand in response. "Some things you do not have control over."

Crissa wasn't yet ready for the hopeful gazes from the many eager young men she knew would notice a new face.

She settled in the back of the buggy with Aigner and Britta on either side and little David nestled on her lap. The crowded buggy rumbled through town as Signe and Lars waved greetings to the curious stares from passersby on the street.

"I wish people weren't so nosy," Signe grumbled.

"Oh, they just want to see our beautiful guest."

"The pasture wall certainly has grown," said Crissa, red-faced. The cement wall bordering the northern edges of the city delineated the pasture from neighboring homes. Brigham Young had sent new immigrants to work on the wall until they could find regular employment. "Are you still working on it, Lars?"

"No, I have been working on the Lindsey Gardens."

"Lindsey Gardens? Is that new?"

"Mr. and Mrs. Lindsey are building a public park. It has a picnic area, a playground for the children, even a private bathhouse. It's nearly finished."

"Father promised to take us there on *Mor*'s birthday," Britta said, then quickly resumed her best Sunday reverence.

"That will be wonderful fun." Crissa wrapped an arm around Britta's shoulders, gathering her close.

Lars turned the buggy in line with the rest of the buggies waiting to enter the churchyard. After inching forward for several minutes, he helped the ladies and children down so they could go inside and find a place to sit while he parked the rig. Normally, two different congregations would use the building each Sunday at different times of day, but today the congregations had been combined for the special dedicatory service.

President Young was a rousing orator, speaking on the early history of their church: the early members; their gathering in Nauvoo, Illinois, and later expulsion; the journey through treacherous lands with unpredictable weather. He spoke of the building up of this valley from barren desert to rapidly growing community and the challenges that lay ahead.

Crissa tried to focus on what was being said, but time and again her thoughts wandered to the events of the last year and a half. And, as always, her thoughts ended on the image of Drake kneeling over her bedside. She had known him for only a few days, yet she felt as though their lives could never be separate. *Does he miss me as I miss him? Or is Suzanna Hampton keeping him busy?* A tight lump formed in her throat as tears sprang to her eyes.

"Through it all, dear brothers and sisters, we must remember 'The meek shall inherit the earth.'"

The meek shall inherit the earth. Suzanna certainly is not meek, yet she seems to hold my whole world in her palm, Crissa thought. She bowed her head to hide the tears that she could not control.

On the train home, the sun overhead, the rhythmic sway of the buggy, and the gentle breeze soon had the children lulled to sleep. The mood was quiet and content as Lars, Signe, and Crissa looked out over the valley. The northeastern portion of the city, where the new meetinghouse was situated, rose on the elevated bench approaching the foothills. From their vantage point, the trio could view the entire valley from where it disappeared on the southern horizon, westward to the Great Salt Lake, Antelope Island, and the Oquirrh Mountains beyond. The sun turned the lake into shimmering silver satin flowing northward as far as the eye could see. Crissa let her thoughts meld with the scene before her and carry her to a feeling of serenity where no harm or hurt could exist.

★ ★ ★

The flower gardens that bordered the Bjorksons' front walk-way burst into a bright array of red snapdragon, pink petunias, and white alyssum as May turned to June. Crissa took on the responsi-bility of tending the family's kitchen garden out back, sewing the children's summer wardrobe, and telling wonderful stories as the family gathered in the parlor each night before bedtime. Indeed, Crissa quickly became as much a part of the Bjorkson family as the Bjorksons themselves.

While Crissa spent each day busily engaged in her new duties, her nights were long—and very lonely. Her thoughts of Willow Springs, of Drake, matured into dreams that robbed her of her sleep many, many nights. She yearned and dreaded to return. Was there any hope her relationship with Drake could continue to develop? Or was he planning a wedding with Suzanna Hampton even now? Would Garth have "simmered off" as Molly had suggested, or would he be waiting to take his revenge? She could not talk to Signe or Lars about her concerns, for they would certainly urge her to stay in Salt Lake, while the key to her happiness remained in Willow Springs—with Drake Adams.

The evening of June 18, 1861, Crissa sat in a rocking chair out on the porch, sewing a pair of britches for David. Turning three next week, he was old enough to throw off the restrictive dresses of toddlerhood and don the drawstring britches of a growing boy. The family had spent that morning and early afternoon at the newly completed Lindsey Gardens, celebrating Signe's birthday as prom-ised. Now, in the peaceful twilight, Crissa sat, rocking gently, loving thoughts woven with each stitch. Lars and Aigner perched in a tree, picking apricots, Signe and Britta sat on the steps pitting the fruit, and an angelic David slept, curled up on a rug at Crissa's feet.

"Mother," Lars called out from somewhere in the tree, "looks as if we may have company coming."

"Company? Tonight?" She stood up, smoothing the wrinkles from her skirt and apron. "Who would be visiting at this hour?"

"I believe it is Charlie Callahan," Lars replied, swinging down from the tree.

"Charlie!" Crissa was instantly off the porch and halfway down the sidewalk, the forgotten britches tumbled in a heap on top of David. "Charlie!"

Charlie urged his horse to a trot when he saw the family out front to greet him. "Whoa, Betsy." He slid off the horse, draping her reins around a tree branch. "Well! This be as fine a reception as I ever have seen. How are ye this evening, folks?"

"We are just fine, Mr. Callahan," Signe said as she took his arm and led him to the porch. "We spent a lovely day at the new Lindsey Gardens. How is Mrs. Callahan?"

"Feelin' a bit greener than she'd like, I'm afraid. Likes to tell folks married life makes her sick."

"Well, give her our best wishes, and tell her she will feel better as soon as her pregnancy begins to show."

"What brings you all the way to Swede-town, Charlie?"

"Well, Lars, I was in town today, passing by the Pony Express Office when Flyin' Saddle Adams came in."

Crissa's ears perked up when she heard the last name. "Flying Saddle?"

"Drake Adams, in fact, ma'am. Folks call him 'Flyin' Saddle' on account o' that fancy saddle he designed for the Express riders. If ye ever saw him whip that saddle off'a one horse and on t'other, you'd be callin' him Flyin' Saddle, as well."

Lars and Signe stared at Crissa who, in turn, stared at Charlie. Three astounded jaws hung limp, speechless.

"Said he was hangin' up his saddle to start up a ranch out in Willow Springs. Can't figure why anyone would want to settle in those godforsaken parts." Charlie looked from face to face, not comprehending the shock registered there. "He brought in a letter for you, Mrs. Bjorkson, so I told the stationmaster I'd bring it by."

"Why, thank you, Charlie." Signe took the letter with a Springville return address, but the name—James Smith—she did not recognize. "I wonder who this could be from?"

"Well, it'll be long dark by the time I get home. I best be on my way."

"May we offer you some refreshment before you go?"

"Thank you, ma'am, but my Maggie'll be wonderin' what came of me if I don't get started."

"Thank you again!" Signe lifted the envelope in the air.

Charlie mounted his horse and waved a final good-bye. He steered around two boys balancing on empty nail kegs as they rolled down the street.

Crissa watched Charlie ride away, too shocked to speak. *Drake Adams is here! In Salt Lake City!*

"There is a letter in here for you, Cristalina. It must be from your parents."

"My parents? They must have used a false name so no one would recognize mine." She read the letter silently.

"A gentleman by the name of Donald Jenkins came to the house yesterday asking about you. He told us that Eric had hired him to find you and the baby, and beg you to come home. Your father told him that you had died in childbirth on the journey across Kansas and that your child also had perished. Mr. Jenkins left his calling card, which I am sending with this letter, in case you wish to contact him. We wish only for your happiness. We pray always that everything is well with you in Willow Springs, and that you are safe. Ever your loving, *Mor*."

She shared the good news with her friends. Lars rubbed his hand along the side of his jaw, his eyebrows raised thoughtfully. "It seems as though your troubles may be over."

"But the law is still looking for her."

"If this Donald Jenkins thinks Crissa is dead, he will tell the marshal, and the search for her will be over."

Crissa looked from Lars to Signe and back to Lars again. "Over? You mean I will be free to live as I please?"

"Exactly."

"I will no longer have to hide?" If this indeed was true, Crissa could return to her parents' house in Springville. *They will no longer be ashamed of me—or afraid to have me in their home.*

"I think it's time to celebrate your freedom," Lars said, interrupting her thoughts. "I'm going into town tomorrow. Would you like to come with me?"

"Oh, I would love to! I have been longing to roam through the shops."

"That is a wonderful idea!" Signe clasped her hands together. "Perhaps you will see your Mr. Adams!"

"Drake? Oh, I do not think so. He will either ride on to Fort Bridger or return to Willow Springs. But I will have a glorious time shopping, or simply strolling along the street with Lars."

For the first time since she left Boston, Crissa slept peacefully through the night, her dreams filled with happiness and hope for the future.

★ ★ ★

The plate glass windows of the shops on Main Street reflected the radiance of the summer day yet could never compete with the brilliance of the young woman standing inside, drinking in civilization.

She clutched her doeskin pouch of money tightly. Though she had led Molly to believe she was sending money home to her parents, Crissa had saved some of her meager salary for just such an occasion. Now she wandered from store to store, mesmerized by the selection.

She chose yards of white dotted swiss for a pinafore for Britta and then bought a little extra fabric to take back to Willow Springs for Amy. She bought toy rifles made of pine for Aigner and David, a clay roasting pan for Signe, and a bolo tie with a ship etched on the silver slide for Lars. She thought of her friends in Willow Springs and bought gifts for them as well. For Will, she bought a polished wood whistle. For Molly, a beautiful gray-and-rose silk shawl made with genuine St. George silk to wear with her "second" mourning dress. And a blue Wedgewood pitcher that she would save for Vic and Marida's wedding gift. She even bought several tins of sardines and herring, delicacies she had missed since leaving Boston.

As she passed the menswear counter in Kimball's, her eyes lingered on a sterling silver mustache comb.

"A perfect gift for your husband," the man behind the counter offered.

"Oh," Crissa stammered, unaware the man had approached her. "I am not married."

"Your young man would certainly appreciate it, then."

"I am afraid not. Thank you." Crissa rushed away. It would never do to give Drake such a personal gift. Besides, she could not consider him her "young man." He had certainly never stated his intentions. She clutched her bundle of packages and rushed to find Lars.

She pushed the heavy glass door open with her shoulder, and then peered over the top of her load to determine which direction to head toward the feed store. She set her bundles on the bench and shielded her eyes against the noonday sun to look in the other direction.

"Crissa?"

The familiar baritone voice sent a shiver down her spine. She whirled to face him. "Drake!" She found herself swept into his embrace, her arms circled about his neck, and her feet lifted off the ground before logic or propriety could prevail.

At last he released his grip and returned her to earth. His eyes roamed her face as though unable to believe it was she. "It's so good to see you. How are you? I thought you were staying in Springville—"

Crissa's laughter interrupted his rambling. "It is nice to see you also. And I am fine, thank you. Now, tell me, how is everyone in Willow Springs?"

"Everyone's just fine. They miss you terribly, though. Widow Henderson says her dinner business has dropped to half since you've been gone. Amy adopted one of the kittens as the official Henders Inn mouser."

"And what about Vic and Marida?"

It was Drake's turn to chuckle. "Marida has planned every last detail of the wedding, but she won't set a date until you come back. Vic's just about fit to be tied."

"Well, you may tell them that I will be home soon. Then the wedding can go on."

"That'll make several people very happy. We've missed you." His finger followed the path of a stray tendril from her temple to her chin. "I've missed you. But what are you doing here in Salt Lake?"

Crissa opened her mouth to speak, then closed it. Her gaze drifted to the hollow of his throat, which was just showing beneath his unbuttoned collar. "I am here visiting friends." Her eyes returned to his.

Drake briefly glanced up and down the street, then in the store entrance behind her before taking Crissa's hands in his. "It's sure nice seeing you again. Are you okay?"

The pain and embarrassment of her encounter with Garth in Willow Springs washed over her, followed by memories of waking to find Drake hovering over her bedside. "I am fine." His eyes were so soft—so full of concern. "Really. I am fine."

He looked off in the distance—not speaking—but squeezed her hands gently. At last he turned back to her, changing the subject. "Did your parents come with you?"

Her mind reeled, reviewing bits and pieces of the story she had told her friends in Willow Springs.

"No, they are in Springville."

"I'd like to meet them sometime."

Crissa shifted her gaze, knowing that would never happen yet not wanting to say it outright. "What are you doing in Salt Lake, Drake?"

"I quit the Express."

"Quit?"

"I got anxious to get more work done on the ranch, so I quit the Express. You should see the house!" His face shone with enthusiasm. "The foundation's finished, and I'm getting ready to start on the walls. It'll be ready to move in by fall, I hope. I just bought me a wagon and two horses. I'll load up with building and housekeeping supplies before I head back. Gosh, listen to me. I sound like a schoolboy, going on like that." Drake took a step backward and rested his hands on Crissa's shoulders, holding her at arm's length. "I've really missed you." He paused long enough to study her face and hair. "Come back with me now, Crissa."

"Drake!"

"There you are, Cristalina!" Lars strolled up behind the laughing pair, a little surprised at the sight.

"Lars! I would like you to meet Mr. Drake Adams from Willow Springs. Drake, this is Lars Bjorkson. It is his family I am visiting."

"You must be the famous Pony Express rider," Lars said, extending his hand.

"Retired Express rider," Drake corrected. "And hardly famous."

"Famous in this town, Mr. Adams. It is a pleasure to meet you."

"The pleasure is mine. Do you live near here?"

"North of here, in Swede-town. Crissa, it is time to go home. Drake, you would honor us if you would come to dinner tonight."

"I'm afraid I have some business to attend to here, and then I head back for Willow Springs in the morning. Miss Engleson, I hope it will not be long before I see you again." He lifted her hand to his lips, bowing stiffly.

Crissa could not stifle her smile. "Good-bye, Mr. Adams."

★ ★ ★

When Lars and Crissa had gathered her bundles and turned the corner to their waiting buggy, a man in a gray worsted suit stepped from the shadows from across the street. He intercepted Drake and guided him in the opposite direction.

★ ★ ★

It was the end of June, and Crissa sat on the front porch, snapping beans and watching the neighborhood children at play. The little girls of the area sat on the porch steps playing dress-up in fancy hats and aprons. Each girl busily sewed a cloth square on which Crissa had outlined a design. This was the day's sewing lesson. The boys, equipped with wooden guns and stick horses, were playing various versions of Pony Express riders and stagecoach robbers.

Crissa looked up from the basket of beans to find a man watching her from across the street. He was dressed in a gray worsted suit—unusual for this part of town, and very unusual for this warm weather. A twinge of panic made Crissa's skin prickle. Bobby Helstrom raced past and shot the stranger with his wooden gun.

"Bang! You're dead, you bandit!" Bobby yelled before racing back to the rest of the boys.

The startled man clamped his lips in a thin line and took a step toward the boys. In the instant his attention was diverted, Crissa darted into the house, unsure exactly why she should be alarmed. She watched him from behind the safety of the lace panels at the window as he turned his attention back to the Bjorksons' porch. His face pinched in a scowl as he muttered something. Then he strode off the way he had come.

★ ★ ★

Crissa spent a restless night pacing the floor and staring from her window into the inky blackness. It must have been well past midnight when a quiet rapping sounded at her door.

"Who is it?" Crissa whispered, half afraid of the answer she might receive.

"It is Signe. May I come in?"

Crissa opened the squeaky door as quietly as she could, admitting her friend.

"I heard the floor boards creaking. Are you all right?"

"I am fine. I am just having trouble getting to sleep."

"Are you worried about that man you saw?"

"No, not much. I just have an uneasiness. Here, in my chest."

"I have a special tea that will help you sleep. The midwife, Marinda Bateman, gave it to me after David was born. I will bring it for you."

Crissa smiled as Signe rustled out of the room and down the narrow hallway. She remembered the first time she had come here; the woman next door was going through a difficult labor, and no doctor could come. Mrs. Bateman had rushed from her home in the south end of the valley to offer what help she could. After much sweat and many prayers, mother and son were delivered safely.

Signe returned with the steaming tea and sat with Crissa while she sipped it.

"This is delicious. What is in it?"

"It is a mixture of chamomile, spearmint, lemon grass, hawthorn berries, and a secret ingredient Mrs. Bateman would not tell me."

"Is it the same tea Mrs. Bateman gave your neighbor when she was having the baby?"

"You mean when she had the fluttering heartbeat? That was foxglove tea. A little bit can cure the heart flutters, but too much can make your heart stop and—" Signe held her hand up and snapped her fingers.

"Goodness! How ever did Mrs. Bateman learn so much about medicine?"

"I suppose she studied about herbs while she was training as a midwife in New York. Well, you should sleep deeply now, my Cristalina. So to bed with you while you are still able."

"Thank you, Signe. I am sure to have sweet dreams now. *God natt.*"

★ ★ ★

Crissa tossed and turned violently while she slept. Images of wild horses with flaming nostrils charged at her. Huge fists flew through the air to pummel her. Men with grotesque faces and shiny star badges chased her as she ran in slow motion. Her father beckoned her from the distance only to raise his whip to her when she at last reached him. Her mother's sad face hovered over all this misery but turned away when Crissa sought her help. And Molly sailed forth, out of the mists, with her arms extended in a welcoming embrace. As Crissa neared her comfort, Molly's body vanished, leaving her gray mourning dress lying in a crumpled heap at Crissa's feet. Will and Amy rushed at her out of the darkness.

With clawing fingers outstretched, they wailed, "Don't leave us! Please don't leave us! Crissa, where are you? What happened to my mama? Please don't leave us here!"

And there, watching over Crissa's horror, stood the man in the gray worsted suit.

A scream pierced through the Bjorkson home as Crissa awoke from her nightmare. Her skin was like ice, her sheets drenched with sweat, her body shaking in spasms. Crissa covered her face with her trembling fingers while terror swept through her body in renewed waves.

"Crissa! What happened?" Signe in her nightdress and Lars, fumbling to fasten his trousers, appeared in her doorway. "Cristalina, are you all right?"

Crissa stared at them with vacant, horrified eyes before shooting out of bed to stand in the middle of the floor. "Molly! Something has happened to Molly! I must leave here. I must get to Molly!"

"Cristalina, *älskling*, your friend is fine. It was only a bad dream."

"No, Signe, it was more than that. It was a warning. A *tecken*. I must get back to Willow Springs immediately."

"Crissa," Lars said, stepping into the room, "it is the middle of the night. Rest for now, and we will discuss it in the morning."

"I cannot wait. I must leave now."

"There are no stages running at this hour. You can do nothing right now, so try to rest. We will help any way you wish, but you must wait until morning."

Crissa gritted her teeth, biting back hurtful words her friends did not deserve. "Of course. You are right." Her voice was unnaturally calm. "I will wait until morning. Thank you for your kindness. I will try to rest for a while." She smiled reassuringly at Lars and Signe, and guided them from the room.

As soon as her bedroom door was closed and the Bjorksons' footsteps had faded down the hallway, Crissa pulled her satchel from under the bed and began packing for the trip home.

★ ★ ★

Crissa had her satchel packed and was pacing the kitchen floor, a letter clutched in her hand, as Signe and Lars shuffled from their room at the first light of dawn. Crissa had laid eggs, bacon, biscuits, and coffee on the table before offering so much as a "*God morgon.*"

"All ready to go, I see," Lars said while stifling a yawn with the back of his hand.

"Lars, will you please post this letter by Pony Express as soon as you take me to the station?"

"Cristalina, please," Signe pleaded, "do not leave in such a hurry.

Send the letter to Widow Henderson, then wait for her reply. It will take you two days to get to Willow Springs by stage. You could have her reply in not much longer. And why do you go? Because of some silly nightmare?"

Crissa glared at the woman. "This was no silly nightmare. Molly is in danger, and I must help her. I will not waste time by waiting for letters she may not be able to send." She turned to a helpless Lars. "Now, will you take me to the station in your buggy, or must I walk?"

"Of course I will take you, but the stage does not leave until eight o'clock. It is barely six now."

"It does not matter how early I am. I must not miss that stage."

Crissa tiptoed into the sleeping children's room and kissed them each good-bye. Her throat tightened. Seeing them asleep like that, she wondered if she would ever see them again.

★ ★ ★

Crissa watched the stagehand load her satchel in the keep of the stage. She pressed the letter into Lars's hand. "Now, do not forget to post this with the Pony Express as soon as you leave me. If Molly is all right, she will want to know I am coming."

"Signe and I will pray that everything is well in Willow Springs. If you have trouble, however, remember that you are always welcome here. And," Lars continued, his voice growing gruff, "we will always love you."

Crissa tried to smile, tears filling her eyes. She hugged him tightly, then mounted the stage for the long journey home—to Willow Springs.

CHAPTER 7

The midday sun hung above the livery, scorching the earth below with its late June intensity. Stepping from the stage platform, Crissa adjusted her bonnet. She looked toward Henders Inn, hoping to see a friendly face or at least a helping hand. Where was everyone? Had her letter arrived? Even with the stage being late, surely Will or Amy would be watching for her. She remembered the dream that brought her rushing back. Panic knotted her chest as she lugged her satchel toward the inn. What has happened? Oblivious to the few women and shopkeepers milling about on the street, Crissa stumbled forward, hampered by the clumsy bag.

She struggled to breathe through the vise of worry that gripped her lungs. The heavy front doors of the inn stood closed, and there were no signs of customers about. *Molly should have opened the dining room hours ago—unless . . .* Crissa slid her satchel across the porch and timidly tried the door. Unlocked, the door swung open to the familiar dining room. *Everything is fine*, she scolded herself. *Do not be such a goose.*

"Molly! Marida!" She stood next to the bar, braced to receive her friends' charge from the kitchen. "Hello? Molly? Marida?" She stepped to the foot of the stairs and called up to them. The knot of panic tightened, and her hands instinctively began to tremble. "Marida?" Crissa's voice was faint as she gingerly pushed open the kitchen doors. "Molly?" Not a soul was in sight. She stepped into

the room, scarcely able to breathe. A noise out on the back porch—
Will and Amy.

She flung open the screen door. "Children!" she cried, tears of relief streaking her dusty cheeks. "I thought no one was here!"

"Crissa!" Will and Amy threw themselves at her so hard she sat down on the step with a thump. "Where've you been?"

"Where have I been?" She pushed Will's hair out of his eyes. "I do not understand."

"Your letter said you was coming last night!"

"We waited an' waited, and you didn't come."

Crissa drew Amy onto her lap. "Oh, dear. The stage had a problem with one of the wheels, so we stayed over at Simpson Springs to get it mended. I am sorry you had to wait so long, but I am here now!" She paused to give each a tight hug. "Where is your mother? And Marida?"

"Mama stayed up later'n we did waiting for you, so she's sleepin' in. Marida says Mama must be awful tired, so's we can't wake her up. After breakfast, Marida went down to Miz Falcone's to get her wedding dress sewed on some more."

"Oh, Crissa." Amy jumped up and down with excitement. "Marida says now that you're back, we're gonna have us a wedding right quick!"

"A wedding! I guess I had better get unpacked ,then, so I can help out around here." Crissa gave Amy a squeeze and turned to leave.

"When you get done," Amy pleaded, "will you fix us something to eat? I'm awful hungry, and all Will knows how to fix is potatoes."

Crissa grimaced at the sight of the dirty, raw potato that Will had been slicing with a pocket knife. "Of course, *min älskling.* I will be right back."

With one hand clutching the banister, Crissa lugged her satchel up the stairs, pausing at the landing to tap at Molly's door. "Molly, it is Crissa. Are you awake?"

No answer.

Well, Crissa thought, *I will just put my things away and then surprise her with a nice lunch.*

Crissa retrieved her room key from a pocket inside her satchel. The door swung open at her touch. Why is my door unlocked? She stepped through the opening and then breathed a sigh of relief.

"Molly?"

Crissa stepped toward Molly, who was lying on Crissa's bed, her back to the door. Crissa looked at the white curtains fluttering at the open window, to the plate of cookie crumbs and the vase of roses, foxglove, and daisies on her nightstand, and back to Molly.

"Molly?" That knot of panic was back. Her face felt numb and tingly as she inched her way forward. "Molly?" she whispered, her eyes locked on the unmoving form.

"Molly?" Gently she touched Molly's shoulder. Ice cold. Shock and fear engulfed her. She shook the stiff shoulder wildly until Molly's body rolled over, eyes fixed on another world.

"Crissa?" Too late she heard the little feet running up the stairs. Too late she darted to block the door. Too late to save the little girl from viewing her mother's cold, gray face. "Mama!" Amy screamed in terror, raced past Crissa, and flung herself at Molly.

"Mama!"

"Amy," Crissa pleaded, "please let go." Gently, she lifted the stunned child, cradling Amy's head on her shoulder.

Crissa closed the door behind her as she carried Amy from the room. Footsteps pounded up the stairs behind her. "Will, quickly, go get the doctor."

"Why? Who needs—Amy! What's a matter with Amy?"

"Just go get the doctor. And bring the sheriff also."

Will's eyes widened at the tone in her voice. The color drained from his face.

"Yes'm." He wheeled on one foot and leaped down the stairs, yelling as he reached the boardwalk, "Doc! Sheriff! Come quick! Doc!"

Crissa sagged against the top step, heedless of any thought other than trying to comfort the stricken child cradled in her arms.

★ ★ ★

"Are you calling it foul play?" Sheriff Hawkes paced the floor, absently stroking the cheroot he held in his fingers but never lit.

"Not at all," Doc Robbins corrected. He sat forward in his chair, leaning on the table, scratching his thick, graying beard. "I'm just saying I never would have pegged Widow Henderson as one with heart problems.

"You are sure it was her heart?" Crissa stood poised between two dining chairs, watching these two men debate Molly's death as though death were a common occurrence in this town. She was not far wrong, what with mining and ranching accidents and the odd drifter shooting his way through a hangover. She glanced from the debaters to the kitchen to the stairs, half expecting to see Molly come ambling in to oversee the noonday meal—just as she always did.

"Well, Miss Engleson, I can't figure what else it could be. There weren't any marks on her body to indicate other injuries."

"What about the whites of her eyes being all yella like that?" The sheriff strode to the table.

Doc Robbins stopped scratching his beard and cupped his jaw in his outstretched hand. "Yeah, there was that, and she was covered in hives, but that don't tell me much. Could be a reaction to medication, but she weren't taking no medication. Unless someone wants to tell me otherwise, I say it was her heart. The flutters, most likely." He looked from the sheriff to Crissa and then placed his pen to an official-looking document. "I'll need each of you to sign as witnesses."

Crissa took the pen and signed Cristalina Karolina Engleson. She wondered briefly if she should sign the rest of her name, but the sheriff took the pen from her and carefully printed his name.

"Doctor Robbins, was . . . was there any time to . . . could I have helped her if I had been here?"

He shrugged his shoulders lightly. "It's hard to say, ma'am. There are folks from the old countries that claim you can steady the heartbeat with foxglove tea, but I don't know nothing about that kind of medicine. For all I know, that kind of treatment could do more harm than good." He stood up and placed his hand on her shoulder. "You were a good friend, Crissa, but I'm afraid there weren't anything any of us could have done. Take care of her babies. That's what's important now."

"What will happen to the children?"

"I'll contact the authorities in Salt Lake," the sheriff offered. "I've got to be going up there in a couple of days. They'll be able to locate any next of kin."

Crissa nodded her head meekly. "Thank you, sheriff. And Dr. Robbins. I appreciate your kindness."

Crissa sat with Will and Amy on the soft patch of grass under the cottonwood by the stream. It was here the *kära barn* had searched for gold, finding new kittens instead. It was here Crissa brought the children to shelter them from the deluge of neighbors and curiosity seekers. It was here she prayed for the strength to deal with the arrangements of a funeral. And it was here, in this refuge, she tried to explain that which she herself had not yet learned to accept.

"Your mother has gone away for awhile, *min älsklings*."

"Where'd she go?"

"She's gone to heaven to live with God."

"Doc Robbins said she had hard tack."

"A heart attack, Will. That means the heart stops beating the way it is supposed to."

"My papa lives with God."

"Yes, Amy, he does. And now your mama will live with God too."

"Well then, me and Will are gonna live there too." Amy's voice was matter-of-fact. No fear. No questions. Crissa and Will watched her weave blades of grass.

★ ★ ★

"I did not know what else to say to Amy, Marida." Crissa ran her finger along the cool rim of her glass of ice tea as she recounted the day's events.

"'Course not. Enough tears will fall in days, years to come. No need look for words make them fall today."

The sun hovered lazily on the western horizon, making the air dry and stale.

"Does Molly have any family we should contact?"

"Haven't heard her talk of any," Marida answered. "I hope sheriff find them."

Crissa stood up and carried her glass to the washbasin. "We should plan a nice funeral."

"I never plan funeral before. I don'a know where to start."

"My pa is buried above Dutchman's Pass." Will was standing unobserved on the porch. "Mama would want to rest near him."

Crissa and Marida exchanged glances.

"Garth Wight was by a while ago," Will added, "and I asked him to start digging the grave."

"Garth was here?"

"I didn't figure you'd be wanting to talk to him," Will said, "so I took care of things. I talked to the bishop when he was here 'bout the funeral. The 'Lief Society will be by to dress Mama in the morning. Now, I guess it would be fitting for Mama to be buried in her gray dress, but I'd like her to be wearing her white lace collar. She covered a little Bible with lace, and I think she'd want to take that with her."

"Will," Crissa interjected, "why are the Relief Society ladies from your church dressing your mother? Wouldn't you rather Marida and I took care of that?"

"That's just what they always do. They like to help out. 'Sides, Amy'll probably need your help getting ready tomorrow." Will sat down at the table and continued, his voice steady, as if he were conducting a meeting of church elders. "Amy can wear the blue dress she got for Christmas, and I'll wear my Sunday go-to-meetin' clothes. I have a string-tie, if one of you could tie it for me. I should get my hair cut to look 'spectable."

A frown of concern creased Crissa's brow. "Will, where is Amy?"

"I put her to bed. I figured tomorrow'll be so busy, she'd best get some extra rest tonight."

Crissa and Marida looked at each other over Will's head. He was so calm and efficient. Not at all like an eight-year-old boy dealing with the death of his mother.

"That was a fine meal the 'Lief Society brung in tonight."

"Yes, it was," the two women chorused.

"I suppose they'll be bringing in food tomorrow after the funeral. And dinner too."

A few moments passed as the three sat in silence.

"Told Bishop Belnap ten o'clock would be just fine for the services."

Another few silent moments lapsed.

"Guess I'll turn in early myself." Will stood up to leave.

Crissa and Marida stood up with him.

"Will?" Crissa took a steadying breath. "Are you all right?"

He placed a hand on the door frame and looked over his shoulder at her. "I'm fine. I just needed to be—doing something." The door swung closed behind him.

Crissa remembered the sampler hanging over her bed.

Vart jag mig i världen vänder
Står min lycka i Guds händer
Wherever in the world I might wander,
My fate rests in God's hands.

She had stitched the sampler before she left Sweden. It was supposed to bring her comfort. It was those two sweet children who would need comfort now. Mere babies who had first lost their father and now their mother. "*Dyr Gud,*" she whispered, "watch over Will and Amy."

★ ★ ★

"Our Father who art in heaven, hallowed be thy name. Thy kingdom come. Thy will be done . . ."

Crissa looked around her at the cluster of townsfolk gathered on the hilltop. Most of the town of Willow Springs had come to Molly's funeral. Grief filled the hot, heavy air. *Molly Henderson had befriended some of the most lonely people in the territory of Deseret,* Crissa mused. Gold miners and ranchers—dreamers who were often forgotten by their own kin—were always welcome at Henders Inn.

Crissa peered through the crowd, at last spotting Drake. He was watching her, and for an instant she wanted to run to him.

She moved her gaze among the other bystanders. Standing next to Drake, dressed in form-fitting black, was Suzanna Hampton.

Crissa clamped her jaw tightly. *She cannot even keep a respectable distance between them at a funeral.* Crissa looked again at Drake, who was standing stiffly, and then turned her head in the opposite direction. Apart from the rest of the mourners, beside a straggly willow, Garth Wight stood turning his hat uncomfortably in his hands. His eyes caught hers for an instant before dropping his glance. Suzanna's mother, Rachel, stood a short distance from Garth, her face covered by a black veil despite the suffocating heat. Her chin jerked up sharply when Crissa looked her way.

"Give us this day our daily bread, and forgive us our debts . . ."

Molly epitomized charity and Christianity, Crissa reflected. *She took me into her home when the world would have me stoned. She knew nothing of my ways or past. To her it did not matter.*

"For thine is the kingdom, and the power, and the glory, forever. Amen."

Crissa added her own silent prayer for Molly: *Please, Lord, bless her in thy kingdom.* Molly was dragged out here as a young bride to run an inn that was struggling to survive. She prayed for years to have babies to bring joy to her harsh life. Then, when she finally knew joy, Indians killed Hank. Surely, after the hardships she had endured in this godforsaken place, Molly Henderson deserved to meet with glory now.

"Lord, we consecrate this piece of thy earth as the final resting place of Naomi Molly Jennings Henderson. We pray that it may be a hallowed ground, protected from the ravages of nature and man until such time as Molly may rise again, to walk among us on the day of resurrection . . ."

Gently, Crissa laid a small spray of wild roses on Molly's casket. The only flowers Molly could coax out of this barren land would go with her to the grave. Bishop Belnap, Doc Robbins, and four other men stepped forward to take up the ropes cradling the casket, push away the wooden skids, and lower the wooden box in the ground.

From the stillness of the group came a tiny voice. "Is my mama gonna stay in that box?"

"Hush now, baby. She will be fine."

"And reach out thy loving hand, dear Lord, to comfort the family and friends assembled here. Let us be assured that thy will has been done. Let us dedicate our memories of this fine woman to thee. In the name of our Lord, Jesus Christ, amen."

Will accepted condolences with dry eyes and a firm handshake. Bishop Belnap put an arm around his shoulder. "Son, you're the head of your family now. Be strong for Amy."

Crissa stood cold and numb as she watched the line of townsfolk file past the lowered casket, dropping flowers in reverence.

"Have you considered your plans yet?" Mr. Potter held her hand in a damp grip. "I expect the inn will shut down."

Crissa looked at him, for the first time aware of how Molly's death would affect her future.

"You know, we will hate to see you go," Mrs. Potter joined in. "We never got a chance to welcome you proper."

Go? The inevitability stunned Crissa. *Where will I go?* "I have not had time to consider my plans." She looked toward the children and felt the impact of her grief at last.

One by one, the mourners returned to town—to their own businesses—to their own lives. Only a small cluster remained on the hillside, reluctant to leave Molly, unsure of how life would continue once they did.

"Let's take Will and Amy home, Crissa." Marida steered Crissa away from the group. "The Relief Society fixed up lunch."

"I am sure we could all use some rest. I will bring the children."

Amy sat at the edge of her mother's grave, her feet dangling over the side, dropping petals on the casket below. Her voice a faint whisper: "Jesus loves me, this I know. For the Bible tells me so."

Crissa sat down beside Amy, carefully tucking her feet under her skirt. "What are you singing, *min kära?*"

"Just a song mama sings to me when I go to sleep."

"I would like to learn your song. Then perhaps I can sing it to you."

Amy looked at Crissa for a long moment. "Are you gonna take care of me and Will while Mama's gone?"

"Of course I will, sweetheart. The sheriff knows people in Salt Lake who can help us find some of your family."

"But I want to stay with you." Amy looked at Crissa, round blue eyes brimming with tears. "You want me to stay with you, don't you? You an' Marida can take care of us."

"Marida's gettin' married." Will stood there, feet planted firmly, arms folded tightly across his chest, glowering down at Crissa. "She's gonna move into her own place." His voice steadily began increasing in pitch. "And you! You'll go running off on us again! Just like you did last time. My mama said you'd worry her right to her grave, and that's what you did! Right to her grave!"

Crissa stood up and reached out to him.

"Well, I'm not gonna let you do it again, that's what!" He started hitting her. "You can just get out now! We don't need ya!"

A strong arm wrapped around Will's waist, pulling him away from Crissa.

"It's all right now, Will."

Will clung to Drake's warm embrace, and finally the tears came. "I don't need her, I tell ya. I don't need no one."

CHAPTER 8

Crissa sat at one of the polished wood tables in the dining room of Henders Inn. Writing paper and envelopes, pen and ink, and a tall glass of icy lemonade were arranged neatly in front of her. Her chores were done, breakfast guests were satisfied, and Amy had coaxed Will into searching for gold again in the dry creek bed. Crissa relished the solitude and the inn's shady refuge from the relentless July heat.

> *Thursday, July 6, 1861.*
> *Dear Lars and Signe,*
>   *How busy I have been since my last letter. Running an inn and taking care of two children is much more work than I had thought it would be. Will is having such a struggle since his mother's death. He has the idea he must be the man of the family now and be in charge of everything that happens around here. He insists on sitting at the desk with me when guests arrive. He checks my shopping list, checks what food I plan to cook, and checks on my housekeeping of the inn. I feel he still blames me for Molly's death. He has taken charge of Amy, bossing her more than her mother ever did, and even tucking her into bed at night. I am afraid I have begun to feel like an unwelcome stranger here. I used to think Will had taken a bit of a fancy to me, but now I think he will be glad to see me go.*

I wait each day to receive some word from Salt Lake about relatives who might be willing to assume responsibility for Molly's children. Despite Will's gloom and suspicion, I love him and Amy deeply. Amy clings to me whenever she can escape from Will. It breaks my heart to think about leaving them. For now I must not think of it. The children need to see happiness.

Willow Springs was full of fun for the July 4th holiday. The Relief Society ladies from the church cooked a big breakfast of hotcakes, eggs, and sausage, to begin with. Then there was a nice parade that traveled from the livery to Potter's store and back up the other side of the street. Just about everyone in town was trotting their horses, playing musical instruments, or marching along with the others. Even the children dressed up their dolls and stuffed toys to ride in wagons.

Will and Amy looked so sad, watching the other children make preparations, but Will said it would not be proper for him and Amy to join in so soon after their mother's death. I suppose he was right, but I helped Amy dress her doll in black ribbons anyway. When Will saw what we were doing, he gave us plenty of talk about it but then could not resist the black netting I had found to drape on his little wagon. He said it was fitting that there should be a mourning float. They looked so sweet parading down the street, trying to be somber but not escaping an occasional giggle.

After the parade, we loaded wagons with more food and traveled to the Deep Creek mountains for a picnic. You would not believe there could be such a beautiful forest here in the middle of the desert. Of course, it is nothing to compare to Uppsala, nor could it compare to the woods in the eastern states, but a very nice place to escape the heat nonetheless. After Bishop Belnap gave a long speech, we had contests and games of every variety.

I brought a herring salad, though I admit it was not easy to part with two tins of my precious herring. I used elk instead of beef for my beef lindstrom, and I made an extra large batch of my mother's soft gingerbread. It was wonderful to once again cook the foods I have longed for.

In the evening, there was a dance at the church house. I have too many painful memories of the last dance I attended there to want to go again. I have thankfully not seen Garth Wight since Molly's funeral. The liveryman told Marida that Garth had taken a team and wagon up to the Adams's mine. But still, I cannot bring myself to go to another dance just yet. I watched Drake arrive at the dance with Suzanna Hampton and her mother. I believe I mentioned Suzanna when I visited you. I know I have no arrangement with Drake, but it still "raises my dander" (as Molly would have said) when I see him with that woman.

Drake and I are becoming very good friends. He has been to the inn nearly every day since the funeral to help out. It is bittersweet for me to have him so near. He speaks constantly about the house he is building, asking my advice. I dream about someday living there, yet he has never given me any indication that this may be. Perhaps I am becoming a foolish old maid. He spends the better part of each day working on the house. He finished setting the rocks and mortar into the foundation a few days ago and already has walls put up as high as my waist. He invited me to ride out and see his progress today, but I made it clear I would not sit in the same buggy Suzanna Hampton had been sitting in just two days before. Perhaps I am being petty?

Drake has been asking me questions about my life before I came to Willow Springs. I wonder just how much I can tell him. I have told him that I traveled with a group of Mormon Saints from Boston, but I feel he is trying to find out more. It would be nice to no longer have anything to hide, but I am still afraid of Eric finding out I am alive. I grow weary of this deception.

Marida and Vic were married on Sunday. Marida spent so much time planning for a beautiful wedding, but when Molly died, a large wedding no longer seemed appropriate. Instead, Vic, Marida, Will, Amy, Drake, and I traveled to Ely to a Justice of the Peace. Marida still wore her white satin dress, but she wove a little black ribbon through her neckline and cuffs to show respect. I gathered some black ribbon into a rosebud, which Marida tucked into her bouquet. Afterwards, the new Mr. and Mrs. Danello continued westward to California to visit their families, and the rest of us returned to Willow Springs.

Crissa put down her pen on the blotter. She picked up her glass of lemonade and walked to the door. The stage from Simpson Springs was just pulling into the station. The street-side door opened, and a lone man stepped out. Crissa's breath caught in her throat, and her hand trembled until lemonade splashed over the rim of the glass. The man wore a gray worsted suit. Crissa watched as he conversed with the stationmaster, looking this way and that as various directions were pointed out to him. She ducked out of sight as the stationmaster nodded toward the inn, and the man turned in her direction. She scurried back to the table, whisked her writing materials behind the bar, and rushed to the kitchen.

It is just coincidence that he is here, she told herself. This is a stage-stop town, and he is just passing through. When the stage pulls out, he will surely be on it. She stood beside the door, hidden from view, gathering her nerve to venture out.

Cautiously, she stepped into the dining room, peering into the corner shadows, then peeked over the top of the swinging doors. He was gone. She placed a hand on her pounding chest and drew a long, slow breath. At the sound of an approaching horse, Crissa stepped onto the boardwalk, hoping it was Drake returning from his homestead. Again her heart quaked. The man in the gray suit slowed his horse a bit and nodded as he passed, the corner of his mouth curled in a sneer around a fat cigar. He continued on down the street, past the paralyzed Crissa, then turned right at the assayer's office and out of sight.

She stumbled back inside the inn, collapsing against the bar as the room swirled and began to turn black. *He is not here for me*, she told herself stubbornly. *This is just a coincidence. Eric thinks I am dead. He is not here for me.* She forced herself to draw a deep breath. *Vänligen Gud, he cannot be here for me.*

★ ★ ★

Crissa finished the letter to the Bjorksons, deposited her stationery in her room, and was tying on an apron to fix dinner when a commotion arose in the dining room.

"Stop messing up the floor!" Will berated his sister.

"You're not my mother. Stop bossing me!" Amy shouted over her shoulder as she continued her trek across the dining room, strewing flower petals as she went.

"Mama's dead, so I'm in charge."

"She's not either dead!" Amy spun on her heel to confront her brother. "She's just visiting God. An' when she gets back, I'm gonna tell her how mean you we are, an' she'll kick you right out of here."

"Children!" Crissa rushed in, pulling the two apart. "Whatever is the matter?"

"Amy thinks Mama is off visiting God, and that you're only taking care of us 'til she gets back."

"Amy?"

"Well, Will says Mama isn't never coming back, and that you're going to die too, then the inn will be his!" Amy paused long enough to wrap her arms around Crissa's waist. "You're not gonna die, are you, Crissa?"

"Of course not, *min älskling*. Will, why would you say such a thing to your sister?"

"Because it's true. Mrs. Hampton told me you're just freeloading here, trying to take all our money."

"Will, that is not true. I will stay here and take care of you children until some of your family can be found. Any money that I make with the inn goes straight to Mr. Cornwall's bank. It will stay there until you are twenty-one years old, and then you may divide the money with Amy and decide what to do with the inn. I loved your mother, and I love you. I would never do anything to hurt you children."

Will scuffed a bare toe along the floor. "But Mrs. Hampton said . . ."

"Mrs. Hampton is wrong."

Amy took Crissa's hand in her own, studying it. "Crissa? Is my mama ever coming home?"

Crissa knelt down beside her and cupped both of her tiny hands. "No, *min kära*. Your mama has gone to live with God and your papa in heaven. She cannot come back. But they will all be waiting for you when it is your turn to go to heaven, and then you will all live together again."

"I miss her, Crissa." Big tears welled up in Amy's eyes, and her lip started to tremble. "Can I go to heaven soon?"

"No one knows when they will be called to heaven, *min älskling*, but I pray you have a long and happy life here first." Crissa stroked the wispy hair from Amy's brow and caressed her cheeks before pulling her to her breast. She gulped past the lump in her throat while her cheek rested on Amy's head.

"Now," Crissa said huskily, brushing the tears from her cheeks, "here are two pennies. Will, take Amy down to Mr. Potter's and buy a sweet for each of you." She scooted them toward the front door.

"Crissa?"

"Yes, Will?"

"I'm sorry 'bout what I said." He looked at his dusty feet, then back at Crissa. "I'm glad you're here, and . . . I love you."

Crissa smiled at the sound of little feet slapping away down the boardwalk.

★ ★ ★

Dinnertime was quiet this time of year. The cattle drivers on their way to California usually didn't arrive until mid-August. Stage travelers were sparse because of the punishing heat. The nearby ranchers who occasionally dropped by for breakfast or lunch while they were in town for supplies had returned home for their evening meals. Crissa was able to keep up with what customers she did have with the welcome help of Drake.

Dressed in a white half apron, he was nearly as handy in the kitchen as Crissa herself. While she was accustomed to cooking fish and beef, Drake knew just how to season wild game to please the most finicky guests. In addition, he was the fastest dishwasher Crissa had ever seen. He hummed while he worked, a rich baritone, and Crissa soon came to love the way he searched for the right key when beginning a new tune.

"Barmaid!" a man bellowed from the dining room.

Crissa's mouth dropped open, aghast. A short laugh erupted from Drake before he could stifle it.

"Barmaid!" the man bellowed again.

"Why . . . ," Crissa muttered from between clenched teeth. She glared at Drake, then stomped into the dining room, coming to a dead stop as she nearly slammed right into Garth and the man in the gray worsted suit.

"Evening, Miss Engleson," Garth said, doffing his hat in mock politeness. "Mind if we have a bite to eat?"

"No," Crissa stammered. "No, of course . . ." Her gaze had locked on the man with Garth.

"Allow me to introduce myself, ma'am. Name's Jenkins. Donald Jenkins."

Crissa's cheeks were flaming. She had to force herself to breathe. *Mr. Jenkins—the man who was asking for me in Springville. He was watching me in Salt Lake, and now he is here.* Crissa glanced away, trying to think of a way to escape. Drake was standing in the doorway, his face dark, his jaw clenched tightly. The look on his face was so full of hatred that Crissa turned away in fear. There was no escape.

"What may I bring you, then?" Her voice was even, her eyes riveted on Mr. Jenkins.

"Whatever's handy, Crissa. And a bottle of scotch." Garth's voice was condescending, even patronizing.

Crissa returned to the kitchen—to Drake's steely gaze.

He turned from her and began heaping pork chops, fried apples, and baked potatoes onto two plates. He scooted them across the table toward her and turned his back again.

"Drake? Is something wrong?" Crissa was stunned by his sudden coldness.

"Wrong? Stacking up beaus is some hobby for a woman."

"What? What are you talking about? You know I have no feelings for Garth."

"Cut the act, Miss Engleson. He told me all about the two of you in Salt Lake. I figured he was lying, but now he shows up here. Your sweetheart is getting hungry."

Crissa felt as if she had just been slapped. How could Drake think Garth was her sweetheart? And when had Garth been in Salt Lake? There had to be some misunderstanding. Donald Jenkins had been in Salt Lake . . . "Mr. Jenkins? You think Mr. Jenkins is my—my sweetheart?" She could scarcely breathe, she was so angry, and she bit her tongue to hold back the vulgarities she had heard Eric shout so often. She stormed out of the kitchen and slammed the two plates down in front of her customers.

"What about the whiskey?" Garth asked.

"Get it yourself," she yelled, waving her arm to the bar. She held her head high as she stomped back into the kitchen.

★ ★ ★

Nary a word was spoken between Drake and Crissa as they finished serving the few remaining customers. Miraculously, no dishes were broken as Drake washed them and banged them on the shelf, still wet. Crissa worked like a whirlwind cleaning tables, scraping pans, and sweeping the floor.

They had just finished with the last customers when they sat down at the kitchen table to eat their own dinners—in silence.

"Drake! Drake! Where are ya, Drake?" Will came crashing through the kitchen doors, yelling like a banshee was after him. "Come quick!"

Drake sprang to his feet and rushed to the panting boy. "What is it, Will? What's the matter?"

"It's Pony Bob!"

"Haslam?"

"Yeah. The Indians got him. He's hurt real bad!"

Drake rushed through the door outside, Crissa and Will running behind him. Doc Robbins was helping the livery boy pull Pony Bob from the saddle as Drake reached him. Already a circle of townsfolk crowded around.

"Oh no." Drake knelt down beside him. "How bad is he, Doc?"

The doctor's brow was furrowed as he deftly felt the Pony Express rider's wounds. He shook his head grimly. "It's not good. You fellas help me get him to the office."

"Adams," Pony Bob whispered, "you gotta take it in."

"The mail? But I can't."

"Sure ya can." He winced as he turned his head toward Drake. "You're . . . Flyin' Saddle Adams."

"But I quit the Express."

"Gotta get through." The weakening man was seized with a fit of coughing that bloodied the corners of his mouth. "Gotta warn the other riders."

Drake looked at the faces gathered around him, waiting expectantly. "Sure, Bob. Sure, I'll do it."

Bob coughed again, expelling blood. "Got ambushed at Dese-toya. Indians . . . from the pass to Eureka."

"Eureka? That's over 150 miles."

"Nobody home 'til here."

"For 180 miles all the stations have been shut down?"

"Not by Indians." The rider shuddered as he tried to breathe. "Relief boys must've seen me and got scared off."

"Drake," the doctor interrupted, "I've got to get this boy inside."

"Well, you just rest easy, Bob. I'll take the run. You let Doc Robbins get you patched up now."

Drake unstrapped the mochila from Pony Bob's exhausted horse and flung it on his waiting bay. Grabbing a couple of apples from a bin inside the livery, he stuffed them inside his shirt. He adjusted the stirrups on the saddle, then cinched up the chin strap on his hat.

From the boardwalk outside the inn, Crissa watched Drake standing inside the musty livery. He hung his head and massaged the back of his neck. His shoulders moved up and down as though he had heaved a heavy sigh. *He looks so tired*, Crissa thought. *He will never make it to Salt Lake City. I should not have gotten so angry with him.* Crissa debated running to the livery to apologize, but before she could take a step, Drake swung himself up into the saddle. Kicking his horse into a mad gallop, he was off.

Crissa stood on the boardwalk, hands clasped to her face and fingertips pressed against the inner corners of her eyes to hold back the tears. She felt as if someone were sitting on her chest, robbing her of life.

"Well, I just knew he couldn't give up riding for long." Suzanna Hampton and another girl were walking along the boardwalk, right toward Crissa. "Now I have the chance to surprise him with those curtains."

"Curtains?" the other girl asked, raising her voice slightly as they approached Crissa.

"Why, of course. For that sweet little house he's building us. I thought white eyelet would look delightful in the bedroom."

As the giddy girls passed, Crissa stood perfectly still, her chin held high, eyes focused on some distant spot across the street. *Sweet little house he's building us . . .*

She turned and bolted into the inn, slamming the big oak doors behind her.

CHAPTER 9

Will, *I* told you to wear shoes today," Crissa scolded as she bustled about the kitchen, fixing a picnic basket. "The grasses are all dried out by now, and you will be crying with stickers in your feet."

"I won't neither. My feet are tough as leather." Will stood with his hands on his hips, slapping one little foot back and forth on the scrubbed pine floor to prove his point.

"And leather is what I am just about ready to put to your backside if you do not get moving." Crissa clapped her hands loudly behind his bottom.

Will shrieked and ran from the room, yelling back at her, "Land sakes! I'm going already! Don't get your knickers in a knot!"

Crissa could not help but smile at this phrase of Molly's echoing out of the boy. "Now, Amy, where is your bonnet?"

"There on the peg, next to yours."

Crissa touched her hands to her head and laughed. Indeed, she too had forgotten her bonnet. "Come, then. I will tie both of them."

Will appeared in the doorway, hopping on one foot as he tried to stuff his foot in a shoe without untying it first. "I got a knot in my lace."

"Then I guess we are even." Crissa smiled as she knelt down beside him. "I have a knot in my knickers." She nimbly untied the knot, then laced the shoe correctly.

Wrapping crisp chicken legs and wings in a flour-sack towel, Crissa placed it on top of the carrot sticks and pickles already lining the basket. She wrapped a still-warm loaf of limpa bread in another towel and tucked it in beside the chicken. Three golden pears were snuggled in as well, to make the picnic complete.

Will reached out to snatch a pear from the basket and received a smart slap on the wrist for his trouble.

"If you eat it now," Crissa chided, "you will not have one for the picnic. Now, we must hurry if we are to be back in time to open for dinner."

Will placed the basket on his arm and followed Crissa and Amy outside, shutting the kitchen door behind him.

The three made a merry picture as they skipped hand in hand, following the creek bed to Dutchman's Pass. The blue sky shimmered in the warm sunlight. Webs of wispy clouds floated high above. The creek was dry, and the wild grasses growing on the banks were yellow and withered. A jackrabbit watched their ascent from the shade of the trees. It was a five-mile hike to the cemetery at Dutchman's Pass—a long, hot, dry five miles. Even Crissa was wiping perspiration from her brow as they crested the hill.

"Crissa," Amy panted, wiping a damp lock of hair off her forehead, "can we please bring the buggy next time we come?" Crissa smiled down at her, too winded to reply.

A trail of willows wove its way up the adjacent, steeper hill beyond, leading to the summit of the pass. At the summit beckoned Dutchman's Spring and the Willow Springs Cemetery. Transplanted cottonwoods outlined the perimeter of the graveyard.

As they approached the edge of the cemetery, Crissa stopped suddenly and motioned the children to the ground. She, too, crouched and placed a warning finger to her lips. Will and Amy were immediately silent and squatted motionless where they were. Crissa raised her head slowly to observe the man she had spied standing over Molly's grave.

"It is Garth," Crissa whispered to the children behind her. She watched as he finished tamping earth around what appeared to be a grave marker. He knelt on one knee and removed his hat, bowing his head over the grave. After a moment, he arose and slapped the dirt from his knees. He replaced his hat, collected his shovel, and returned to a horse tethered opposite Crissa's hiding place. He swung himself into the saddle and turned the horse northward, urging it to a canter.

When the sound of Garth's horse had faded into the distance, Crissa, Will, and Amy approached the newly tended grave. "Well, for Pete's sake," Will muttered in amazement.

Crissa knelt down to examine the beautiful marker. It stood about two and a half feet tall and was finely polished. An engraved arch of roses, foxglove, and daisies followed the graceful curve of the top. Beneath the flowers, Molly's and Hank's names, dates of birth, and dates of death were engraved. And at the bottom, "Your names were loved—sleep tenderly."

"It is lovely," Crissa spoke quietly. "I wonder why Garth would—"

"He was Pa's friend," Will said, anger snapping through his words. "He never did nothing to my ma and pa. When my pa died, he was right there, helping out. He wasn't one to turn and—" Will's voice caught in his throat and he turned his back on Crissa, finishing his sentence in a hurt whisper. "And run at the first sign of trouble."

That explains why Molly never threw him out, Crissa thought. Crissa looked at Will, standing there with his back to her, and wanted to cry. *Garth stood by Molly when she needed him. And I ran away . . .* "Will, you seem to know a side of Mr. Wight that I have not known," Crissa said. "I am glad your mother had such a generous friend to rely on when your father passed away." She knelt beside Will, her hand on his shoulder, and spoke to the back of his head. "It was very kind of Garth to buy such a lovely marker."

"I bet he didn't buy it," Will mumbled, turning his head slightly toward Crissa. "Prob'ly carved it hisself."

"He carved me a bunny once," Amy piped up. " 'Member, Will? That year Mrs. Hampton tried to take the inn?"

"Sure. He carved stuff for us all the time."

"I just wish he wasn't so mean to ever'body now," Amy said wistfully. "Can't stand to look at him anymore."

"Yeah, well . . ." Will's voice grew defensive once again. "If ever'body'd quit bad-mouthin' him, maybe he wouldn't be so ornery."

Amy put her little hands on her hips, elbows akimbo, just as she had seen her mother do so many times. "I don't know why you're stickin' up for him, Will. He treats you as bad as he treats the rest of us."

"I dunno," Will muttered. "Doesn't matter."

From the dejected look in his eyes, however, Crissa could tell that it did matter. It mattered very much.

The long meadow grass was moist and tender, shaded from the heat by the sentinel trees. Will, Amy, and Crissa laid the picnic out next to the graves and spoke in hushed tones as they ate. Sitting on the quilted picnic blanket, Will and Amy began recalling some of their memories, and through this, some of the pain at their loss began to ease.

Crissa privately reflected back on the picnic she had shared with Drake—the sweet smell of spring in the tender meadow grasses, the way Drake's eyes sparkled while he described the house he would build, and when he kissed her . . .

"Remember when the prairie hens wandered into the dining room?" Will said, interrupting Crissa's daydream. "And Mama was chasing them around with the broom?"

Amy laughed. "She hit one of them so hard she killed it."

"Yeah, and we served prairie hen soup for supper that night."

"Only Mama made us promise not to tell anyone it was prairie hen. And remember when you sassed Mama," Amy continued, "an' she sent you out back for a willow switch?"

Will blushed at the memory. "But I was so scared I climbed near to the top of the tree and got stuck. Mama had to get Mr. Potter to come help me get down."

The two children chattered on while they ate, but Crissa had other things on her mind. Something about that grave marker made her uneasy. Something seemed to familiar.

The summer sun was well past its zenith when Crissa packed the remainder of the picnic into the basket. Will had fashioned a basket by weaving leaves and grass, then filled it with wet mud from the spring. Amy gently poked what few wildflowers she could find into the mud.

"I'm glad Mr. Wight made flowers on the marker," Amy said.

"Now I won't have to worry about dressing the grave so much for Mama." She headed off down the hill. Will and Crissa trailed after her.

"Mama brought us up to Papa's grave a lot," Will explained. "She told us it's a sign of respect to keep a grave dressed proper."

★ ★ ★

A crowd of people were gathered at the stage coach station as Crissa, Will, and Amy returned from their picnic. Dr. Robbins came running from his office, bag in hand. "Let me through!" he yelled. "Stand aside now."

Crissa stood on tiptoe, trying to see what was happening, and Will wiggled through to the front of the crowd. There lay the stage driver on the ground with his shirt torn open. His face was drawn and gray. He did not move. The doctor frantically jerked the stethoscope from one area of the driver's chest to another, listening intently. With his lips set in a grim line, he held a palm-sized mirror to the man's mouth. Doc Robbins stood up, shaking his head. "Sorry, folks. There's nothing more I can do. A couple of you men help me carry him to my office."

The crowd started dispersing, and Will appeared at Crissa's side. "Dead as a doornail," he pronounced, slapping the dust from his knees.

Amy hid her face in Crissa's skirts. Her little body shook with remembered anguish.

"Will!" Crissa admonished. "Hush up now. Help me get your sister back to the inn."

Amy pulled her head from Crissa's skirt, still holding the fabric in one clenched fist. "I'm okay, Crissa. I just got sorta scared. That's all. But I'm okay now."

"All right, *min älskling,* but I think you should lie down for a while." Crissa lifted the little girl into her arms.

"I wanna stay with you."

Catching snatches of conversation, Crissa learned the driver had slumped in his seat on the stage just before it reached town. He held the reins long enough to get the stage to the station, then tumbled, dead, from his perch. The passengers were stranded in Willow

Springs until the next stage came through. No one knew when that would be.

Stages departed from major cities only when every seat was filled or when there was a special mail delivery on board. Departures ranged from once a day to once a week. On top of their erratic schedule, breakdowns and Indian attacks added to the uncertainty. The only thing that was certain was that Henders Inn, the only rooming house in town, would be full to bursting tonight.

Crissa bustled around, situating the newly arrived guests in rooms and starting dinner. She made a fire in the stove before setting Will to work peeling potatoes and Amy to scraping carrots. The haunch of venison she had planned to serve would never be enough to feed nine extra people, so she sliced it into cubes for stew. She stirred together a batch of biscuit dough and set it on the sideboard to rest. Quickly, she sliced fresh peaches, laid them in a baking dish, and dusted them with cinnamon and sugar. She used two knives to cut flour, cinnamon, and lard into a crumb topping and sprinkled it over the peaches.

Will and little Amy worked right alongside her as she served up dinner, refilled coffee, and scooped the dirty dishes away from the tables. Unscheduled visitors were rare in Willow Springs, so many of the townsfolk and ranchers came to dine at the inn as well. Crissa was kept at a trot throughout the evening until, at last, the guests seemed satisfied enough for her to sit for a moment to enjoy her own dinner.

Crissa pulled a chair up to the little serving table tucked partially under the stairs just outside the kitchen. She was too tired to make conversation with the guests tonight. Many had already retired for the evening, but Will and Amy were holding court on the far side of the dining room, entertaining those that remained with tales of the Wild West.

It would have been nice to have Drake's help tonight, Crissa mused, sipping the last of her coffee. *He has been gone nearly three weeks. I wonder if anyone has heard from him? Will he even come to see me when he does return?* Her throat began to constrict. *Well, he was the one who said such hateful things before he left. He had no cause to say what he did.* The change in thinking worked, and Crissa felt the familiar sense of indignation return. *He'll have a lot of explaining to do when he does get back.*

"May I join you, Miss Engleson?" The deep, gravelly voice spoke so close to her ear that Crissa nearly jumped from her chair, but a determined hand kept her anchored to it.

"Garth," she said, trying to keep her voice from betraying the hammering in her chest. "What do you want?"

"Only to enjoy a moment of your company." Though his skin was leathery, he was clean-shaven and bathed. He smelled of bay rum. Smiling slightly, revealing nearly straight white teeth, he pulled a chair up next to hers. "May I?"

Crissa looked around the room, ready to refuse. Several of the diners were watching her intently. There was no way she could turn him away without appearing rude. "Just sit down," she said, her voice flat, no emotion showing on her face. "Now what do you want?"

"I thought it was time we got to know each other."

"I already know you better than I would like."

"Is that any way to talk to a fella come a-sparkin'?"

"Come a-what?" Her voice rose, edged with disbelief.

"I come to court ya, Miss Crissa. Figured maybe you could give me a second chance."

"Second chance!" She was incredulous. "I think you have already had one chance too many." She stood up to leave, but he placed his hand on her wrist, restraining her.

"I'll bet you'd give Eric a second chance, wouldn't you, Mrs. Lundstrom?" Beneath a casual smile, his voice turned threatening. "Now why don't you sit down and stop causing a scene?"

Stunned, Crissa looked around the dining room. No one gave any indication of having overheard their conversation. *Has Garth heard from Eric?* she wondered. The panic swelled in her chest, and Crissa found it hard to breath.

Garth tilted back on his chair, crossing his foot over his knee, and pulled a cigar from his vest pocket. He nodded toward the opposite chair, gesturing at it with his cigar. Slowly, Crissa lowered herself to the chair. Garth struck a match and sucked lightly on the cigar several times, waiting for it to catch the flame held before it, then took a long drag, and blew the smoke slowly toward the ceiling.

Crissa watched him intently. Questions and fears chased themselves around inside her head, and she felt her face growing numb,. She concentrated on breathing. At last she leaned forward, her hands braced around her coffee cup. "What do you know about—" She bit her lower lip, unable to speak his name.

"About Eric Lundstrom?" Garth leaned forward as well, smiling rakishly. "I know you're married to him. And I know you're running from him." He took another puff from his cigar, letting the smoke snake from the corner of his mouth

Crissa felt the blood drain from her face and prayed she wouldn't pass out. She glanced about the room. Guests turned away when she looked in their direction. She hoped they were out of earshot, but it was obvious she and Garth were being watched now that he sat at her table. She felt bile swimming in her stomach. Her mind began to race. There had to be some way out of this.

"How did you come by your information, Garth?" Her voice, still barely audible, was firm and demanding.

Garth smiled at her then, cocking one eyebrow. He inhaled deeply of his cigar, letting the smoke slip lazily skyward. "Mr. Jenkins is a very good investigator. And a very good businessman."

Jenkins? Of course—that man in the suit. "Businessman?"

"He knows how to make the most of his information."

"You paid him, then?"

"Well, no, not myself."

"Then who?"

"I can't tell you that."

How far has this gone? Crissa wondered as nausea began to churn in her stomach. "Garth," Crissa pleaded, leaning closer to him over the table. "I must know who else knows about this." She could feel his gaze making its way down her neck.

"You should never have gotten sweet on Drake, Crissa." Garth spoke to her without bothering to take his eyes from her chest. "You got in the way."

"Got in the way?" Crissa was stunned. "Are you telling me Drake hired this man?"

Garth looked up at her then, mischief glinting in his eyes, his lips spread in a gleeful smile. He took her hand in his, caressing each knuckle. He raised his shoulders innocently. "I told you, Miss Crissa, I can't say."

She snatched her hand away. By not saying, Garth had said enough.

The smile faded from Garth's face. Grinding his cigar on the bottom of his boot, he let it fall to the floor.

"There's another thing I know, Miss Crissa."

The suffocating knot rose in her throat again. *Dyr Gud*, she thought, afraid to ask what else he had learned.

Garth leaned in until his face was mere inches from hers. He wrapped his hand tightly around her wrist. His breath stank of the cheap cigar. "I know you're wanted for the murder of the woman your husband was . . . seeing."

Crissa sat stone still, her eyes fixated on him. She didn't blink, she didn't breathe, and she didn't utter a sound. Her mind spun, but no thoughts coalesced. Whiteness blanketed her peripheral vision, closing in on the cruel face staring back at her. With tears welling up in her eyes, Crissa clenched her teeth, struggling for air—struggling not to cry in front of him.

At last he dropped his gaze to the table.

She sucked in a great breath. Terror yielded to anger. "Why did you come here, Garth?"

He raised his eyes to meet hers.

"How much do you want?"

"Want?" The puzzled expression on his face was genuine.

"Money, Mr. Wight. Is that not the custom with you people? Find some kind of damaging information and then make me pay for your silence?"

Garth cleared his throat and looked about the room nervously. His voice was not as discreet as before. "I want you."

"What?" Crissa screeched. Instantly the room hushed and every head turned toward them.

"I want you to be my wife."

"You must be out of your—" Crissa became aware of how loud

she was in the silent room. She lowered her voice to an angry hiss. "You are out of your mind."

"Now, just think about it a minute." Thankfully, Garth kept his voice hushed as well.

"I will not think about it! You tried to . . . have your way with me. You tried to kill me! If it had not been for Drake—"

"And where's Drake now?"

Crissa felt the tears rising again. Her lip started to quiver as she struggled with the memory of their fight before Drake left. Garth laid her hand in his, gently stroking the length of each finger before kissing the back of her hand.

"If you marry me," he whispered, "I can keep this information quiet. If you don't . . . well, Crissa, I doubt a judge will be so forgiving."

Tears splashed on the hands clasped in front of her. *Is this what Drake meant before he left?* Crissa wondered. *Was he trying to arrange for Garth to be my "sweetheart" all along? Why did he not just tell me he did not want me? Why did he have to dredge up my past? Did he think that if he dishonored me, I would run away again?* It was all starting to make sense. Twisted, painful sense. *If I ran away, he would be free to marry Suzanna Hampton, and he would never have to look at me again. Well, the devil with you, Drake Adams! You can rot with the devil!*

"Well?" Garth held out a dingy handkerchief. "What's your answer . . . honey?"

Crissa dabbed her eyes with a corner of the handkerchief before wiping her nose, then carefully folded the cloth to provide a clean surface. *My answer is that you can rot as well,* träsk hund. *Jenkins found me once. He will not find me again. I will be gone before you have a chance to—* She looked across the dining room to where Will and Amy had their audience laughing so hard that many of them held their sides or pounded their fists on the table. And she realized that she could not leave Will and Amy unattended.

Stall until Marida gets back, then disappear, she reasoned. But this inn had become her home—these children, her family. She felt despair setting in, but there was no other way. She was lost already.

She inhaled slowly before beginning her negotiations. "When Molly died," Crissa said, "I promised Will and Amy that I would look after them and the inn until some of their relatives could be found. I cannot just leave—"

"There's no problem with that. I thought we could live right here 'til I find us a nice place of our own. The shack I live in now is, well, a shack. It's barely big enough for me, let alone a family."

"A family!" Despite her plan to leave, the panic-stricken words escaped before Crissa could check herself. *No! He would not expect me to—of course he would. Oh, but I could never—* "Garth, I cannot be your wife."

Garth's face turned menacing. "We just went over that. You can and you will."

"No. I mean . . . I cannot love you."

He relaxed a bit. "Maybe not right away, but you'll grow to love me in time."

He does not understand! "I cannot . . . make love to you."

Garth let out the loudest guffaw Crissa had ever heard. He leaned forward, wiping tears from his eyes with his shirtsleeve. "Now, Miss Engleson." He chuckled again. "Since you've been married before, I'm pretty well certain you're capable of making love. And, as you were made aware at the dance, I am fully capable of living up to my husbandly duties."

Crissa gasped at his crudeness.

"Furthermore, ma'am, I wouldn't bother making you my wife if I weren't gonna get my rights." He twisted a tendril of her hair around his finger, pulling her painfully toward him. "Now, do we have an agreement?"

It does not matter, she reminded herself. *I will be gone before he gets his chance.* Crissa meekly nodded her response.

Garth stood up and bellowed, "Ladies and gentlemen, we're gonna have us a wedding . . . tomorrow!"

"Tomorrow! Garth, no! We have to wait for—"

"Tomorrow," he insisted. His fingers bit into the flesh of her arm as he pulled her up to stand beside him. "The lovely Miss Crissa here has agreed to be my wife, and you're all invited!"

CHAPTER 10

Crissa tossed and turned violently as she slept. A familiar dream haunted her throughout the night. Wild horses with flaming nostrils . . . Huge fists flying through the air . . . Men with grotesque faces and shiny star-shaped badges . . . slow motion . . . Her father . . . his whip . . . Her mother's sad face turning away . . . Molly . . . a welcoming embrace . . . vanishing . . . Will and Amy rushing . . . clawing fingers . . . "Don't leave us! Please don't leave us! Crissa, where are you?" . . . A man laughing, his face changing from Eric to Garth, laughing louder and louder. Even in sleep, Crissa clasped her hands to her ears, sure she was going mad. And there in her nightmare, leering at her, the man in the gray worsted suit.

Crissa bolted up in her bed, drenched with sweat and shaking like an aspen leaf. She could not calm her terror. Had her mind snapped? Had she gone insane? She peered through the darkness of her room, trying to regain her bearings, her courage.

She tied her wrapper around herself as she walked to the window. The blackened sky above the livery was warming to gray in the false dawn.

Today is your wedding day, Cristalina. Feelings of dread overwhelmed her as she reflected on the nightmare and contemplated the day ahead. *My wedding day. Dear God*, she prayed, *how can I marry him? How can I not? I cannot leave the children. Why did Drake betray me like this? I thought he . . .* She sat on the windowsill with her knees drawn up beneath her nightgown. With her cheek resting on her knees, she watched the night fade. *I imagined he cared for me. He was being nice. That was all. He never said what I hoped he felt. And now I know.*

She hugged her knees in the chill air and allowed her thoughts to wander back to Eric. *There was no reason for Father to make me marry Eric in the first place,* she thought. *We were not so crowded in our berth on the ship. That was just his excuse to get rid of me. "Marry her off. Then her husband can pay for her keep." If Mama were not so afraid of Father, she would not have made me marry Eric. Mama even left her own son behind to appease Father.*

Crissa reflected on the day her family moved from Sweden. Grendell and Wilmina, two of her three older sisters, were already married and staying in Sweden with their husbands. Celeste, the third sister, was engaged and had already left for America with her fiancé's family. Crissa and three-year-old Simon were the only children left to make the trip. Simon was dragging everything he could find and throwing it into the small trunk the family was allowed to carry. Everything he put in, his mother took out. And everything his mother put in, Simon took out. Finally, in exasperation, Crissa's mother took Simon to a neighbor's to play while she and Crissa finished packing. The neighbor refused to return the boy "to meet his death on shipboard" when it was time for the Englesons to leave. Crissa remembered the anguished cries of her mother pleading for her son and her father's outraged bellows about missing the boat. Without further argument, Crissa's father threw Simon's few belongings from the cart and headed off for the docks. Simon's cries faded into the distance, but her mother's sobs accompanied the family to the promised land.

Even now Crissa remembered Simon's beguiling smile and the empty place she felt within her heart. *Mother, how could you not fight for your son? And why did you not fight for me?*

A horse whinnied from the stable. *Well, wedding or no wedding, I have an inn full of people to feed.* She rubbed both hands over her face, trying to knead some of the tension away. *I wish Marida was here. No, I am glad she is not. Whether I get married or run away, she will be disappointed in me. It is better this day be over with before I spoil her happiness.* She stood up with a great sigh, letting her wrapper fall to the floor, and dressed for the day ahead.

Crissa tiptoed down the stairs to the kitchen, willing her guests to sleep as long as possible. Quietly, she arranged ingredients on the kitchen table, then mixed up bread dough and set it to rise. She pulled a knitted shawl around her shoulders and carried the egg basket out to the coop.

The rounded hills in the west were silhouetted against the purple dawn. *You are not mountains,* she thought, suddenly homesick. *You are hills—tiny mounds compared with my mountains in Sweden, in Särvattnet or Hede. Those are rugged and mighty mountains. Rugged and mighty like Drake.* The familiar knot tightened in her throat as she allowed herself to dream of what could have been: keeping house in the beautiful home he had built just for her, tending a garden out back, visiting in town with the rest of the respectable wives, laughing with her babies, waking up each morning in his embrace and going to sleep each night knowing he loved her as much as she loved him. *Dear God,* she prayed, *you are a loving Father. I have agreed to be Garth's wife, and I will try to be a good wife. Please do not let it be Drake who has betrayed me, and please, Father, take away the pain I feel in my heart.*

The hens set to squawking as Crissa opened the door to the coop, but they quieted down quickly as she carefully plucked the bounty from each nest. She chatted softly with each hen as she gathered the eggs. She breathed deeply the musky scent of warm hay. *A cozy coop smells the same in America as it does in Sweden.* She tucked her shawl about her shoulders, then latched the door securely as she left.

Thoughts of her grandmother played through her mind as she walked the few yards back to the kitchen. *Mormor* always had a fond saying to lend comfort in any situation. *Mormor, are you watching me now? Can you see what lies before me today?* Almost as if in answer, Crissa remembered two phrases: *liv vilja forsätta*—life will continue, and *ju lycka du sa idag vilja kyssa du två i morgon*—the happiness you sow today will kiss you twice tomorrow.

Oh, Mormor, can there be happiness today? Will I ever know happiness again?

She braced the door behind her, careful not to let it bang shut, and then set the egg basket on the counter and untied her shawl. She lifted the shawl to the peg, then let it slip to the ground. She was not alone in the kitchen. She whirled around, certain it must be an apparition.

"Marida? Is that really you?"

"No, silly child, is my great aunt Sofia." Marida grasped Crissa in a great hug. "Of course is me!"

"You are home!" The relief of seeing her friend again caught Crissa off guard, and a flood of tears bore evidence of her pent-up emotions. "You are home!"

"Crissa, why ever you cry? You not glad to see me?"

"Of course I am glad to see you!" Crissa brushed away the tears and forced herself to smile. "I cry for joy, Marida. I am so happy to see you home. Now," Crissa said, holding Marida's hands in hers, "tell me everything. How was your wedding trip? You look wonderful. Did you get to California?"

"Ah, you ask so many questions! Where do I start?"

"Why don't you start with what a great husband I am?" Vic strode into the kitchen and wrapped his strong arms around Crissa's waist, lifting her in the air with his friendly bear hug.

The sureness of his friendship set Crissa's emotions flowing again. The tears bubbled once more to the surface as she felt the warmth of his embrace.

"Crissa?" Vic released his hold on her. "You're crying?"

"But he is great husband," Marida teased, trying to coax a smile on her friend's face. She put her arm around Crissa's shoulders and steered her to the table. "Twice you cry this morning. Something must be wrong. You tell me. Now."

"I am sorry to cry like this. It is just that, just—" Crissa sagged into a chair. With Marida home to watch the children, Crissa could flee. But it was daylight now. Someone would see her, or if they did not, she would be too easily found. The wedding was just a few hours away. *There is no time. I have lost my chance.* She covered her face with her hands and sighed. "Oh, Marida, so much has happened."

"What has happened make you cry?" Marida sat in the chair next to Crissa.

"I am to be married."

"Married! But when?"

"This afternoon."

"Oh no! It cannot be! Drake say he wait 'til I return!"

"Drake?"

"He told me the day of our wedding that he make changes for you. I never thought he marry foreigner girl, but I was wrong. Oh, Crissa, he does love you! I am so happy for you!" Marida squeezed Crissa's hands and kissed her on the cheek. "But I thought he wait for me to get back." Marida pouted. "Now here you have wedding planned without Marida."

"But—" Crissa was growing confused trying to follow the conversation. "I am not marrying Drake."

"Not marry Drake!" It was Marida's turn to be stunned. "But of course you marry . . . Crissa? You not marry Drake? Then, who?"

Crissa sat, chewing on a fingernail. Her muffled reply was barely audible. "Garth."

Marida's hands fell to her lap. She shook her head back and forth, her mouth wide open. "I not hear you right. You marry Garth?"

Crissa nodded her head.

Vic sat dumbfounded in the chair next to his wife.

"Garth Wight?"

She raised her chin, looking at Marida defiantly.

"But I thought . . . you, Drake . . ."

"Drake is gone."

"Gone? You mean dead?"

"No, not dead. Just gone." Crissa stood up and moved across the room. "Would you like some coffee?"

"Coffee? I don'a want coffee. I wan' some answers." Marida took Crissa firmly by the arm and set her back in her chair. "Now, what you mean, Drake's gone?"

Crissa sat with her back rigid, trying to hide her emotions as she condensed the story. "Drake and I had an argument. He took a Pony Express run, and I have not seen or heard from him since."

"But, Crissa, that just silly man pride. Drake will be back. He ask me about you, your feelings for him. I thought he going to marry you."

"Well, he is not. He has betrayed me. He has put me in a position such that I must marry Garth."

"What d'ya mean he betrayed you?" Vic's brow was furrowed as he pulled a chair out across from the ladies and sat down.

Crissa dropped her head and contemplated her next words. "It is a personal matter which I do not want to discuss."

"Tarnation!" Vic boomed, slamming his fist on the table. "Drake's got it worse for you than, than . . . I don't know what! And you don't want to discuss it?"

"Drake has feelings for me?"

"Aw, Crissa," Vic folded his arms on the table. "Ever since he first saw ya here. Why else would he be rushin' to finish that house he's building? And why else would he be spending all his spare time here with you an' the kids?"

With all her heart, Crissa wanted to believe what Vic was saying, but logic and hurtful memories prevailed. Suzanna walking down the street describing the bedroom curtains—*he is building the house for Suzanna.* His jealous outrage that last day in the kitchen—*he was only spending time with me until he could find out about my past. And when he did, he paid that man and told Garth! But why?* It still made no sense to her, but the mixture of hurt and anger was so raw that she nearly blurted out the depth of Drake's betrayal.

"I know he is your friend, Vic," Crissa said at length, "but that does not change what happened between Drake and me. Since then, Garth came to . . . court me, and I have agreed to marry him."

Marida shoved her chair back from the table and crossed the room. She yanked a griddle from the shelf. "Crissa, I thought we friends. You told me nothing. How long is Drake gone?"

"Nearly three weeks."

"When Garth come courting?"

"Last night."

"Last night!" She banged the griddle down on the stove. "Drake love you for months now, and you give up on him to marry Garth?"

Tears welled in Crissa's eyes and spilled down her cheeks. "No, Marida." She stood toe-to-toe with Marida. "Drake does not love me. Maybe he did once, but . . . I wish you would try to understand. He only wants to hurt me."

"How can you say such things?"

"Because it is the truth."

"Crissa?" Will burst into the kitchen, dragging Amy with him by the hair, effectively putting an end to any further discussion between Crissa and Marida. "What can I use to tie back Amy's hai—Hey! Marida! When d'you get back?"

"Oh, Marida," Amy wailed, pulling loose from Will's grasp. "Did you hear?" She buried her face in Marida's skirt, bursting into tears.

"This not over, Crissa," Marida whispered from between her gritted teeth. "We finish this later." Marida knelt down to hold Amy's face in her hands. "Hear what, *mi bambina*?"

"Crissa's runnin' off'n gettin' married!"

"Running off? You not get married here at inn?"

"Well, yes . . . I am getting married here."

"She's gettin' married so she can leave us!" Amy's tearful face was set with determination, and sobs erupted anew. "She don't love us no more!"

"Oh, my Amy!" Crissa knelt down to join Amy and Marida. "I cannot leave you."

"See! I told you, you stupid girl!" Will scolded. "Now stop your blubbering. Crissa's gonna stay right here in Willow Springs with Garth."

Amy stomped on Will's foot and pulled free of Crissa. "I hate Garth! He's a mean man now. He won't never let Crissa visit us. I hate him! I wish he was dead too!"

"Amy!" Marida grabbed her by the arm. "You don'a ever say such a thing!"

"Amy," Crissa said patiently, taking her from Marida, "I told

Mr. Wight I would marry him only if we could live here with you." Crissa tried hard to accept her own comforting words, but the black pool of desperation inside of her would not be suppressed. "I could never leave you. I love you."

"Honest, Crissa?"

"Cross my heart, *min älskling*."

"Well, now that settled, we have breakfast to serve." Marida planted a kiss on the top of Amy's head and turned to the stove.

"Marida," Crissa said, "you just got home. You do not have to fix breakfast today."

"I heard 'bout stage stranded here. You have hands full. And wedding too! How you plan take care of everything if Marida not help? I had honeymoon; now, business as usual." She snatched an apron off a nail by the stove and began issuing orders as she tied the apron on. "Will, you run over to stage station and see if there's news about next stage. Amy, you go with him. Vic!" Marida snapped. "You not have things to do?"

Vic sprung out of the chair, chuckling. "My Marida. So long the bride, so soon the wife." He kissed Crissa on the cheek and patted his wife on the bottom.

"Vic?" Marida said meekly. "You be close if I need you?"

"Sure," he said, returning to peck her cheek as well. "I'll be right back."

"Now," Marida said, straightening her apron, "I have inn full of hungry people to feed. Are you going to help me?"

"Of course." Crissa reached for the basket of eggs, still warm from the nest. The dark abyss of depression yawned before her. She worked mechanically, without thinking or feeling, but with renewed hope. There was no escaping the wedding, but with Marida back to take care of the children, it was only a matter of time before she would escape the marriage.

Marida slapped slices of salt pork on the hot griddle, jerking her hand away as the greasy fat sizzled and spat. Now and again she turned to say something to Crissa, then clamped her lips together again. Her tight lips worked against each other, her jaw clenched, her eyes narrowed to slits of concentration. Still, she cooked as brusquely possible without ruining the fare, unwilling—unable—to speak her mind.

Crissa cracked eggs onto another griddle, scrambling some, leaving others to simmer in a gold-and-white pool. She watched Marida's emotions playing on her face. Crissa herself vacillated between anger, shame, and despair. *Well, this is my life!* Crissa thought in frustration. *She has no right to tell me who I may or may not marry . . . but she is my best friend. She may well be the only one in America who does love me . . . but she said Drake . . .* Crissa glanced at Marida again, trying to read what was not said. *What if Drake does love me?* She shook the tempting thought from her mind. *It cannot be true, or he would not have given that information to Garth.* As she pondered her predicament, she realized that Garth had never admitted that it was Drake. *But if not Drake, then who? It does not matter; somebody gave Garth that information about me. Even if it was not Drake, there is no way he could love me when he learns about my past.*

Crissa pulled a large bowl from the shelf and measured flour and water into it for hotcakes. A twinge of guilt twisted her stomach as she thought about the children under her care. *I promised Will and Amy I would never leave them*, she thought with anguish. *But I cannot live with Garth. I have to leave. But if I leave, he will tell the sheriff about Boston. And if I do not leave, how long will it be before Garth gets angry or drunk and tells someone about me anyway?* In every scenario Crissa could imagine, her secret would be found out. *I will be put in prison, or . . .* Her hands started shaking so violently she dropped the egg she was about to crack. It broke on the edge of the bowl, scattering pieces of shell throughout the hotcake batter.

"*Mamma mia!*" Marida growled, stepping in front of Crissa to salvage the eggs. "If you going help, help. If you not, get out of kitchen."

Crissa stood watching, her bottom lip quivering, tears swimming in her eyes.

Marida clamped her lips shut again but did not turn away. At last she spoke. "I'm sorry, Crissa. I don'a want you leave. It's just that . . . I feel like I been hit in head with horseshoe, and now my mouth, it talks without listening to brain first. Let's get breakfast over with. Then we talk, no?"

Crissa nodded, then silently helped Marida retrieve the shards of shell from the batter.

Vic returned and sat on the kitchen porch, his back propping the door open, mending a ragged saddle blanket. He watched the women working for quite some time before finally speaking. "Miss Crissa?"

"Hmm?"

"Y'know, Garth Wight's not such a bad sort of fellow."

Crissa wiped her hands on her apron and went out to sit on the step beside him.

"What I mean to say is . . ." He pushed the yarn-threaded needle in and out of the blanket. "Garth's got a demon inside of him that hankers for a shot of whiskey now and then."

"I do not understand."

"He's a boozer, is what Vic try to say," Marida interjected. "He's a drunk."

"Well, sure, he likes to drink enough, but when he isn't drinking, he's a right decent sort of man." He brushed some straw off the blanket.

"Decent!" Marida bellowed. "There no decent thing in him! D'you forget he attacked Crissa? That no decent! If not for Drake, well, you know what would've happened. D'you forget Crissa's bruises and cuts? You call that decent?" Marida looked like she might take a swing at her husband, but then her voice softened and tears came to her eyes. "D'you forget that 'cause of him, Molly, God rest her, worried herself to the grave?" Marida swiped at her eyes. "There no decent thing in him."

"That's all true," Vic said, "but that all happened because he was drunk. I guess what I'm trying to say is, if you can keep him away from his liquor, maybe you could learn to be happy bein' his wife."

Marida stood in the doorway shaking her head, dark eyes blazing. "Garth's got bigger demon in him than just liquor. He's got demon in his soul. You make big mistake to marry him, Crissa. You never be happy with him."

"My friends," Crissa said, standing up and walking back into the kitchen, "I do not expect to be happy with him, so I do not expect to be disappointed." She turned to the stove and poured another batch of hotcakes.

"I don' understand you!" Marida yelled, following Crissa inside. "You say you don' love him. You say you not be happy with him. Why in name of all that's holy do you marry him?"

All that's holy? Because I have already been bound by all that's holy! "Because—because I made a bargain—" Crissa bit her lip, realizing she had said too much.

"Bargain! What you mean, bargain?"

"Marida, please," Crissa pleaded. "I agreed to marry Garth, and I intend to do it. Please do not fight with me today. I need . . ." Her voice caught in her throat. *I need someone to be on my side for once*, she silently finished.

Marida's lips twisted as she fought to control her frustration. "You need friend to stand by you," she said at last, her voice husky as she wrapped her arms around Crissa. "I'm sorry I fight with you. I want you be happy." She moved the browned slices of salt pork from the griddle to a waiting plate, then added more pink strips to the hissing fat. A sly smile spread across her face. "Remember when you dumped Garth's dinner on him?"

"I remember," Crissa said without smiling at the memory.

"I told you then, if he gives you any more trouble, I wring his neck." Marida mimicked the familiar gesture. "I still do this for you."

Crissa smiled then. "I will remember."

"Now, we have lotsa work to do. Vic, tell Mrs. Potter we could use help decorating for wedding."

"Decorating!" Crissa interrupted. "I do not want any decorations. I just want a small, quiet ceremony."

"With inn full of guests, is not goin' to be small ceremony. We decorate dining room. Vic, you go now."

"I do not want decorations," Crissa repeated emphatically, as Vic sauntered out the back door. "I do not want a party."

"Crissa." Marida's quiet, determined voice precluded any further argument. "I plan nice wedding for Vic and me, but such sadness happened that was not good time for party. It was enough just to marry man I love. You and I both know you don'a love Garth, but you marry him anyway. Nice wedding give you good start on marriage. Give you good memories when—if—Garth give you sadness. Besides, will be good for children see you be happy tonight. Will bring them happiness."

There it is again, Crissa thought, *it will make Will and Amy happy. It will make Marida happy. It will make the guests happy. If only something could make* me *happy.*

★ ★ ★

Crissa watched as Marida, Vic, Will, and several of the stranded passengers bustled about arranging sprays of roses and wild grasses tied with ribbon in porcelain vases throughout the room. The same blue-and-yellow bunting she had seen at so many dances cascaded from the wrought-iron chandelier suspended in the middle of the dining room, creating a canopy around the room. Gathered in a bow above the staircase, the bunting was draped to form an archway at the base of the stairs. Crissa stood under the arch, surveying the transformation of the simple dining room. The tables had been moved out back, and two rows of chairs were clustered around the stairway in a semicircle. The bar was laden with Molly's china, crystal, and genuine silver plate for the buffet afterward.

This is the wedding I have always dreamed of, Crissa mused. *But, once again, I am not marrying the man of my dreams.* Crissa slipped into the kitchen, not yet ready to face the ordeal ahead. The image of Drake wrapped in an apron and drying dishes tickled her memory for just a moment before she firmly thrust it from her thoughts. She heard humming from outside and walked to the porch to investigate.

"Amy? Why are you out here?" Crissa asked.

"I dunno."

"Why are you not with the others decorating?"

"I dunno."

Crissa sat on the step beside Amy, letting a few moments pass in silence.

"Why do you have to marry Garth?" Amy asked quietly.

"I . . . do not understand, Amy."

"Garth isn't a good man anymore. He scares me. I don't want you to marry him."

"Mr. Wight has had many sorrows in his life, *min älskling.* Perhaps, if I am a good wife, he can be a good man again."

Amy looked at her skeptically.

"Amy, do you know what a flower girl is? When I was a child in Sweden, all of the little girls from my village would walk down the aisle in front of the bride, scattering rose petals and rosemary."

Amy furrowed her brow, but kept her eyes focused on some far-off point. "Why?"

"To bless the marriage."

Amy looked at her then. "What do you mean?"

"Well, many people think that rose petals give feelings of love and peace, and the rosemary makes you live a long time. By sprinkling the petals on the floor, we were blessing the couple with love, peace, and a long life."

Amy sighed.

"Amy, would you please be my flower girl?"

"Really?"

"Really. We have no fresh rosemary, but I am sure Marida could make you a pretty bouquet of roses to carry."

Amy thought for a few moments. "But that'd only give you love and peace."

Crissa folding her arms around Amy, breathing in deeply the spicy scent of her freshly washed hair. "If I have your blessing for love and peace, then I can ask for nothing else."

CHAPTER 11

Crissa viewed herself in front of the full-length mirror she had dragged from Molly's room to her own. The plain woman staring back showed belligerent approval. She was dressed in the gray cotton dress she had worn most of the way across the prairie. She plucked at the folds that had once hidden her swollen belly. As her hands slid down her now flat abdomen, she remembered the last time she had worn the dress.

The handcart company they'd been traveling with was anxious to cross the Great Divide into Wyoming. The perilous journey that had stretched through months of pulling heavy carts across flat plains in the blistering heat, crossing roily rivers in torrential downpours, and passing over jagged mountainsides was nearing its end. It was imperative to make the last leg of the trek before the cool autumn turned to frigid, deadly winter.

Crissa, in her seventh month of pregnancy, had been duti-fully taking her turn pulling the handcart piled with her parents' belongings. Each new day brought her closer to a new home, a new life, and a sweet new baby to give meaning to this difficult trek. It seemed her belly grew larger each day, and with each kick of a tiny leg, Crissa thought her ribs would crack. Thankfully, the child had been quiet for several days. With every step the pain in her legs and back increased, yet she could not complain or turn the wagon over to her father. He would likely whip her if he felt she was not doing her duty, and in her condition, she could not afford this abuse.

Only when her waters broke shortly after midmorning did she realize her pains were not from exhaustion but from the impending birth of her child. Word quickly spread to the front of the hand-cart company, but the company could not afford to lose time for childbirth. Leave her to deliver as other women had done, they said. She and her family could catch up later. A young woman named Sarah who had assisted a midwife a few times stayed behind to help. Crissa's father dragged the cart off the trail and under some trees, then stomped off, leaving Crissa, her mother, and Sarah to fend for themselves and the early birth.

With each agonizing hour that passed, Crissa became more frightened that something was not right with the child. She lay on the back of the handcart, knees akimbo, screaming with each tor-turous contraction. The top of the baby's head was in sight, but Crissa lacked the strength to push it out. Sarah had never experi-enced a difficult delivery and had no idea what to do. She paced back and forth, wringing her hands or clapping them over her ears to shut out Crissa's screams.

Just after sunset, Crissa watched a lone horseman approach. Although scarcely a man, he had the air of confidence peculiar to the expedition's scouts. As he came closer, Crissa realized it was Charlie Callahan, come back to check on the young mother. Crissa greeted him with a guttural scream as the next contraction seared its way through her womb. He jumped off his horse, peeled off his jacket and shirt, and pushed Crissa's skirts out of the way. His Irish brogue was so thick that Crissa couldn't understand what he was about to do until she felt the pressure of his fingers slid-ing inside of her to grasp the baby's head. The next contraction began immediately. Crissa bit her lip to hold back the screams as her mother pushed on Crissa's belly to force the baby down. With one steady pull, the horseman drew the baby's lifeless body from its nest.

"A sore cross to bear, that it is," Charlie said, "but judging from his color, I'd say the good Lord took the wee bairn home of his own accord. 'Twarn't nothing to be done about it. Your lad's been in heaven for several days now."

Crissa caressed the little curled fingers that lay still to her touch. Except for the blue-gray tinge to his skin, he could have been a beautiful little boy asleep in his mother's arms.

For the remainder of the night, Mr. Callahan stayed with Crissa and her mother. He pulled a flask of whiskey from a small bag of bandages, sulfa powder, and other simple first-aid supplies and instructed Mrs. Engleson to wash Crissa thoroughly to guard against infections. He wrapped the baby boy in the blanket Crissa had knitted for his christening and allowed Crissa to cradle the bundle in her arms until the night faded to dawn. As the first rays of the sun peeked over the eastern horizon, Charlie Callahan took a small spade from his saddlebag and began digging a grave for the child.

Please forgive me for leaving you here, in the ground, without a proper burial, she silently pleaded. Crissa stroked her son's furrowed brow and kissed his little pursed lips. *It was for you I made this journey, and now I fear it was the journey that stole you from me. I loved you with each kick you made in my womb—you were my promise of love in return. I leave you now, my angel, but I do not leave you alone. My heart, my very soul, will lie beside you to keep you company until we meet again.*

Crissa's father emerged from the cover of the trees, walked past his wife and daughter, and took the shovel from Charlie's hands. He finished digging the grave without a word. Lifting the small bundle from Crissa's arms, he knelt and gently placed the child in its grave.

The grave was filled in, then covered with rocks to protect it from scavenging animals. Charlie Callahan accompanied Crissa's family as far as Fort Bridger. No word was spoken of the unnamed child again.

Crissa's gaze returned to the present—to the dour-looking bride standing before the mirror. "Not exactly the typical bridal gown, but it will have to do. No sense getting all fluffed up anyway," she told herself sternly. She went to the window and watched buggies rolling into town, bearing unwanted guests. *Go away*, she thought longingly. *You have only come to gawk and laugh in the foreigner's face, so just go away.*

A tapping at her door interrupted her thoughts.

"Crissa? You need help dressing?" Marida stuck her head in the door and then let out a loud gasp. "Heavens, girl! You dressed for funeral, not wedding!"

"Oh, Marida, just leave me alone."

"I will not leave you alone," Marida said emphatically. "You said you want get married: people waiting downstairs to see wedding! Garth just came in with new suit on and hair spit-shined. Now take off sackcloth-and-ashes dress and put on nice dress for to be married in."

"I have nothing nice!" Crissa shot back. "Look for yourself! I have this or my work dress. The only fancy dress I had was torn apart by Garth at the dance!" Crissa gulped past the tears.

"There now, we think of something." Marida paced back and forth. "How bad is fancy dress torn?"

"It is torn where the buttons were ripped open, and one sleeve is torn loose. It is hopeless, Marida."

"Nothing ever hopeless. I take look at it." She pulled the skirt and shirtwaist from the wardrobe and laid them on the bed, then stood back surveying the damage. "I have just the thing!" she said, snatching a pincushion and thread from the nightstand. "You start mending. I be right back."

"There are people waiting!" Crissa started to protest.

"You mend!" Marida ordered as she dashed from the room.

Where do I even begin? Crissa wondered as she sifted through her trinket box for ten buttons that would match the blouse. *We can never get this repaired in time. Everyone will see the stitching and remember the night I wore it to the dance. Why does Marida have to be so bossy, anyway? I should just put my foot down and tell her to mind her own—*

"Voilà!" Marida exclaimed as she appeared in the doorway, brandishing a lacy bodice. "This do the trick!"

"Lace!" Crissa bolted from her seat on the edge of the bed. "Marida, I am not wear—" She paused long enough to gain control of her anger. "I do not want to get all gussied up today. I do not want Garth to think I—I cannot wear lace today."

Marida's lips were set in their familiar firm line. "You not want to look like bride today. But if you be bride today, Garth will see you as every man see his bride. He treat you with love and respect. You want married life begin with love and respect. At least try it on."

Crissa agreed, and the two worked fast and furiously to finish the repairs. A few moments later, Crissa stood with the peach skirt and white shirtwaist on. She waited impatiently while Marida laced the front of the bodice and pulled the laces tight against her rib cage. At last Crissa was permitted to turn and view her reflection in the mirror.

The bodice had a high neckline with ruffles at the top to frame Crissa's face. The lacy sleeves floated just below Crissa's shoulders like angel wings. The midriff was laced tightly, holding her bustline high. Cleavage peeked out above the shirtwaist's round neckline, but was sheltered demurely by the sheer fabric of the bodice.

Marida's mouth hung open in an expression of awe. Crissa looked at her reflection in the mirror. "It is beautiful," the bride whispered. "Thank you."

"Now we do hair," Marida whispered in return. "I be right back." She returned in a moment with a haircomb embellished with pearls. "I found this in Molly's drawer one day while I clean. She would want you to wear it." She skillfully picked up tendrils of Crissa's hair, guiding them to the top of her head to be entwined in the comb, and left them to fall in curls down Crissa's back. Marida pinched Crissa's cheeks to color them, then stood back to admire her handiwork.

"I glad Vic marry me first," she teased. "I not want him single and see you like this." She kissed Crissa on each cheek. "You ready now. I tell Amy start throwing flowers." She bustled out of the room, and Crissa heard the murmur of voices from below subside.

Someone was playing Mendelssohn's "Wedding March" on Molly's piano, and Crissa's stomach churned to each new chord. She turned for one last check in the mirror. *How I wish Drake could have been the one waiting for me downstairs.* "I will stand with Garth," Crissa whispered, as though Drake were in the room with her, "but it is to you I speak my vows."

The crowded guests in the dining room fell silent as Crissa

stepped to the head of the stairs, framed by the archway of ribbons. "Gosh!" escaped from Will , who waited at the bottom of the stairs for Amy to finish with the flowers. Amy paused to turn and look at Crissa until Crissa prompted her to continue. And standing before the bishop, Garth looked up at his bride waiting to descend. His face was pale, his amber eyes wide. He wetted his lips nervously. Crissa couldn't recall ever seeing a grown man with such a boyish demeanor.

Crissa began her descent, feeling every bit a princess, stepping softly on the sprinkled rose petals and smelling their sweet fragrance wafting after her. She held her eyes fixed on Garth, standing straight and tall and looking for all the world a gentleman. *Why could you not have married someone else?* she wondered. *Someone who would love you. Someone who would feel joy to see you walk through the door. Someone who would not think of another when she lay beside you at night.* This last thought sent a shudder up her spine as she stepped off the final stair. She stood beside him in front of the bishop and felt Garth's sweaty hand cradle her icy one. She wanted to pull away and run, but it was too late. *I am as a lamb to the slaughter.* She gave a great sigh and held her chin high to receive her sentence.

"Dearly beloved," Bishop Belnap began, "we are gathered today to witness the joining of this man and this woman in holy wedlock . . ."

Crissa closed her eyes, trying to block out the sound of his voice.

"Who gives this woman to be wed . . . ?"

Crissa's eyes flew open. *I did not ask anyone to give me away! Perhaps if no one gives—*

"I do, on behalf of her father."

Crissa spun to look over her shoulder at the person who had spoken. Mr. Potter stood there, smiling benevolently. He winked at Crissa when she turned his way, then sat again beside his wife.

Crissa turned back to the bishop, an objection forming on her lips, but he had already continued with the ceremony.

"Are there any among you who have any reason why this man and this woman should not be joined?"

Someone please say something.

"Let him speak now or forever hold his peace."

She heard someone shifting in a seat. She waited breathlessly for a voice to proclaim her freedom but was met with silence.

"Well then," the bishop said, "let us continue. Garth, take your bride by the right hand. Do you, Garth Warren Wight, take this woman . . ."

Crissa was scarcely aware of the words that Garth spoke. It was so hard for her to breathe that her head began to swim. *Garth Warren. Warren is Drake's father's name. I wonder what Drake's middle name is. Where are you now, Drake? The next time you see me . . .*

Crissa felt Garth squeeze her hand as he said, "I do."

"Do you, Cristalina Karolina Engleson, take this man . . ."

Dyr Gud . . .

"To have and to hold, for better, for worse . . ."

Crissa felt the blood draining from her face.

". . . for richer, for poorer, in sickness and in health . . ."

She began to wobble and Garth put his free hand beneath her elbow to steady her.

". . . to love and to cherish for as long as you both shall live?"

From somewhere within the darkness surrounding her, she heard a voice whisper, "I do."

"Then by the power vested in me as a bishop in Zion in the Territory of Utah, I now pronounce you man and wife. You may kiss your bride."

Crissa felt Garth's dry lips close over her own before her knees buckled and her world turned to black.

★ ★ ★

"Crissa? Crissa? Wake up, darling."

The woman's voice invading her sleep was not welcome.

Let me rest awhile longer, Mama.

"She'll be fine," a man's voice joined in. "Prob'ly just a case of wedding jitters."

Wedding. Crissa felt herself cradled in strong, warm arms as her mind struggled to return to consciousness. *Drake. You have come back.* She nestled in closer to his chest before opening her eyes. It was not Drake's face she stared into, but Garth's. She struggled to sit up.

"Where?" The room began to spin, putting an end to her struggle. She sank back into Garth's cradling arms.

"You're here in kitchen." Marida stood over her, along with Vic, Mrs. Potter, and Doc Robbins. "You blacked out, honey."

"How're you feeling?" The doctor placed a hand on her forehead, then onto her wrist.

"I will be fine. I am just a little dizzy."

"Betcha haven't had much to eat today, have you?"

Crissa thought back on the hectic day. She couldn't remember having eaten at all. "I am sure that is all it is."

"Well, you rest a spell, then come out and get yourself something to eat." Doc Robbins patted her on the cheek and then went out to the dining room. The others remained with her, reluctant to leave.

"I am fine. Really."

Marida, Vic, and Mrs. Potter began moving toward the door. "I fix you plate," Marida said, then waited for Crissa and Garth to follow her.

"We'll be right out, Marida," Garth said. "I'd like a minute alone with my wife first."

"You don'a be long. She need to eat." Marida shut the kitchen doors softly behind her.

"Your wife," Crissa whispered.

Garth raised his eyebrows and smiled at her—a smile of pure adoration. "It's gonna get pretty *loco* out there, and I won't get much chance to talk with you. Well, I just wanted you to know that I . . ." He paused to clear his throat. "I, you're . . . you're the most beautiful woman I've ever laid eyes on, and I'm honored that you're my wife, and well . . ." He cleared his throat again. "I'm gonna try to be the best husband a woman could have."

Crissa smiled at his gush of emotion. "Thank you," she said simply, then stood up to straighten her dress. "We have guests to greet."

CHAPTER 12

Applause erupted as Crissa and Garth emerged from the kitchen. "Congratulations!" "Best of wishes!" "You make a beautiful bride!" The crowd closed in around the couple as they inched their way toward the bar laid out in an array of potluck dishes. At last the crowd parted.

"Crissa, you eat this," Marida commanded as she thrust a heaping plate into Crissa's hands.

Crissa gasped when she saw the mounds of food collected for her. "Marida, I could not possibly eat this much."

"You will eat this, and you won'a argue."

"Thank you," Crissa replied meekly, feeling quite overwhelmed.

"Now you," Marida commanded again, waving her arm at Garth, "go fix plate you'self."

Garth grinned good-naturedly and bowed to his bride. "By your leave."

Crissa watched him walk away and had to smile at his attempt at humor.

"That's first time I see you smile all day," Marida said.

"Marida!" Mrs. Hampton's loud voice scolded as she marched across the room to Crissa. "It's not polite to keep the bride from her guests!"

Suzanna held her head high as she trailed behind her mother.

Layers and layers of stiff ruffles surrounded Suzanna in a cloud of ivory organdy. Her exposed head and neck, and arms were the only indications that she was not, in fact, a huge tumbleweed just blown in. Even her elegantly coifed hair had a mound of green netting fastened to one side. "Crissa, you look positively sweet," she said. "Doesn't she look sweet, Mother?"

"Yes," Mrs. Hampton said, sneering, "very nice. It's a shame you didn't have time to order a real dress, what with you and Garth having to get married so quickly." She raised her eyebrows and let her gaze fall to Crissa's abdomen.

Crissa bristled at the insinuation. She stood tall with her shoulders back and purposefully smoothed the dress over her flat stomach with her free hand. Several men stared as her figure was fully displayed. Crissa blushed and let her shoulders relax in modesty. She smiled sweetly at Mrs. Hampton and her fluffy daughter. "Thank you for coming."

"Just a moment," Mrs. Hampton snapped as Crissa began moving away. She regarded Crissa through angry, beady eyes, her mouth pinched in a bitter knot. "We brought you something."

"Oh, yes," Suzanna chorused, "a wedding present. Come and see what it is." She took Crissa by the arm and began pulling her across the room. "Look, everyone, Crissa's going to open a present!"

Mrs. Hampton took the uneaten plate of food from the beleaguered bride and laid it on a table as they passed. She picked up a gaily wrapped box from another table and lifted off the lid for Crissa.

"Oh, little tiny cups." Crissa lifted one of the delicate china cups for the crowd who had gathered. "How . . . quaint."

"Demitasse." Mrs. Hampton sniffed.

Crissa turned the cup around in her hand. It was glazed a light shade of pink with a spray of flowers painted on one side. "They are lovely."

"They're from my own personal collection," Mrs. Hampton boasted.

Crissa studied the painted spray of flowers. *This is the same design that Garth carved on the grave marker.* She looked at Mrs. Hampton quizzically, uneasy with the association. "You are very kind."

"Well, I felt you should have some little thing."

"Rather like a consolation gift," Suzanna cut in. "Wouldn't you say, Mother?"

Crissa gasped.

"Rachel! Suzanna!" Garth snapped as he shoved his way through the crowd. "Nice of you to come," he said through clenched teeth. "Too bad you can't stay." He took Mrs. Hampton and Suzanna each by an arm and brusquely steered them toward the door.

"Some nerve!" Suzanna tried unsuccessfully to wrench her arm free. "Standing up for that tramp!"

"I'd be careful who you call a tramp."

"Garth!" Mrs. Hampton hissed in a loud whisper. "Remember who you're talking to!"

"Ain't no one gonna talk to my wife like that," he barked in return. "Not even you!"

Crissa was stunned with the fury in Garth's voice as he defended her. *My wife. My wife.* His words echoed through her mind.

Garth led Crissa back to the buffet table, and the party resumed. Picking up a plate, he spooned small portions from the dozen or so dishes. He led Crissa to an empty table at the front of the room and held out a chair for her. He retrieved her plate of food and set it in front of her, then slid her chair closer to the table. "Now don't you move, and don't you talk to no one until you've eaten your fill." Placing a finger under her chin and tilting it up, he tenderly kissed her on the lips.

Crissa watched him as he walked outside, pulling uncomfortably at his collar. Is this the "right decent fellow" Vic described? *I haven't seen him drinking today, and he has been kind.* She saw him run his hand nervously through his hair, then draw a cigar from his pocket. As he walked past the window, he drew a flask from his vest pocket.

Crissa busied herself nibbling food and chatting with the roomful of guests. Marida hovered nearby, whether to make sure Crissa was eating or to protect her from any more unkind confrontations, Crissa didn't know. She watched the door anxiously, waiting for Garth. Where could he be for so long? At least he could be polite enough to speak with his guests. Vic would occasionally walk outside and, when he returned, speak privately with Marida. Both of them looked increasingly worried about something as the afternoon wore into evening.

"Crissa," Vic said, his voice quiet and somber. He sat down beside her. "Me and Marida are thinking that . . . well, that . . . maybe——"

"You stay here tonight," Marida broke in impatiently.

"Stay here? Well, of course we will stay——"

"Where is she?" Garth burst into the dining room, resting his hand on a table to steady himself. "Where's my woman?"

"*Dyr Gud,*" Crissa murmured, rising to her feet. She hadn't considered that, with Vic and Marida to watch the children, Garth would expect her to go elsewhere tonight.

Garth staggered to where she stood and took her by the arm. "It's time to go, wife."

Her eyes watered with the putrid smell of cigars and whiskey. "Garth, please . . . ," she whispered.

"No need to say please, darlin'. We're married now."

Crissa turned pale as she was led from the room toward his waiting buggy.

From the silence of the dining room, Crissa heard Amy's plaintive cry, "Crissa, please don't go!" And Will's disgusted reply, "Aw, let 'er be."

Lifting Crissa, Garth tossed her up on the seat of the buggy, then hauled himself in beside her. Clicking his tongue, he urged the horse to a trot.

"At least let me get my overnight things," Crissa snapped.

"Won't be needin' 'em."

Crissa's face grew hot with the realization of what was coming next. "But you did not even let me say good-bye."

"No need for that neither. They knew'd you was goin'."

"Garth! I am your wife now. I will not allow you to treat me so rudely!"

He pulled the horse to a stop and turned in the seat to face her. "That's right, lady. You're my wife now, and I'll treat you any way I feel like. And right now I feel like"—he paused long enough to let his leering gaze make her uncomfortable—"I feel like honeymoonin'."

Crissa gasped and turned her head in embarrassment. Feeling vulnerable, she folded her arms instinctively across her chest. She huddled as far from him as she could on the narrow seat for the remainder of the journey.

At length, a shack came into view as Garth steered the horse to the far side of a hill. Crissa bit her lip in disappointment. Her new home was nothing more than a dilapidated barn perched on the western side of the hill. Situated far enough from the trail and sheltered by the hill, passersby on their way to or from town would never realize the shack was there unless they were deliberately looking for it. The isolation was overpowering. About twenty-five feet from the house, a patch of weeds rimmed by a rickety picket fence could have been a flower garden in years gone by. Somewhere farther downhill, Crissa heard a stream trickling.

She climbed down from her perch as soon as the buggy came to a stop to avoid having his hands on her again.

"In a hurry, darlin'?" Garth tied the horse to a tree without bothering to unhitch the buggy.

Crissa turned around on the doorstep just long enough to glare at him before stomping into the house and slamming the door. She stood with her back braced against the door, trying to still her pounding heart. The shack was only one room. A fireplace, a table, and two chairs occupied one side of the room. Shelves hung on the wall next to the door. There were a few tin dishes and even fewer provisions for meals. An ornate glass-front cabinet stood in the corner of the room proudly displaying rifles and pistols of every description. Several boxes of cigars were stacked on the single shelf in the case. *It is obvious where he spends his money*, Crissa mused in disgust. *He lives in squalor yet displays his guns and tobacco like fine china. Will he expect me to live in poverty, or will I be part of his prized collection?*

Reluctantly, her gaze moved to the other side of the room. Rough-hewn logs lashed together with rope made up the bed. A plump patchwork quilt hid the mattress, and two fat pillows were covered with crisp, white pillow slips. A crude nightstand stood next to the bed. On top was a tin pitcher and bowl. A bouquet of wild roses lay next to the pitcher.

Crissa regarded the efforts Garth had made to make this shabby cabin comfortable for her. *Who is this man I have married? One moment he acts like a wild animal, and the next . . .* She glanced again at the new pillow slips. *He is as a man with two souls. But which soul belongs to Garth?*

She lifted an edge of the potato sack that acted as a curtain over the cabin's single window. Garth stood on the porch, sucking on the stump of a cigar. He ground the spent cigar under his boot, then turned to a nail keg filled with water. She could hear him splashing, and occasionally he would submerge his entire head in the barrel, then shake his head wildly like a wet dog. He leaned his head back and gargled with the same water he had just bathed in, then spit it off the side of the porch. She watched as he threaded his arms through his suspenders, picked up his coat, and turned toward the door, scratching either side of his buttocks.

She held her icy hands to her throbbing head. *You are married to him, Crissa. You have to go through with it. Just get it over with.* She groped in the pocket of her skirt for the silk hanky Marida had given her. *This had better work, Marida.* She mentally went over Marida's instructions on how to prevent a pregnancy. She heard Garth's footsteps on the step, and she quickly moved away from the door.

Stepping inside, he shut the door behind him and hung his jacket on a peg. He lit the oil lamp on the bedside table and turned the flame to a soft flicker. Without a word, he faced his bride. His face was bathed in the gentle glow of the lamp as he moved toward her. Carefully, he drew the pearl-studded comb from her hair, letting soft tendrils glide from their moorings. He knelt, tenderly unbuttoned her shoes, and guided them from her slender ankles. Slowly, he stood, his golden eyes warm in the lamplight.

"I don't 'member much about that night, Crissa, but I'm powerful sorry that I hurt you. I'm gonna stop drinking. I promise." The rest of his words were muffled in her hair as he began to kiss her.

The twisting sensation in her stomach grew with each kiss, each caress, and it climbed steadily toward her throat. Dry heaves pulled at her gut, and she struggled not to vomit. He removed his shirt and draped it on the bedpost, then wrapped his arms around her. In desperation, she shut her eyes and replaced Garth's face with the images of Drake—the first time she saw him at Molly's, him kneeling beside him at the water's edge, their picnic together, the soft caress of his lips on hers . . .

Garth lifted her hair and gently kissed her neck. The sound of horses pounding up the path interrupted his kisses. Garth bounded to the door, opening it just a crack. The door crashed open, sending Garth flying. His head slammed against the corner of the table. Crissa screamed.

"There she is!"

"Got here just in time!"

"Grab her quick before he comes to!"

Crissa clutched Garth's shirt to her thin chemise and cowered in the corner of the bed as a gang of drunken men streamed through the door. One of the men, Garth's friend Wakelin, slung her across his shoulder. He sprinted from the room and flung her up to another man waiting on horseback.

"Ya'll git outta here now!" Wakelin yelled. "Frank 'n' me'll take care of Garth."

"No! Garth!" she screamed. Through terror-filled eyes, Crissa saw Garth lying on the floor of the cabin, unconscious. She turned to the man holding her on the horse. Pummeling him with her fists, she screamed again. She tried to wrest herself free and was nearly thrown from the galloping horse.

"Yer gonna get yerself hurt now! Be still!" He tightened his hold on her and yanked her closer into his body.

Crissa struggled to keep her seat on the racing horse. She clung to the horse's mane. Frantic, she looked around. They were heading northward, into the foothills of the Deep Creek Mountains. *Where are they taking me? What will they do to . . . I must find a way to escape! If I jump, I could be trampled. If I do not . . .* She played out several possible scenarios in her mind, each one more frightening than the last. As much from terror as the chill air whipping around her, she trembled uncontrollably. "*Gud som haver barnen kär, Se till mig som liten är,*" she whispered. "God who loves little children, watch over me, for I am small."

For a long time they galloped. Crissa wasn't sure how long, but the dusk had turned to darkness before they finally drew into a stand of trees and dismounted. Crissa was pulled from the horse. She pushed her arms into the sleeves of the shirt she still clutched around her nearly naked form. The scant covering did little to stop her shivering.

"That's right," one of the men said, sneering at her, "you bundle up now." He pulled a blanket from his saddlebag and walked toward her with it. "Garth'd kill us if you caught yer death out here."

Crissa backed away from the cluster of men. "What do you want? Leave me alone!"

He plucked at a button on her shirt as she backed against a tree. "Don't fret, honey. Don't none of us wanna hurt ya."

"Leave 'er alone, Harris," another man said, taking the blanket and wrapping it around Crissa's trembling shoulders. "Let's get her tied up and get outta here."

"I sure as blazes don't wanna be around when Garth finds her." A third man stepped forward with a piece of rope and began tying her hands. "D'ya reckon we ought'a tie her feet?"

"Naw, leave some fight in 'er for when Garth catches up."

Crissa gagged as she finally grasped what the men were debating. "This is Garth's doing?"

The men broke out laughing. "Not hardly! This here's a shivaree, lady. Jest a little harmless funnin', less'n you're the bride or the groom, o'course."

"But how will he find me?"

"Wakelin stayed behind to tell him where to find ya."

"Yeah—after we get a good head start, o'course."

Fingers of terror clawed through Crissa's stomach. "But you cannot leave me out here alone! It is dark! There are coyotes and—and—wild animals!" She felt herself growing dizzy as the blood drained from her face.

"I'll stay with you." Another of the men stepped forward, striking a match to light his cheroot. The light bathed his face in an eerie glow. Though he was dressed in denim trousers and a cotton shirt like the other men, Crissa recognized him: Donald Jenkins, the man in the gray worsted suit.

CHAPTER 13

Cottonwoods edged the clearing Crissa and her captors stood in. Soughing in the wind, the trees lent an air of doom. With tiny hairs rising on the nape of her neck, Crissa stared, transfixed, at Donald Jenkins.

Images from last night's dream swirled around her, cruel, haunting specters of her greatest fears. It was him. Jenkins. Always nearby when Crissa's tormentors were upon her. "You—you were the one who—" Crissa sucked in a ragged breath. "Please—" She turned to the man who had wrapped her in the blanket. "You cannot leave me here! Not with—not alone!" Terror pounded in her temples with every heartbeat. She swept beseeching eyes from man to man. "Please . . ."

"She's right." The man who had carried her on his horse stepped forward. "The six of us been riding together since we were kids, and I wouldn't trust a'one of you alone with her. An' we hardly even know Jenkins here. Garth'd string us all up if'n anything happened to 'er. We'd best leave one of us to stay with 'em to chaperone."

"Chaperone? What for?" The man called Harris thrust his finger at the group. "You s'pose a chaperone could be trusted anymore'n Jenkins?"

"We'll leave Carter with 'em." The first man grabbed a short, stocky fellow by the collar and dragged him into the circle. "He's so drunk he couldn't stand straight, let alone hurt the lady. Jenkins ain't gonna try nothing anyway. We just gotta make it look right when Garth shows up."

"It will not matter how it looks when Garth arrives," Crissa said through gritted teeth. "You have abducted me. You have terrified me. And now you leave me alone in the dark with two of your ruffians. Garth will not be amused with your prank."

"Yeah, well," another man said, chuckling, "he'll have to catch us first. And, with all due respect, ma'am, he'll have other things to keep him busy once he finds you."

Crissa gasped, too shocked embarrassed by the truth to reply. Amid guffaws and more crude remarks, all but two riders mounted their horses and galloped into the black chasm of night.

Pulling the blanket more securely around her, trying to trap what body heat she had left, Crissa turned her attention to the two men left to protect her. Carter stood next to her, so drunk he could scarcely keep his balance. Jenkins carefully avoided her glance while he piled dry twigs and leaves, then struck a match to start a fire. Carefully coaxing the blaze, he added one stick after another to the growing fire.

Clasping the blanket around her, Crissa inched her way to the edge of the fire's glow. *Why is he here?* she wondered. *I have married Garth, and surely he has received his payment. What more does he want?* Gliding unseen through the leafy canopy overhead, a screech owl cried out, sending an eerie shiver racing up Crissa's spine. Licks of firelight beckoned her to draw nearer. Fatigue pulled at her limbs, begging her to sit, relax and sleep. Yet tension kept every nerve taut, anxious, and waiting. Straining to hear Garth's approach, willing his arrival, she felt as tightly wound as her father's pocket watch.

Carter grunted something unintelligible and shuffled off into the bushes. Looking up from where he crouched over the fire, Jenkins motioned Crissa to join him. "Might as well sit a spell, Mrs. Wight."

"I prefer to stand."

"Suit yourself." Shrugging, Jenkins stirred the fire once more, then sat down opposite Crissa. "No tellin' how long it'll take before your husband figures out where you are."

"He will not be long."

"Might be morning 'fore he can pick up the trail."

"But Mr. Wakelin is going to tell him where to find me."

"Maybe. He'll give his friends enough time to cover their tracks, though."

"Surely he would not wait until morning."

Jenkins shrugged again.

Several minutes passed with Crissa shifting her weight from foot to foot. Certainly she could not remain standing until morning. Brushing leaves and pebbles away with her bare foot, she settled in front of the fire to await her rescue.

Crissa peered in the direction the drunken Carter went. "I wonder why Mr. Carter has been gone so long."

"Aw, he's just waterin' the bushes."

"Do you suppose everything is all right?"

"Guess I could take a look-see." Jenkins stood up, stretched, and adjusted his gun belt. "You okay alone?"

Crissa scooted closer to the fire. "I will be fine." She heard something scuttle off the path as Jenkins made his way after Carter. Muffled voices were carried on the wind, followed by a grunt, the rustle of leaves, and then silence. From several miles away, the lonely cry of a coyote drifted back to Crissa. A shiver crawled down her back as she watched Jenkins return alone.

"Did you find him?"

"Yeah. He's asleep."

"I heard voices."

"I tried to wake him." Jenkins smiled a crooked smile at her. "He's sleeping like the dead."

Something in his voice prompted Crissa not to ask any more questions.

Surely two or three hours had passed since her abduction, and still no sign of rescue. Crissa studied Mr. Jenkins from across the fire. This seemingly innocuous man had invaded her refuge, revealed the past she had so meticulously evaded, and indeed precipitated her marriage to a consummate drunk and womanizer. Why? Why her? Why now? Why him? And why was he still here after she had fulfilled her agreement to marry Garth? "Why?"

"Ma'am?"

She had spoken her last thought aloud. Thudding in her chest, her heart tried to choke off any more conversation. The question hung in the air, waiting for all the answers to her past, her present, and her future. She drew a deep breath and plunged into her interrogation.

"Why are you still here, Mr. Jenkins?"

"'Cause you were scared to stay here alone."

"No—I mean, why are you still in Willow Springs?"

Jenkins studied her from across the fire. He scratched his chest and rose to a squat to stir the fire. His eyes were narrow beads when he again looked at her.

His cold look of hatred was nearly overwhelming, but there was no turning back. Her questions must be resolved. "You have exposed my past, you have forced me to marry one of the vilest men in Willow Springs, and you have been paid for your trouble. What more do you want? Why are you still here?"

He remained in his squatting position, his coal-black eyes penetrating hers. Slowly, his tightly drawn lips spread in a self-satisfied smile. Lowering one knee to the ground, he chose his words carefully. "I have been paid for my trouble. By a most generous . . . person."

"Who paid you?" Crissa demanded.

"But she only bought information," Jenkins continued. "It was someone else who sent me out here to find you."

"Then please tell me who sent you," Crissa pleaded again.

"Y'know, Mrs. Lundstrom, for some reason your husband—your real husband—was worried that some bounty hunter would bring you back to Boston."

"But . . . you told my parents the charges against me had been dropped."

He smiled. "Didn't s'pose they'd tell me where you were otherwise."

"They told you where to find me?"

"Naw, they just pointed me in the right direction. It was my own doin' that found you."

"But what does Eric have to do with this?"

Jenkins smiled again, obviously well pleased with himself. "Y'see, you being such a pretty thing and all, Eric was concerned the law just might believe you were innocent of that lady's murder. Then who would be left to point the finger at? So you see, he paid me right handsome to make sure you never got found." Jenkins stood up, rubbing his knees.

Crissa struggled to make sense of what he was saying. "Never get—you mean to . . . You are here to kill me?" She frantically scrambled, trying to gain her footing on the gravel. She watched his hand drop to his gunbelt. He unbuckled it and lay it gently across a broken tree stump.

"Aw, honey, I been watching you such a long time now. There's only one more payment I'm lookin' to collect 'fore I finish up with my business here."

Backing away from him, Crissa tried to think of some way out—some way to reason with him, but her terrified words sounded like gibberish. With the fire barring her escape on one side and Jenkins steadily advancing on the other, Crissa turned and bolted through the brush. "Carter!" Her scream vanished in the dark. She must find Carter! "Help!" She could hear Jenkins's mocking laughter as he thundered after her.

The canopy of trees overhead forbade the moon from lighting her way as she struggled through the dense underbrush. At last, she saw Carter hunched beside a tree. Rushing to him, she shook his shoulders.

"Carter," she begged. "Wake up!"

He toppled limply to his side, revealing the gaping slit in his throat. Recoiling, too terrified to scream, she cast about for somewhere to hide, some way to defend herself, something . . . In Carter's gunbelt, she found his revolver still wedged in its holster. She grabbed the gun, pulled back its hammer, and rolled to face Jenkins looming above her.

"No!" Screaming, she closed her eyes and fired a shot.

Silence hung heavy in the dark forest. With her head buried in her arms, Crissa couldn't hear any sounds of movement. After a long moment, she dared to look up.

A lifeless Jenkins was sprawled on the ground, inches away from where she crouched.

"No . . ." Her voice was a whimper. Tears sprang to her eyes as she crawled slowly toward the lifeless body beside her. "I told you no."

Icy sweat shimmered on her arms as she knelt over her victim, waiting for him to move, to groan, to breathe. Engulfed by the realization of what she had done, she knelt beside a scrub oak and vomited.

Struggling to her feet, she looked around trying to find a path. If Garth's friends had followed any kind of trail to bring her here, that trail had been lost in the darkness. Oblivious to the gun she still clutched in her hand, she turned to what she believed to be south and began pushing her way through the brambles. Twisted branches of dry pinion pine were interwoven with lithe willows that slapped about her as she forced them aside. She had lost her blanket while fleeing from Jenkins and was clasping Garth's inadequate shirt about her. Falling into a clearing, she gasped for air, scorching her lungs with each breath she gulped. "I have got to get home," she said to herself. The sound of her quivering voice reverberated through the stillness surrounding her. "Vic and Marida will help me find Drake." She felt as if she were suffocating as hopelessness threatened to choke her. "He will know what to do. He simply must."

Tears strayed down her cheeks as she tried to replace her terror with logic. The moon was to her back, which meant she had been traveling eastward. She found a creek a few yards from the clearing. It was no more than a trickle, but it was flowing to the south. If she followed it, and if it didn't dry up too soon, she should be able to find her way back to town—and safety.

Weaving her way along the wash, dodging tree limbs, and slipping on loose rocks, she was able to maintain a good speed despite her bare feet. Her thoughts were consumed by what she would say in her defense when Jenkins's body was found. And what about

Mr. Carter? Would she be blamed for his death as well? It was self-defense—she had heard lawyers in Boston use that term. But Garth had said that Jenkins was a Pinkerton man. Would they believe that he had tried to kill her? And she was already wanted for another murder. Would they assume she'd killed Jenkins when he tried to take her back to Boston? She replayed her statement of self-defense over and over as she ran, and each time it sounded less believable. She needed Drake to help her sort things out. But he wasn't there. Would he even return to Willow Springs before the marshal came to arrest her? She swiped at the tears blurring the path before her.

A horse whinnied somewhere ahead of her and to the left. Crissa darted from the streambed, hiding herself behind a bush, waiting . . . for what? For whom? Frantically, she cast about, searching for more secure cover. Nothing.

"Crissa!" a man yelled. "Crissa!"

Drake? She was too weak to return his summons. She stumbled from her hiding place, clambering over the streambed, dodging scrub brush to reach him. He was there, in the distance, urging his mount toward her. No, it wasn't Drake—she could see that now. It was Garth. Her lungs exploded, and stars tumbled to engulf her. Just as she fell, Garth caught her and held her securely in his arms.

CHAPTER 14

Crissa awoke to the soft scraping sound of a door opening. She turned her head toward the sound but couldn't focus her eyes. Drawing the heel of her hand across her forehead, she winced as she passed over a tender welt above her right eye.

"Leave it alone," a male voice spoke from across the room. She heard the heavy thunk of a man's boots come toward her. "Don't go messing up that salve I put on it."

Crissa felt the mattress sag beside her as he sat down. She lifted her head, trying to fix her sight upon him. Her eyes felt as if they were glued shut, allowing her to glimpse only a fuzzy image through painful slits. A rough hand slipped under her head, lifting it enough that she could sip from a cold metal cup. After the first painful gulp passed down her throat, she realized just how thirsty she was. She sucked in great mouthfuls of the sweet, cool liquid before the cup was pulled from her grasp.

"Slow down now. Just sip it." He stroked her face with a damp cloth, freeing her lashes from their crusty tears. At last she could open her eyes enough to view him.

"Garth!" Her hoarse exclamation came out no louder than a whisper. She drew away from him. "Where—?"

"Take it easy. You're home now."

Home! Twisting away from him, she was seized with pain

131

scorching her stomach. She clasped her hands over the site, which only made it worse. She cried out with the pain, clenching her hands into fists suspended over the wound.

"Don't touch it," he commanded. "You've got powder burns all over your middle."

"Burns?" She struggled to clear away the remnants of a deep sleep.

Garth took her hands in one of his, then with his other arm around her back, helped her sit up. He dabbed at her eye with the moist cloth. "Got one heck'uv'a welt there too."

Welt? How did I . . . ? Like vague snatches of a nightmare, convoluted images ripped through her mind, at last slowly organizing into the memory of last night's ordeal. Remembering what she had been wearing the night before, she clutched her hand to her throat, closing her garment tightly about her neck. Gingerly, Crissa inspected her apparel. Garth's tattered shirt had been replaced with a sackcloth nightshirt. The neck buttoned up the front, and it extended well past her knees. Unable to remember what had happened after Garth found her last night, she pressed her hand to her bosom, thankfully feeling the lacy edges of her chemise slide under her touch. She wanted to get dressed in her own clothing, but she did not dare disrobe in front of him yet. She looked at Garth, her husband, and all the angry rebuffs knotted in her throat. Silently, she let the tears of fear, hurt, and anger course down her cheeks.

He reached out to touch her, then pulled his hand back. Folding his arms across his chest, he leaned forward, resting his elbows on his knees. At last Garth stood, pacing back and forth, avoiding Crissa's confused stare, his hands flexing into fists at his sides. He snatched the tin cup from her grip and slammed it on the table.

What on earth?

He strode to the fireplace, poking angrily at a smoldering log. Facing Crissa, his arms folded tightly, he opened his mouth to say something and then clamped it shut again, lips twitching angrily.

Perplexed by his rage, Crissa's own indignity mounted. "What is the—"

His angry glare cut her short. Crossing the room again, he

marched outside, banging the door shut behind him, only to return a scant moment later.

"What is the matter with you?" Crissa snapped, coming to her feet. "I am the one who—"

"That's right!" he barked. "You are the one—" Through gritted teeth he tried again. "You are the one who—" Whirling around, he slammed his hand on the mantle of the fireplace.

Fearing he'd hit her next, Crissa leaped for the door and bolted from the cabin. Light-headed, she stumbled down the hill, collapsing in the soft weeds and clover that had overgrown the flower bed. The sweet aroma enveloped her but did nothing to soothe her frustration. *I have done nothing! But I have. I killed a man. Surely Garth would not have found him already. Why else would he be so angry? He has no right to treat me . . .*

She lay there, panting, debating whether she should try to make it to town—to Vic and Marida—or if she should hide until nightfall, steal a horse, and just disappear.

The early morning sun cast Garth's shadow long before him, revealing a wide stance with his hands on his hips. Several minutes passed before he finally sat down beside Crissa. He drew his knees up and braced his feet against the downward slope of the hill. The dry grass rustled in the slight breeze, and the feeble stream gurgled as it meandered its way past the base of the rise. The rest of the world was silent while Garth and Crissa each waited for the other to speak.

"Why didn't you just leave?" He didn't look at her. Rather, his words were more of a gentle rumination to whatever lay in the distance.

Leave? "I had to come back. I did not know what else to do."

"What else to do!" Garth clenched his teeth; a muscle began twitching above his lip. Obviously struggling to control his anger, he asked her, "What more was there to do?"

Crissa stared at him, trying to read what lay behind his brooding eyes. Was he angry that she had escaped her attacker last night? "I . . ." she stammered. "I thought Vic and Marida might—"

"Might what? Give you more money? Shoulda known you was a gold digger."

"Wha—?" She tried to comprehend what he was saying. Confusion swirled so thickly she had trouble sorting her own thoughts, let alone his.

Garth chewed the edge of his thumbnail and peeled a slice of it away. He spat the nail out in front of him, then watched as a drop of blood beaded on the corner of the tear. He looked off into the distance again, wiping his thumb on his pants. "Why didn't you and Jenkins just take the money and . . . go?"

"Jenkins?"

"Stop playing the innocent, Crissa!" Garth yelled, the flush of anger staining his cheeks scarlet. "Your game is over! If the two'uv you have done anything to Carter, I'll hunt you down faster'n—"

What little shred of sense Crissa had clung to vanished completely, along with her forced patience. She jumped to her feet, her own fists clenched. "What in heaven's name are you going on about?"

He matched her stance, towering over her, eyes glaring from beneath knotted brows. "You and Jenkins," he said in measured tones, "traipsing off together like a couple of—" Crissa's brutal slap across his face interrupted his tirade.

"How dare you!" Crissa bit off each word, trying to disguise the tremor in her voice. "How dare you stand there and accuse me of that! It was your friends who abducted me! Your friends who left me out there. And you . . . you *ynkrygg*, who could not be bothered with coming after me."

"You're lucky I came lookin' for you at all! Wakelin told me all about Jenkins's little scheme to get you alone. Way I figure, you were in on this all along. Play the fair maiden in distress, cheat innocent people outta their hard-earned money to protect you, then run off with your lover in the dead of night with us none the wiser."

"You thought I ran off with those hooligans on my own?" Crissa pulled her captive hand free, massaging the blood back into her tingling wrist. "You thought Jenkins and I were partners?"

"Can't figure why you went ahead and married me, though. Jenkins already had his money. Why didn't the two of you just hightail it right then?" Garth's voice softened as he spoke, his personal loss evident in his soft brown eyes. "What did you think you could gain by it, Crissa? I ain't got no thing that would interest you."

"You know why I married you. You are the one who black-mailed me." Crissa felt drawn to comfort him, yet she still bristled at his conniving and his accusations. "Mr. Jenkins and I were not . . . together. I had never met him before you brought him into the inn. I do not know where you got such notions."

"You sayin' you 'n' Jenkins weren't . . . that you didn't . . ." He took a step back from her and dragged both of his hands over his face and through his hair. "Wakelin filled my head with so much talk . . . got me in such a lather . . . I set there and stewed a long time just trying to sort things out. By the time I set off after ya I figured you owed me. I was aiming to collect."

"Collect what?"

"It was my wedding night too, y'know!"

Crissa looked at him in shock before bursting unexpectedly into peals of hysterical, surprised laughter. After all of the trauma they had each experienced the night before, it was the lack of consumma-tion that had made Garth the most indignant? Clutching her hand to her mouth, she tried to regain her composure as she glanced at him. A look of astonishment was evident in his eyes. He obviously was not sharing her mirth. "I am sorry," she said, but her amusement was not willing to be contained.

He gripped her shoulders tightly, turning her toward him. "I swear, Crissa, when I finally found you, and you purt' near leaped into my arms, I thought my heart would bust wide open."

Sobered by his words, Crissa looked in his warm honey eyes. Finally understanding his pain, she was confused by her own response to it.

"And then, when I lifted you up on my horse and you were holding Carter's gun, and powder burns all over your middle, I . . . didn't know if I was comin' or goin'."

The thought of telling Garth his friend was dead brought an ache to Crissa's throat that could not be soothed. Biting her lip she swiped at her tears.

"I gotta know, Crissa," he whispered, brushing the rest of her tears with a rough paw. "Did you kill Carter?"

She shook her head slowly. She rested her small hand on his large one, pressing it gently to her cheek. "Jenkins killed him." His hand stiffened, but he left it in her grip. "Please, you must believe me. I did not want to go with the men. You saw them grab me. I did not even realize Jenkins was with them until we stopped in the woods where they left me. I was frightened beyond words. Jenkins offered to stay with me, but your friends did not trust him alone with me, so they left Carter also. He was terribly drunk. He went into the bushes but did not come back.

"Jenkins told me Eric had paid him to kill me. He made advances on me, and I ran into the woods. I found Carter with his throat slit. When Jenkins caught me and tried to force himself on me, I . . . I . . ." Her body slackened, and she cupped her hands to her face, sobbing.

Garth pulled her hands away from her face, forcing her to look at him.

"Shot him," she whispered.

"You—" Garth stammered. "I didn't . . . I thought . . . Oh, Crissa." Garth wrapped his arms around her, stroking her hair with one hand.

Crissa allowed his warmth to encompass her, knowing that only too soon they would have to go into town and deal with her latest crisis. She moved in closer to his embrace, feeling his arms tighten around her.

Finally Crissa lowered herself back to the clover carpet, tucking her knees under the nightshirt she still wore. "How did you know it was Carter's gun?"

"I carved the grips," he answered idly. "Put my mark in the butt." Garth sat beside her and toyed with his wounded thumb.

The sun rose steadily behind them, nearing the midmorning point. At last, trying to bridge the uneasy silence between them, Crissa nodded toward the rickety fence that might have once delineated a garden. "Is that a garden?" The tangled mess of weeds bore little resemblance to anything cultivated now.

Garth gave a halfhearted chuckle that sounded more like a snort. "Used to be. We et what we grew, not much more. Guess when my pa died, there weren't anything to leave to my ma. She owned the inn for a while." He raised his eyes to Crissa long enough to make sure she understood. "Henders Inn. But, well, the incoming never did catch up with the outgoing, and we ended up here."

"I am sorry," Crissa murmured. "I did not realize you had—"

"Well, I's a pretty little sprout, back then. Can't say as I remember ever having anything extra on my plate, but I never went hungry."

"How did your father . . . ?"

"'Fore I was born. He was a sailor—died at sea."

"How very sad."

At length, Garth rubbed his hands across his face and exhaled a frustrated sigh. "So, how're we gonna get you out of this one?"

"Get me out of this one?" She eyed him suspiciously. "We will just tell the truth."

"The truth?" he bellowed, incredulous. "Lady, you're already wanted for one murder. Once those bodies are found, you can bet you'll be accused of them, as well. You tryin' to make me a widower before the week is out?"

The reality of what faced her if—no, when—the law caught up with her left her stunned. *Garth is right*, she thought. She had run instead of coming forward. She had destroyed any chance of proclaiming her innocence. An innocent person wouldn't have run. But her dad had convinced her that because she was a foreigner, the law would certainly convict her.

"So, what do you propose we do?"

"What do *we* do?" He glared at her with fierce amber eyes, stalked off a few paces, returned, and glared again. "Look," he said finally, "let's just settle down and think this thing through. First off, we've got to figure out what to do about Jenkins and Carter."

"I do not understand. What can we do?"

"Well, if you can remember where they are, I'll go up and bury the bodies. Carter's people are in Denver. I don't know where Jenkins's from, but it'll be a while 'fore anyone misses them."

"But Carter works at the mine. Will he not be missed?"

"Well . . . no one saw him after he was dropped off with you. I'll just say I found you wandering in the woods alone. I do think we ought'a head away from here for a spell, though." They started back toward the house. "I've already talked to Mr. Adams about taking an advance on my salary to build us a decent house."

At the mention of the Adams name, Crissa's chest tightened. She looked at Garth, trying to see anything beyond the man who had destroyed her life. *If it were not for you*, she thought, *Drake never would have left, and I would not be in such trouble now. This is all your fault.* She nearly gave voice to her thoughts, but it was Garth, after all, who was here now, trying to help her.

"I think we ought'a take the money and move on. New Mexico . . . or Texas, maybe. I can repay him later, when we're situated."

Crissa spun abruptly on the porch. Facing Garth as she was—he on the bottom step, she two steps higher—she looked him square in the eyes. "I will not run again. I did not kill that woman in Boston, I did not kill Carter, and it was in self-defense that I shot Mr. Jenkins. I have not committed any crime. I will not run." She strode to the rain barrel and scooped up a double handful of water, then flung it back in the barrel in disgust.

"Crissa—"

"And I will not bathe with insects."

Erupting in laughter, Garth leaned against the wall of the house for support. His sudden outburst startled a family of wrens from their home in the rafters. "I'll fetch some fresh water from the crick in a minute," he said, still chuckling and wiping tears from his eyes with the back of his fist. "Crissa," he began again, more soberly, "you've got three killings hitched to your name. A judge ain't gonna believe they was all self-defense."

"I told you," she huffed impatiently, "I shot Jenkins in self-defense. I am not responsible for the other two."

"And I told you," he shot back, matching her tone, "no judge is gonna buy your story."

"Then I will hire a . . . solicitor—a lawyer."

"A lawyer!" Again he guffawed. "We got no lawyers in Willow

Springs! Closest lawyer would be . . . I bet there's not a good lawyer any closer'n Salt Lake!"

Standing toe-to-toe with Garth, Crissa spoke quietly, her jaw firmly clenched. "I should have known you would not try to help me." She stepped inside and closed the door between them.

With her back purposefully to the door, Crissa sat at the small table, waiting for Garth to follow her inside. Peeling small wooden slivers off the table, she listened intently for the sound of Garth's approaching footsteps. Several minutes passed before she heard a step on the porch. She sat up straight, folding her arms tightly in front of her, but no one entered the room.

Waiting did nothing to ease her temper. They had things to discuss. What was taking him so long? *Surely, he does not think I . . . well, he has got another think coming.* She poured herself a cup of lukewarm coffee. Grimacing at the pan of biscuits covered with congealed gravy, she scanned the shelves looking for anything resembling food. A lump of rancid butter, a sack of rock-hard biscuits. He had obviously brought in only enough fresh provisions for one breakfast. *Does he never eat? How does he expect me to . . .*

Furiously, she yanked the door open. "If you think for one minute—" Seething with rage, she stared at the empty steps. "Garth!" She stomped to the edge of the porch, leaning over the rail to peer around the side of the house. "Garth!" she yelled again. "Answer me this minute!" Save for a jackrabbit leaping through the brush downhill, all was silent. There was a bucket of fresh water on the porch, but no sign of Garth. "Garth!" Nothing. "Well, if that is the way he wants it." She stomped into the house, slamming the door behind her.

Crissa found her wedding clothes folded neatly on a stool at the end of the bed and quickly put them on. Pulling her hair into a single, tight braid, she wound it around her head once and twisted the excess into a knot on her crown, securing it with Molly's pearl comb. She moistened her fingers with her tongue and plastered her bangs flat, effectively covering the welt on her forehead.

"Now what do I do?" she said aloud. As if in answer, a mouse darted across the room, disappearing into a hole by the fireplace.

Sawdust puffed out of it, adding to the tiny heap already in place. "Ugh," she said, grimacing. "Looks as though this 'house' has not seen a good cleaning since who knows when."

After looking about for a moment, she grabbed the nightshirt to use as a dust-rag, then spent the better part of the next hour chasing cobwebs from the exposed rafters, sweeping mouse droppings out from under the bed, and beating several years' worth of dust out of every nook and cranny in the cabin. As she worked, she reviewed her dilemma, grasping for anything that might be able to ensure her freedom. Each direction of her thoughts carried her back to the same spot. She was stuck in the cabin with no idea where Garth had gone or when he'd be coming back. She sought solace in slapping filth around with a nightshirt.

The only piece of furniture that had seen any kind of care was the beautiful gun cabinet in the corner. From top to bottom there was not a speck of dust on it. The leaded glass front sparkled, the wooden shelves gleamed, and even the thick, forest-green velvet lining the shelves was meticulously brushed so the nap was perfectly smooth. Each gun on display was carefully polished and poised— except one.

Her hands trembling, Crissa lifted the .41 Colt from its resting place. With a flick of her thumb, she snapped the cylinder open, revealing six empty chambers. She peered down the empty barrel before rotating the cylinder back in position. Running her hand along the sleek handle, she felt a carving under the butt. Peering closely, she could scarcely make it out. The letters BEC were carved inside an inverted triangle, and a small feather dangled from the upper-right corner. She pondered its significance: BEC would stand for Boyd something Carter, but she could think of no meaning for the triangle and feather. Garth said he had carved it, and Crissa had to acknowledge that he certainly was a master at his craft. The workmanship was incredible. After thoroughly dusting the revolver, she laid it back in the cabinet, wrinkling her nose at the foul odor emanating from the tin of expensive cigars.

Standing on the porch, she viciously shook the nightshirt,

slapping it against the railing to beat the dirt out. Mother always said that idle hands were the devil's workshop. After beating the nightshirt, Crissa stood with her back against the railing, mopping the sweat from the back of her neck. "Well, Mother," she said aloud, "you know my hands have not often been idle, but I do certainly seem bedeviled."

She sauntered back inside the house, looking for anything to wile away the time. *I cannot stand to just wait for him. Why, he did not even tell me where he was going. I will not stay here waiting for him. I can take care of myself. How dare he—*

The hoofbeats of an approaching horse interrupted her reverie. Before she could get to the window, someone stomped up the steps. She flung the door open. "It is about time!"

"What's the meaning of—"

"Drake!" Crissa gasped, pressing her hand to her chest. His clothes were dusty, his hair long enough to curl over the top of his collar, and he sported a thick black beard, but there was no mistaking the azure eyes gleaming from the depths of his ruddy face. The pungent smell of sweat, mixed with his hot, musky aroma, wafted around Crissa as she struggled to keep from throwing herself in his arms. "So. You are back," she said coolly.

"So. You are married," he returned, walking past her into the room. "Where is he?" His hands hung loosely at his sides while Drake peered nervously about the room, as if expecting someone to jump out from a darkened corner.

"Where is who?"

"Who? Garth!"

"He . . . is not here. I . . . do not know where he is."

With arms folded snugly across his chest, Drake leaned against the crude table and stared at Crissa through narrowed eyes. "Sure didn't take you long."

"Long to what?"

"To run off with Garth as soon as my back was turned!"

"Run off! Why, you are the one who ran off!"

"I didn't run off. That express rider was injured, and I had to finish his route. You know that!"

"What I know is you accused me of some terrible things, then left town at the first opportunity and did not come back. You did not even bother to send word if you had arrived safely." She struggled to speak the last few words with the realization that he was here, safe. He *had* come back.

His tensely narrowed eyes relaxed a bit, revealing those Swedish-night eyes Crissa so wanted to trust. He chewed on his lower lip, showing his white teeth. Resting his hands on his thighs, he studied her hair, her eyes, her mouth, and then stared at the floor. "I missed you." He took a step forward, lifting his hands to pull her into his embrace.

"You would not dare!" she scolded, taking a step backward. "I am married!"

"That's right," he said with a humorless chuckle. "You are married. Must've shown you some pretty fancy footwork to get you in his bed."

The slap she administered to the side of his face left her hand tingling smartly. "I have not been in his bed—as if you cared," she snapped.

"Who said I cared?" he retorted, rubbing his cheek. "Just 'cause the whole town's jawin' about it. Pretty little foreigner girl leading me on a merry chase, only to marry the town drunk soon as my back was turned."

"So that is it. I am a foreigner . . . not good enough for you."

"Not good enough! I built a house for us! Doesn't that tell you anything?"

"You built that house for Suzanna!"

"Suzanna!" He spun on his heel to face Crissa. "Where'd ya get an idea like that?" The angry furrows between his eyebrows eased, and he nodded his head knowingly. "From Suzanna."

"Well, what was I supposed to think?" she retorted. "Leaving town like you did, not bothering to write or anything. Three weeks you were gone! Three weeks!"

Placing his hands on her shoulders, he drew her nearer. "Two weeks. I've been back nearly a week now, finishing the house. The house I built," he said huskily, "is—*was* for you."

"You have been back a week?" Crissa asked. Her chest felt tight. "But why did you not come to see me before now?"

"I figured if other men were to start sparkin' on you, I'd better be able to offer you something they couldn't. So I finished our house."

"But—"

"'Course, I didn't plan on coming back to find you married to someone else."

Eyeing him warily, she asked, "How did you find out I was married?"

"I didn't want to come into town until the house was finished, so I've been taking my meals with the Hamptons. Rachel told me this morning."

Crissa's eyes bulged with shock. She felt a vein in her neck rapidly pulsing. "She has known for a week that you were back, and she did not tell me? That . . . that . . . *woman* came to my wedding and *still* did not tell me!"

"But why should she tell you?" Drake asked, truly puzzled. "You were marrying Garth. Why should she think you'd care where I was?"

She swept her bangs off her sticky forehead. "You think I wanted to marry Garth?"

His eyes fixed on the revealed welt. "He hit you!"

"No! It was not him!" Crissa jerked her hand to her head, trying to cover the rapidly bruising welt. "I was . . . there has been . . ." She gripped his rough hand between her two delicate ones. "I need your help."

CHAPTER 15

Seated in the shade of a willow at the edge of the creek, Crissa tried several times to begin her tale. Was it trust she saw in Drake's baleful eyes? Doubt? Despair? She sat with her hands cupped, one inside the other, unconsciously pushing back her cuticles while considering her words.

"At the beginning, Crissa," Drake urged patiently. "When did you first become . . . sweet on Garth?"

Her head snapped up, ready to let loose a barrage, but the kindness in Drake's eyes quickly quelled her defensive temper. "I was never 'sweet' on him."

Drake only lifted one eyebrow in response.

"He came to the inn the day before yesterday," she told him, amazed by what she was saying. *Has it only been two days since then?* she wondered in astonishment. "He had some information about me that I did not want to . . . become common knowledge." She paused, trying to read some clue in Drake's gaze. "I agreed to marry him in exchange for his silence."

Drake sat unblinking and then finally nodded. "Go on," he urged, his tone wavering slightly.

Am I making any sense? Crissa waited. Watching shimmering ripples of heat rise from the meager stream, she felt perspiration gathering under her folded knees. *How much do I tell him? How much can he accept?* Still she waited, listening to his steady breathing, his occasional heavy swallows.

At length his questions began, slowly, carefully phrased, as if he needed more information but didn't really want it. "This information was about you?"

"Yes."

"Before you came to Willow Springs?"

"Yes."

He shook his head, then wiped the dampness from the back of his neck. "What could he have possibly said to make you marry him?"

Somehow she must find the words to explain.

"How could you think I wouldn't come back?"

Find the courage to try . . .

At her continued silence, he heaved a loud sigh in frustration. "Crissa, if this information is as serious as you believe it is, you need to tell me. I don't think I can help you much if you don't confide in me."

Looking at him, she was seized with the urge to ask him to run away with her. She could be with him then, and he would never have to know about her past. "I am afraid," she whispered.

"Afraid! Crissa, you can trust me a heck'uv'a lot more than you can trust Garth! I'm not going to tell anyone."

"It is not that," she said, wrapping her arms around her knees. "I am afraid you will no longer care for me."

A look of alarm raced across his face before Drake answered her. His voice was calm, but the muscles in his arm were taut as he plucked at a clump of clover. "I love you. Nothing you can say will change that."

"You love me?" The joy that raced through her chest died and plummeted to her stomach as she realized how impossible a life with him was. "I am wanted by the federal marshal. If I am arrested—"

"Arrested! What in heaven's name?"

She forced herself to utter the damning words. "For a murder in Boston."

Drake's mouth dropped opened, and he sat very still. The only indication that he was not as composed as his stillness implied was his rapid breathing. He clamped his jaw shut again.

"And," she rushed, closing her eyes tightly, "I am married to another man, also in Boston."

He stared at her for a long moment, his dumbfounded look dissolved into skepticism then twisted into jealous fury. "So I was wrong. You don't go tramping around the country collecting beaus. You collect husbands!"

"No! That is not—"

"And who was this person you killed? A jilted lover, maybe?"

"I—"

"An unsuspecting sap who caught on to your dupe?"

"I did not kill anyone!" Crissa shouted emphatically, rising to her knees. Her shoulders slumped, and she looked out beyond the creek. "I was right. I knew I should not tell you. How could you possibly love a woman such as I?"

"How indeed!" he snapped. He also kneeled and turned Crissa to face him. "Do you have any idea what you've done to me?" he asked, jabbing a finger at his chest. "I adore you, Crissa. Yet every time I think I've cleared an obstacle for us to marry, I'm hit with another one. How long were you going to wait before you told me you were already married?"

"You wanted to marry me?"

"Of course I did, you *dum gosse*!" Drake tried to repeat the phrase that Crissa had so often used. "Why else would I have quit riding with the Express? Or beat myself half to death finishing our house?"

Giggles burst from Crissa before she could contain them.

"What's so funny?" he demanded.

Crissa scrunched her mouth together trying to suppress the giggles. "You called me a *dum gosse*. A silly *boy*!" The giggles spilled forth once more.

"You told me that meant 'silly goose.'"

"Oh, dear," Crissa said, gently rubbing her side. "*Goose* is pronounced 'goase.' 'Goss-eh' means *lad*."

"Well, that still doesn't change the fact that I've been turning head over heels for you since we first met, and now I find out you've got a husband in Boston waiting on you to come home."

"I do not intend to go home. I left my husband, and I will not go back."

Drake shook his head again and blew out a deep breath. Sitting back on the saddle blanket, he pulled her down beside him. "Is it possible to tell me about your husband, about the murder charge, why you married Garth, and who gave you that knot on your head in one story . . . without getting me too confused?"

Looking at him doubtfully, Crissa gave him a weak smile. "I will do my best."

Crissa settled herself cross-legged on the blanket, arranging a pile of dry grass on her skirt. Drake lay beside her, arms and legs dangling off the blanket, idly plucking long grasses to add to her pile.

"My father met Eric aboard the ship we sailed to America on. Father had lost a good amount of money gambling but had no funds with which to settle his debt. He arranged for me to marry Eric in exchange for payment." Shuddering with the memory, she fumbled with the mound of grass before continuing. "It was not a happy marriage, but Father was satisfied. We arrived from Sweden with no money and few skills. We lived in a tenement next to the fish market, and I worked in the market each day in exchange for our rent. Eric could not find a job. Each night he would go out—I supposed he was drinking with his friends—and then he would sleep all day, not bothering to even look for a job. He would get out of bed only after I had lain dinner on the table. Every night it was the same. He would eat dinner, smoke a cigar, and . . ." A shudder snaked its way down Crissa's spine as she remembered. The familiar nauseating sensation welled up in her stomach.

Crissa looked over at Drake, but he gave no reaction. He did not speak, did not look at her, but he had stopped picking grass, his hand frozen on a slender stalk. She picked up three shafts and began braiding them. "After he was . . . finished, he would leave. He never told me where he went, and he would not come home until nearly time for me to go to work the next morning. We began to argue whenever we were together. The fight would continue until he would hit me, and then he would leave again. Perhaps I was not a good wife. I have difficulty apologizing when I have done nothing wrong. One night he did not stop hitting me. He hit me until I fell to the floor."

Drake clenched the stem of grass in his fist until his knuckles shone white.

"When he left, I ran after him. I was so angry. My neighbor across the hall tried to stop me, but I screamed that I was going to kill Eric, and I tore myself free of her. I followed him to the wharf. That is where the bar girls live. He went up some stairs behind a boarding house, into someone's room. I saw her red dressing gown before she shut the door. I sat on a step across the street and waited for him. I was not going to kill him, but I wanted him to know that I knew what he had been doing. A light came on in the window of the apartment, and I saw them there, their shapes, as . . ." Crissa could say no more as small sobs escaped from her throat with the memory.

Drake sat beside her, cradling her head in the hollow of his shoulder.

As her pain eased, she sat up straight and brushed the tears from her cheeks. "I left him then. I went back to our place only long enough to gather what belongings I had brought with me from home—from Sweden." Crissa sat back and exhaled deeply, trying to dispel the pain of her memories.

"So where did you go?" Drake prompted. "Did you have friends you could stay with?"

"I went to my parents and told them what had happened and that I was coming West with them. My father is a very strict man. I was afraid that he would not allow me to come with them."

"But surely—"

"In his mind, a woman belongs with her husband regardless of how he treats her or how miserable she is. But he also believes that adultery is an abomination before God and that any man who is unfaithful does not deserve a wife."

"You mean to tell me," Drake asked, aghast, "that if you had not caught Eric in the act, your father would have allowed him to continue beating you?"

"The Bible says, *'Och din änskan ska vara i din äkta man, och han ska styra där du.'* 'And thy desire shall be to thy husband, and he shall rule over thee.' My father takes great stock in the Holy Bible—as long as it supports what he believes." Crissa stretched her neck from side to side and gingerly pulled the damp fabric of her dress away from her burned midriff. "It is the woman Eric was with that night who I am accused of killing."

"But I thought you didn't go into her room."

"I did not. I did not even get a good look at her."

"Did anyone see you waiting across the street?"

"Yes, several people stopped to chat. All the fishermen the market buys their fish from live near the wharf."

"That might explain why you were accused of her murder."

"I do not understand why they would think I—"

"How long was it before you left town with your parents?"

"Two days."

"They may not have found her body for two or three days, and when the police came to question you, you were already gone!" Drake jumped to his knees and grabbed her hands. "Of course they would suspect you! They thought you were running from them!" Drake squeezed her hands tightly. "When did you find out about the murder?"

"When our wagon company arrived in Fort Wayne. Mr. Stanton, the wagon master, saw a notice posted at the livery. I was wanted for the murder of Miss Sheila Langston, Adventuress, of Boston, Massachusetts. It was only a drawing, and it used my married name, but Mr. Stanton knew it was me."

"If he knew it was you, why didn't he take you to the sheriff?"

"The poster said I had slit this woman's throat. According to Mr. Stanton, it takes a good deal of strength to do the job properly. He did not believe I could have done it. My father wanted us to continue on to Minnesota until he realized that Eric might have known our plans. He was worried that Eric might send the law after us, so the wagon master arranged for us to come to Utah with a Mormon handcart company instead."

Drake placed her hand inside the crook of his elbow and sat down again beside her. Looking off toward the next rise in the foothills, he continued his questions. "Why didn't you just go back to Boston and clear your name?"

Crissa chewed on the inside of her lip before answering. "I was afraid," she said. "In Boston, there is great hatred toward foreigners. It is feared we will come in and cheat Americans out of their good-paying jobs. In Boston, we are all from different countries. Whoever steps off the boat last is the new foreigner. I was afraid that since I had so little English then, I could not make the authorities believe in my innocence. And," she continued, looking at Drake, "I was afraid if I went back I would have to remain with Eric. I had discovered that—I was . . . in the family way."

Drake's mouth again fell open, his shock registering as a scarlet flush on his cheeks.

"I felt it would be better for my baby if he thought his father was dead than to live with . . . such a man."

"Oh, my sweet Crissa," he murmured, holding her palm to his lips. "What you've gone through."

"So many times I have wanted to tell you," she said, her eyes pleading for understanding. "I have lived in such fear."

"And where is your child now?"

Tears sprang to her eyes with the memory of that lonely glade. "He is buried just east of the Great Divide. He came too early. Winter was coming, and we had such a long way yet to travel." Squeezing his hand, she choked out the words, "I did not even name him."

Drake kept one arm around her shoulders, sharing her pain in silence.

"I stayed in Salt Lake with friends for a while, then came to Willow Springs. I hoped to begin a new life. I never dreamed anyone would look for me here."

"Most likely no one would have."

"I beg your pardon?"

Shifting his weight uncomfortably, Drake cleared his throat before looking at her again. "That fellow, Jenkins. I, uh . . . told him you were here."

"What?"

"He approached me after you and I saw each other in Salt Lake."

Drake picked up a handful of pebbles, tossing them one at a time into the water. "Said he had been your beau back East and would like to see if you still had feelings for him."

"And you believed him?"

"Had no reason not to. Said he just wanted to write to you, and if you were no longer interested, he would go on his way. That's why I flew into such a pucker when he came to the inn. I thought you and I had an understanding. When he showed up, I just figured you had given him some kind of encouragement."

"And you did not even bother asking me about him?" Hard lines etched the corners of her mouth as Crissa glared at Drake.

"I'm not one to step aside once I've set my cap on a woman. But when I thought someone else might come between us . . ." Drake touched her hand, which was idly worrying the hem of her skirt. "I'm sorry."

"That does not do me much good now."

"Why would Jenkins give any information to Garth?" Drake puzzled out loud.

"It was not Jenkins who gave it to Garth."

Drake raised his eyebrows in response.

"Jenkins told me someone paid him a large sum of money for the information on me. I do not think Garth would have any money. Someone else paid Jenkins and then told Garth. You were so angry when Jenkins came to town, I thought you were the one who paid him. I thought you knew about my past and despised me for it."

Glinting like cold steel, Drake's eyes were narrow slits. "I'm willing to bet I know who's behind this."

Crissa looked at him in surprise. "Who?"

"My father." Drake's voice was low and soft and frightening. "He's been meddling in my life for as long as I can remember, but this time he's gone too far." He stood up and pulled Crissa along with him, precluding the rest of her tale. "It's time I have a few words with him."

CHAPTER 16

Drake, please do not leave," Crissa begged. She watched him swing into the saddle, his blue eyes cold and unforgiving and his chin thrust out proudly. "You cannot be sure your father paid Jenkins."

"There's not another man in the territory with the gum to sell out his own son, 'cept for Warren Adams. It's time he owned up to his chicanery, and I aim to see he makes it straight."

"Then at least let me go with you," she called.

Without answering, Drake turned his horse from the porch railing and cantered down the hill. Effortlessly, the bay mare leaped the creek and made her way up the opposite hillside, turning north toward Gold Hill.

An ill feeling crept through Crissa as she watched him disappear over the hill's crest. "Drake!" she screamed at the empty horizon. "Drake!"

Sitting down on the porch steps, she took long, slow breaths, trying to cleanse the fear that enshrined her. A small lizard poked its head up from under the porch and eyed her nervously as it inched farther into the sun. Crissa picked up a slender stick and gently stroked her visitor. "He left before I could tell him about what happened last night," she explained to her timid friend. "He does not know about the men who tried to hurt me. He does not know that two men are dead because of me. He does not know that I killed one of them."

Tears slipped down her cheeks as Crissa confided in the lizard sunning itself by her feet. It felt good to cry. She had cried so much in the last two days, but these tears were different. Her fear, her guilt, all of the emotions she had been struggling to force down were allowed to bubble to the surface and fall away.

The lizard turned his head to one side and stretched his neck, allowing Crissa to scratch it with the stick. Crissa scooted down another step. She tried to imagine what Drake would say to his father. Nothing could change the situation now. Two men were dead. She was married to Garth. Would Drake demand the marriage be annulled? But that still left Eric and the murder in Boston she was charged with.

Garth would never let her have an annulment anyway. He had been very kind to her once he understood what had happened last night, but she still feared his volatile temper. Was he angry when he left this morning? Where could he be? He said he would bury Jenkins and Carter, but could he find them without her help? Then he was going to ask Mr. Adams for an advance on his salary. Crissa sucked in her breath sharply. *If Garth and Drake have both gone to see Mr. Adams . . .* Crissa jumped to her feet, sending the lizard scurrying for cover. "I must stop them!" The sound of her cry broke the desolate silence around her. A barn swallow fled from the rafters in response. But without a horse . . .

Walking to the south end of the porch, she peered in the direction of Willow Springs. How could she explain that not only was she wanted for one murder, but now there had been two more? She wrung her hands as she paced to and fro. *I cannot involve Vic and Marida in this. They must take care of the children if I don't come back.*

Hot tears streaked her cheeks as she thought about her young charges. How could they ever understand? Would they forgive her? *So young, and already they have been through so much.* In despair, she retreated inside the cabin and lay on the bed, burying her head in the soft comfort of the downy throw. Letting thoughts of Will and Amy mingle with the few happy memories she had of her own childhood, Crissa at last slipped into a dreamless sleep.

★ ★ ★

Judging from the harsh glare of the sun streaming in the door, it was about two o'clock when Crissa awoke. Figuring she had been asleep maybe three hours, she tried to calculate when Garth or Drake might return. With little idea where either man had gone, it was an impossible task. Her stomach gnawed painfully as she stood up and straightened her skirts. Despite the emotional turmoil she had been in when she had lain down, she awoke feeling refreshed and capable.

"I cannot just sit here waiting for . . . who knows what, nor can I hike back to town on an empty stomach." She opened this morning's coffee pot and grimaced at the soggy grains clumped in the bottom. She replaced the lid with a shudder. Stepping outside, she picked up the dipper from the rain barrel and wiped it in the folds of her skirt. The bucket of water Garth had left was now warm, and flies buzzed lazily about it. With a disgusted heave, Crissa tossed the water out to the dusty earth beside the porch. Peering into the distance, she set her sights on the creek bed and trudged down the hill toward it.

The stream, shallow enough to be warmed by the sun, was not as cold as Crissa had hoped, but she eagerly sucked great gulps of cool water nonetheless. Stripping off her alberts and stockings, she let the water trickle over her feet. Marida's silk hanky made do as a sponge, and Crissa wiped her sticky skin beneath her clothes. Unbuttoning her shirtwaist just far enough to expose her midriff, she examined the powder burns and sponged them with the hanky as well.

"Yes, yes," she grumbled in response to her empty stomach's insistent pangs. "Garth said they had once lived on what was planted in the garden. I wonder if there could be anything worth eating still growing there." Crissa rebuttoned her dress and replaced her stockings and shoes, and then made her way back up the hill to where the abandoned garden waited.

Famished, she hoped to find volunteer onions or carrots or anything to quiet her rumbling stomach. Lifting her skirt a bit, she tied it together to form a small pouch. She munched on wild parsley while she searched through the matted weeds for a more substantial feast. At last she unearthed some forgotten potatoes that had, thankfully, resown themselves. On her hands and knees, she began pulling up great clumps of weeds to expose the bounty below the soil.

The blistering sun was nearing midafternoon when she had her makeshift pouch full of potatoes and parsley. If she could find some wild onions at the water's edge, she could make a stew for dinner. She chose a small potato from her stash and rubbed the dirt off. Taking a bite of the hard tuber, she sat down in the shade of a cottonwood with her back propped against a—

"Grave marker!" she gasped, bolting from her resting place, dropping her afternoon's find. She looked again, stooping over the marker to read the engraved name. "Ruth Elsbeth Wight, 1808–1852, Devoted Mother, Beloved Sister." *Garth did not tell me she was buried here!* Crissa thought in amazement. The marker bore the same carvings as those on Molly's marker, and there, tucked among the curve of foxglove, was Garth's mark of an inverted triangle with a feather dangling from the top corner.

Crissa smiled to herself, picturing the many hours Garth must have spent carving this final memorial. *Who ever would have thought that Garth Wight would do something like that?* A small corner of her heart ached, remembering the gentle side of Garth that she was coming to know. *What is to happen to you now? To us? I do not mean to hurt you.* But how could she have a life with Drake without hurting Garth? And how could she possibly stay with Garth and live in the same town as Drake? "It is an endless riddle, Cristalina," she scolded herself. "You are not free to have either one."

Crissa pondered on the woman who was Garth's mother. How long was she married? Why would she stay in such a godforsaken country, newly widowed and with a baby on the way? Did her sister live nearby? Was she happy here? Did she leave anything for Garth to remember her by? Crissa couldn't recall seeing anything in the house that might have belonged to Garth's mother. Surely he would not have thrown everything out. *I hope you only saw the gentle side of your son. Would you have approved of me? Could we have been friends?*

Standing, Crissa looked about the tattered garden for some remnants of the flowers immortalized on the markers. *Those are such beautiful flowers on your headstone, but where would Garth have seen such unusual flowers?* A scraggly pink rosebush leaned against the fence, but there were no signs of foxglove or baby's breath. "You must have been a lovely spot in your day," Crissa murmured as she refilled her makeshift pouch with potatoes. "Perhaps you will be again."

★ ★ ★

After scraping the lump of biscuits and gravy out of the frying pan, Crissa peeled and sliced the hard potatoes and set them simmering on the stove. She rummaged through the few tins that were left on the shelf and discovered a chunk of jerky to flavor the potatoes. *I hope this hasn't been sitting here since Ruth died*, Crissa thought with disdain. She lifted another tin, hoping for another meager treasure. The tin was empty, but behind it was a small, stoppered glass bottle. A long-handled spoon lay on the shelf beside it. Pulling the bottle free of an old spiderweb, Crissa dusted the bottle on her skirt and read the handwritten label: Foxglove—one spoonful in tea at bedtime. Gently removing the stopper, she tentatively sniffed the whitish powder inside. A mildly sweet fragrance still lingered, but there was also just a hint of something . . . bitter? Tangy? Tiny black speckles were mixed in with the powdered foxglove, but they were a mystery. *I wonder where Ruth got this?* It did not look as though she grew it in the garden. Replacing the stopper, Crissa returned the bottle to the shelf. *Surely that is not the only memory remaining of Garth's mother.*

Aside from the gun cabinet and the mantel, there wasn't much left in the room that Crissa had not already cleaned over, under, or around. She had made the bed, fluffing the quilt and pillows, but common sense told her not to venture under the bed while she had nothing more than a dust rag to defend herself. She had dusted the nightstand, straightened its lace covering . . . but what was underneath? Lifting the lace, she inspected the shelf hidden beneath it. A porcelain pot, empty but badly stained, had been used as an ashtray. Several musky cigar butts lay in the pot. Crissa crinkled her nose, replaced the pot, and straightened the lace cloth in place. *I am certainly not going to spend the day after my wedding cleaning his chamber pot!* She had to laugh at herself then. *You will not throw out a few cigar butts, but you will rummage through his house searching for his dead mother's treasures.* She shuddered with the thought, but nonetheless got down on her hands and knees to peer under the bed skirt.

No beady eyes peered back at her out of the darkness, thankfully. A dark shadow in the far corner was the only something under there. Lighting the candle from the nightstand, she looked under the bed once again. The shadow-shape looked like some kind of satchel. Tucking the bed skirt up under the mattress so it wouldn't block the candle's meager light, Crissa scooted under the bed. With a nervous hand, she tried to pull the satchel toward her. It didn't budge. She tried again and failed. Scooting closer to it, Crissa took hold of the bag with both hands and tugged—steadily, firmly. At last it gave ground, and she dragged the bag into the room. It was a large, floral carpetbag. Not terribly heavy, the bag was thickly mildewed on the bottom, adhering to the floor for who knew how many years.

Crissa stood and wiped herself free of any errant spiders or cobwebs that may have stuck to her while she was under the bed. A single hair tickled her cheek, sending shivers through her body. Sitting on the edge of the bed, Crissa clasped her hands between her knees and considered the mysterious satchel before her. *Should I open it now or wait for Garth? But I do not even know where he has gone. And it has been under the bed all these years, and I am his wife now.* She drew a deep breath in anticipation and sat down on the floor beside the bag.

A leather flap, held in place with a brass clasp, secured the carpetbag. The rusted clasp finally yielded under Crissa's insistence, and she slowly pried the bag open, revealing a fascinating array of women's belongings. An ivory satin bonnet sporting a cluster of rose-colored ribbons and ivory lace rested on top of the carefully packed pile. A gossamer satin dress lay neatly folded underneath the bonnet. The ivory fabric had yellowed to a rich, creamy hue. *How lovely! A party dress? Or were you a dancing belle?* she wondered. A delicate lace fan with ribbons matching those on the hat was tucked in beside the dress.

A gilt frame protected a daguerreotype of two young girls sitting side by side on a porch swing. *Ruth and her sister? I wonder which one is Ruth?* Dressed in long, dark skirts, both girls wore dour expressions. Each of them wore their hair braided, but the younger girl had tucked a limp flower behind her ear. She held one of the older child's braids fast in her chubby hand. *Just like sisters.* Crissa smiled, remembering her own sisters' love-hate relationship.

Setting aside the photograph, Crissa looked inside the carpetbag for the next treasure. Lifting out a plain wooden box, she placed it reverently on the floor in front of her. The box had no lock.

A bright playbill announced the Philadelphia debut of *She Stoops to Conquer* in 1818. "Smash hit of the century," the playbill proclaimed. Crissa had to smile—by 1859, when it was revived for audiences in Boston, the Saturday Evening Post she had read dubbed the play "a yawning bore." Two train ticket stubs from Philadelphia to St. Louis, dated September 26, 1838, were tucked inside the playbill. *1838. Garth would have been born right about that time*, Crissa mused. *Why would Ruth be going to St. Louis when Garth was a baby? Maybe he was not born yet and Ruth was traveling with her husband.*

Crissa tried to imagine what Ruth might have been like as a young woman in 1838. Was she a girl who liked fancy parties and dances? How could she have given up such fun to come to such an uncivilized place as Willow Springs? Was Ruth, perhaps, an actress, traveling through the States, performing with a theatrical company? But why would she stay here?

Crissa picked up the satin bonnet, turning it around in her hands. *More likely you were a sweet little girl dancing your way through a line of beaus until one swept you off your feet and carried you to the West.* Crissa smiled at the image she had conjured. In place of Mr. and Mrs. Wight, however, it was the image of her and Drake waltzing through a swirling mist. She slipped the bonnet on her head, savoring the feel of the cool satin as it brushed her cheek.

Something scraped her ear when Crissa tied the ribbon under her chin. Something stiff and crackly. Pulling the bonnet from her head, she examined the lining. A few of the threads had broken, exposing the corner of a piece of paper. *Well, Mrs. Wight, just what was it you were trying to hide?*

Drawing a folded, yellowing letter from the bonnet lining, Crissa turned it over carefully in her hands. No envelope, no return address. Not the fine stationery a lady would use. *I really should not,* Crissa told herself as she unfolded the letter.

May 10, 1838
My Darling,

    Imagine my surprise when I received your letter. I have wanted so much to see you again—to hear your voice, to hold you in my arms. You must realize my joy when I found your letter waiting for me in Ely. You must understand how deeply I care for you, but you must also understand the position you put me in. I have a wife in Gold Hill and a son. Claire carries another child who will be delivered toward the end of next month.

    I never meant to find you, to care for you, but I cannot do right by you now. But I am also not a man to ignore my responsibility. I have staked out a few hundred acres near Willow Springs, which is not far from Gold Hill. I have hired some men to construct a house for you there. You may furnish it any way you like. I told Claire that you are the widow of my boyhood friend and that you are with child. If you will come out here on the condition that no one ever finds out that I am the father of your child, I will do whatever I can to give you a good life.

    It is best that our relationship not continue. However, I employ several men that you might find suitable to marry. Perhaps I can offer some cattle to help you and a husband to get a ranch started up.

    I am enclosing a voucher for you to take to the Pennsylvania State Bank, where I have a bit or two set aside. I'm certain it is more than enough for you to purchase passage out here and whatever you need to make the trip. If you travel by rail to St. Louis, you can hire an Overland Stage to bring you the rest of the way.

    Write me with your arrival plans, and I will arrange to have someone meet you in Willow Springs.

    Warren

Had Crissa read correctly? She stared at the name, Warren. *Warren.* There were only three people in Willow Springs who owned that much land: Zedekiah Bagley, a young rancher who had settled further west than the main body of Mormons in the Salt Lake valley, but he couldn't have written the letter—he would not have been more than a toddler in 1838. The Hamptons owned a large spread, or rather Rachel Hampton, since her husband up and ran out on her several years ago. And her husband's name had been Kurt, not Warren. That left only—"Warren Adams," Crissa said aloud. "Drake's mother's name is Clairice, but she may be called by Claire." A hazy passage of her wedding ceremony flit through her mind: *Garth Warren Wight, do you take this woman . . .*

"Garth is the child," she whispered.

She had supposed the child was Garth, of course. The letter was in Ruth's bonnet, and Ruth was Garth's mother, but voicing her conclusion made it concrete. There was no mistaking the signature. Warren Adams, Drake's father, was Garth's father. Crissa set the paper down. With trembling hands, she tried to smooth it back into its original folds. All the while, one thought chased all else from her mind—*Garth thinks his father died at sea. He does not know about Warren.* The realization formed a knot in her chest like a python crushing the life from her heart.

Crissa wondered what had become of the ranch Warren had offered Ruth. Garth said his mother had owned the inn. Had Ruth refused his offer? *But why would she come out here, then?* A new picture formed in Crissa's mind—a picture of a young woman heavy with child, making her way across the plains, desperately clinging to the hope of a life somehow better than the one she had left behind. Was it Ruth she grieved for now, or her own dejected specter?

This is not your time to grieve, Crissa, she reprimanded herself, trying to shake off her own dark mantle. Should she tell Garth? Leave the letter out where he could see it? What would his reaction be? Would it be better if he never knew the truth? "Ruth," she said aloud, "knowing your son's temper, I believe it is better that you died before he found out." *And what will Drake do, knowing Garth is his brother?*

The far-off plodding of a horse's tired stride interrupted her musings. *Garth or Drake? They cannot know. Not yet.* Frantically, she replaced the articles back in the carpetbag, not bothering to stuff the letter back inside the bonnet's lining, then scooted the bag under the bed.

With her heart pounding and her hands shaking, she lifted back the potato sack curtain enough to see Garth ride up to the house, dismount, and tie his horse to the side of the porch. While the horse snorted in the rain barrel, Garth uncinched the saddle and slung it over the railing.

Be calm, Crissa. Act natural. She turned to the stove and was adding a handful of chopped parsley to the stew when Garth came through the door.

Looking at her, a tired, peaceful expression softened the lines on his face. The hint of a smile lifted the corners of his lips. He removed his hat and hung it on a nail, then leaned against the open doorjamb. "My wife, in my house, fixing supper at my stove. Mind if I just stand here awhile and enjoy the moment?"

Crissa smiled at him, saying nothing, then turned back to stirring the stew to hide the tears in her eyes.

Garth encircled her small body with his arms, resting his chin on the top of her head. "I been missing you something awful. Put down that spoon, Mrs. Wight," he murmured, nuzzling in her hair. "Supper can wait."

Dizzying fear swept through Crissa. Turning to escape his embrace, she was met head-on with the stench of a filthy, sweat-drenched man. "Garth!" Crissa gasped, clasping a hand over her nose and mouth.

Anger flashed for a moment in his eyes, and then it was gone. "Hang it all, woman! You're my wife! But every time I try cozyin' up to ya—" He yanked a chair out from the table and hunkered down in it, waiting for his plate.

Crissa didn't dare ask him to go wash. An uneasy heartbeat of a moment passed in silence. "You were gone a long while." The casual conversation she had rehearsed came out awkwardly, despite the lightest tone of voice she could muster. "Are you hungry?" She chanced a smile over her shoulder at him. "I am afraid it is not much, but considering what I had to cook with, I think I have done rather well." Crissa held her lower lip between her teeth, willing herself to stop this mindless drivel. Hoping Garth's sigh was from fatigue rather than irritation, Crissa kept her back to him, busying herself with dishing up the stew.

"I spent most of the day hunting up those bod—friends of ours, and the rest of the time trying to find someplace secluded enough to bury them." Garth's voice sounded tired, with just a hint of frustration.

"I would have thought the woods where you found them would have been secluded enough."

"Well, yeah, 'ceptin' they was smack in the middle of Drake Adams's new spread. Couldn't have dug them deep enough that he wouldn't roust 'em eventually."

Carefully keeping her back to Garth, Crissa clenched her skirt in one hand and clung to the spoon with the other, disguising their tremors.

"And, yes, I'm purt' near starved half to death. Compared to the swill that ol' dough-belly up to camp serves, this couldn't smell any finer. I'll take you back to town in the morning, but right now, alls I want is some hearty grub and a good night's sleep."

Turning toward him, her composure regained, Crissa laid a plate of sliced and boiled potatoes on the table. "Since this is our first meal together as husband and wife," she ventured demurely, "may I make two requests for the future?"

"Such as?"

"One is that we say grace before we sit down to a meal."

"And?"

"And that you never set foot in my house so filthy dirty as you are right now."

Garth's familiar guffaw shook the tiny cabin to its very roots. With a gallant sweep of his imaginary hat, he backed out of the room. Crissa watched from the doorway as he shoved his horse away from the rain barrel. "Get outta my way, you ornery old nag. We've got us a new boss."

CHAPTER 17

Crissa studied Garth eating his potato stew. He used his fork like a shovel, scooping great mounds of food into his mouth rather than piercing a few slices of potato at a time. His teeth, powered by massive jaws, chomped noisily as he chewed, as though he were afraid the potatoes might grow legs and dash away if he did not smash them thoroughly. Smiling at her imagined potato rebellion, Crissa sat with her forkful of stew suspended halfway between her plate and her mouth.

"Something funny?" Garth demanded, thrusting his fork toward her. A drizzle of white oozed from the corner of his mouth before he could slurp it back in.

Shoving her mouth full, Crissa shrugged and shook her head innocently. She carefully avoided watching him for the remainder of the meal.

"What's that?" Garth rocked back on the rear legs of his chair and nodded toward the bed where the satchel was just showing. With his tongue curling from one side to the other, he sucked the last vestiges of potato from his back teeth. "Someone bring your satchel over?"

"No! It is not mine." She mentally rehearsed what she would say to Garth about its contents, but how Crissa didn't know how to begin. "I . . . found it under the bed. I believe it was your mother's."

"You been snooping around my place?" His chair crashed down on its four legs. He sat for a moment, hands planted firmly on the table in front of him, glaring at Crissa. "I'm sorry," he said at last. "I'm not fit company when I get tired."

Crissa nodded her head, keeping her eyes averted. With her emotions running from fright to anger, it was probably best to just keep quiet.

"I had no right," Garth said after a moment. He sounded chastened. "This is your home too now." He walked over to the satchel and stared down at it. "Haven't looked at this stuff since . . ." He blew out a weary sigh. "Well, then." Taking Crissa by the hand, he led her to the satchel. They both sat on the floor with the bag between them. "When my ma died, I gave her belongings to Rachel Hampton."

"Oh?"

"Rachel is—*was*—my ma's sister." Garth shook his head and chuckled halfheartedly. "Though you'd be hard pressed to tell they were two peas from the same pod. Anyway, after Rachel went through what I gave her, she came over here demanding that I give her the rest of ma's things. She was screaming and hollering to beat the devil. She tore through things like a whirlwind, but I wouldn't let her take anything from the bag. Can't figure why she'd want an old carpetbag, though. Nothing in here 'cept some old clothes." Garth gingerly stroked the leather handles. "Ma called it her treasure chest. Used to tell me that one day the things she kept in here would change my life." He smiled skeptically at Crissa. "Hmph. 'Magine that."

"Have you ever seen what is inside?" she asked.

"Yeah, went through it when she died." Inspecting the closure of the bag, Garth ran his finger along the newly cracked rust of the clasp. "Looks like you did too."

Crissa blushed, embarrassed that she had invaded his only memento of his mother. "I did not realize what it was."

Lifting the treasured dress and fan, he let them fall to the floor, not much interested until he came across the daguerreotype. He smiled at the picture resting in his hands. "This is my ma and

Rachel. Ma's the older one. The sensible one. See the flower in Rachel's hair? Ma says Rachel always did have highfalutin ways. She was always making trouble for my ma, too, then conniving her way out of it."

"It seems she passed that onto her daughter," Crissa murmured.

"Yeah, Suzanna's a hellcat all right," Garth agreed. "Used to make all sorts of trouble for me when I was a kid. 'Course, I'm quite a bit older, so she was more of a nuisance than anything. This is the only picture I've got of Ma. Sure likely I weren't gonna let Rachel have it."

Looking at the daguerreotype now, Crissa could see a resemblance between Garth and Rachel—the same square jaw, the cowlick above the left temple. Ruth's face was more angular, the hairline perfectly smooth. Crissa smiled to herself. *He looks more like Rachel than like Ruth.* Unmistakably missing on either girl, however, were Garth's deep-set eyes—the eyes that looked hawkish on Garth and brooding on Drake—a legacy of the Adams's line.

He set the picture down and inspected the bag, lifting out the wooden box. "You look in here too?"

Crissa nodded.

Opening the box, he thumbed through the playbill and glanced briefly at the railroad tickets. "Ma loved to read fancy books to me late at night. Taught me how to read them too," Garth boasted. "She used to make up different voices for all the characters. Said the greatest thrill of her life was when she got to see this here play, real live on the stage." He added the playbill to the pile of belongings at his knee.

The last item in the satchel was the satin bonnet. "S'pose it's foolishness for me to keep these old things." Picking up the bonnet, he held it out to Crissa. "Reckon you'd have any use for such a thing?" The letter slid from the bonnet's shelter. Touching the folded letter, as if afraid to pick it up, Garth looked at Crissa. She dropped her eyes and bit her lip.

"I never seen this before."

"It . . . it was sewn in the bonnet. The lining was coming loose. It just fell out. I did not mean to—"

"This must be what Rachel was after."

Stabs of pain hammered her temples while Crissa watched Garth study the letter. He read with his brows knit together in concentration. As he read the letter, his face was an unreadable mask at first, draining to a deathly pale when he reached the last few lines. He laid the letter in his lap, his fists still clenching its sides. He began to shake.

Kneeling beside him, Crissa stroked his sweat-dampened hair. The muscles of his face and neck contorted under her touch, as if he were fighting some demon in his mind. At last she felt him relax, and his breathing returned to a steady pace.

"Y'know," Garth murmured, crossing the room to stare out the window, "from my earliest memories I can recollect boys ribbing me about not having a father. Got in a dang good many fights over the matter. Drake was in on it. Oliver too. Saying my pa up and run off when I was born 'cause he couldn't stand the sight of me. Well, I'd beat them bloody and blue most of the time, and then go home to my ma."

A small spider ventured from its hiding place to the edge of the shelf by the window. Garth pressed the life from it with his thumb.

"Ma used to tell me wonderful stories about what a brave and handsome man my pa was. We were certain he must have died trying to save the lives of his shipmates. I was so proud of him. As dirt poor as we were, I had something none of those other boys ever had—my pa was a hero."

Crissa watched in silence as Garth clenched and unclenched his fist around an empty whiskey bottle with a candle stuck in the top.

"Hero, my eye!" Garth whirled around to face Crissa, his face stained with anger.

"My pa is a lyin', cheatin', son-of-a-whoremonger. Got my ma knocked up, then promised her a grand old life to come out here. Look at this place!" he yelled, flinging his arms wide. "Some grand ranch house this is! She spent every penny she had in the world trying to keep that inn open, only to end up here. Where was he when Ma fell from the buggy and broke her arm and still had to keep the inn running? Where was he when the snow piled up so high we couldn't get the door open?"

Garth stepped to the fireplace and leaned with both hands on the mantel, reliving his pain. "We sat here nearly three weeks chewing on raw potatoes and turnips 'cause we had no wood for a fire. Where was he when Ma took sick and couldn't even afford a doctor?" he asked quietly. "She had to rely on Rachel's folk medicine 'til she finally died. And where was he when I carried her out to the garden to bury her? Didn't even bother to come by and pay his respects."

Garth turned to Crissa, angry, hurtful tears spilling onto his cheeks. "Drake and Oliver have been living like kings while I grew up with nothing and watched my ma work herself to death." Clenching the letter in his fist, he shook it in Crissa's face. "Well, Warren Adams didn't own up to his responsibilities. Now it's time to settle up." Garth grabbed his saddle as he bounded from the porch and slung it across his horse's back.

"Garth, please wait," Crissa begged.

He yanked viciously on the saddle strap, cinching it tight around the horse's girth. "I been waiting twenty-three years for my due. I ain't waitin' any longer."

"You cannot confront Mr. Adams while Drake is up there."

"I don't give a demon who's up—Drake's up there?" He spun around and grabbed Crissa by both arms. "Drake's back?"

Crissa gasped.

"How do you know?" he demanded, shaking her. "How do you know?"

"Garth! You are hurting me!"

"Has he been here?" He shook her again.

"Yes!"

"What was he doing here? Soon as I turn my back, he comes after my woman!"

"He did not—"

"So did he bed you, wife?"

With all her might she slapped him. "How dare you!"

Cupping the back of her head in his bearlike paw, tangling his fingers in her hair, he pulled her to him, gripping her wrist behind her with his other hand. His face pressed close to hers in a malevolent grimace. In dreadful silence she stood, rigid, fighting her quaking nerves.

It could have been the devil's own voice that punctuated each of his words. "You are *my* wife now." He flung Crissa to the side and stalked into the house, emerging a moment later with his pistol pulled from its holster while he checked the chamber. He cradled a rifle in his other arm.

"Garth!" Those awful eyes stalked past her, intent on revenge. Fear twisted her courage, sucking the breath from her lungs. "What are you going to do?"

"I'm gonna kill the son of a . . ." He shoved the pistol back in its holster and rammed the rifle into its sling on the saddle.

"No! You cannot!" In vain Crissa pleaded. "There has been too much killing."

Towering over her, Garth glared at her, speaking in a low, controlled, ominous voice. "He's taken everything I ever had growing up, and now he's after you. I'll kill the both of them."

"Garth!" Crissa cried. "You do not know what you are saying!"

He tried to push past her. "I know full well what I'm saying." Crissa stood between Garth and the horse. "Get outta my way, woman."

"I will not!" She clung to his arm with both hands, trying to push him back.

"I said move!" Lifting her by both shoulders, Garth slung her aside like a bag of feed. With one foot in the stirrup, he swung himself into the saddle and looked back down at Crissa. "Don't you leave this house. I'll take care of you when I get back."

Kicking his horse, he galloped off in the direction Drake had gone. "Garth!" She ran after him. "Garth!" Frantic to stop him, Crissa grabbed a fistful of rocks and hurled it at him. Ignoring her screams, he crossed the creek and mounted the opposing hillside. Crissa stared after him, watching him pull a silver flask from his saddlebag.

CHAPTER 18

Crissa watched the horse and rider grow smaller and smaller, then disappear over the crest of the hill. "Don't you leave this house," he had said. "I'll take care of you when I get back." A shudder prickled up her spine while she considered what Garth had in mind. Beat her? Kill her? *No*, she thought, *first he will have his way with me. Then he will beat me near to death.* Memories raced through her mind of submitting to Eric's drunken advances—advances that would leave her black and blue. It was not difficult to imagine Garth using her in the same way, perhaps even killing her afterward. But first he would kill Drake and his father.

Somehow, she had to get to Drake and warn him. Garth certainly would not come to his senses before someone got killed. She had to warn them. She had no way of knowing how far the mines were, and there was only an hour or so of sunlight left. Without a horse, she could not get there. She had to find help.

Hitching her skirt, Crissa ascended the hillside behind the house. It may have only been Garth's temper threatening her, but Crissa wasn't about to stay and find out.

From her vantage point on the hill, she had a clear view of the valley before her. The well-worn path following the foothills between Willow Springs and Gold Hill was deserted for as far as Crissa could see. The path southward, to town, was also barren, disappearing in the curve of the foothills. *How far is it to town?* Crissa wondered. *I should have paid more attention when Garth drove me out here.* She scanned the path to the north again. *Can I make it to town before Garth returns for me?* To the east, Crissa found the wider path of the Overland Trail, the route used by the Pony Express and the Overland Stage. That road was deserted too.

I must get to town. I must get help.

Scrambling down the hillside, Crissa raced back to the house. If Garth did catch her, she had to have some kind of protection. Scanning the contents of Garth's gun cabinet, she grabbed a little pistol, not much bigger than her palm. This would fit neatly in her pocket and not weigh her down. *Bullets. Where are the bullets?* The gun rested atop a small wooden box filled with ammunition. The bullets looked roughly the same size as the single round in the chamber, so Crissa stuffed a handful of shells in her pocket.

Ruth's belongings were still heaped on the floor where Garth had piled them. "For heaven's sake," Crissa muttered. "Has he no respect for the dead?" She considered for a moment whether she should put them away. *No time,* she decided. *Garth can do it himself.* The bouquet of wild roses still lay on the bedside table.

Shutting the door behind her, she thought of Garth—the tender way he spoke of his mother, his quick temper, his lovingly carved grave markers, his angry threats, his stricken look when he read the letter—

"The letter!" Crissa dashed inside again, searching for the letter Warren Adams had written. She could not just leave it out in the open, but where was it? She sifted furtively through Ruth's belongings. Under the bed? The table? Her searches were fruitless, and she realized Garth must have taken it with him. Closing the door once more, Crissa started for town.

With her skirts clutched tightly, Crissa jogged as much as she could, slowing to a walk when her breath gave out or the stitch in her side became too intense. She kept alert to the sound of an approaching horse. The few potatoes she'd had for dinner did nothing but make her ache for more.

Curving away from the foothills, the path to Willow Springs

led Crissa out in the open, away from the shelter of trees or brush. Despite the pockets of green along the creek bed, this was the desert. Dry, hot, unyielding, and unforgiving. Whispers snaked by her, coaxed by the unearthly silence that enfolds the desert. Prairie grass swished with her passing, brushing her ankles. Piles of gray clouds clustered over the hills, blanketing the heat with humidity.

When her breath started coming in jagged snatches, she slowed her pace. The narrow path joined the wider Overland trail now, but Crissa still could not tell how far she was from town. The last time she had traveled this road had been on her return from Salt Lake City. She had arrived just in time to find Molly dead. "Please, God," Crissa whispered, "do not let it happen again. Do not let Drake die also."

Tears trickled down her cheeks as she recalled her short friendship with Molly. *She was so kind to me, taking me in, making me feel like part of her family. If only my stage had not been delayed.*

She remembered the curtains fluttering in the breeze, such a contrast to the uneasy feeling Crissa had had when she'd walked into her room at the inn. Seeing Molly lying there so peacefully the pretty bouquet of flowers, the spicy scent of roses—Crissa froze. *The flowers! Where had the flowers come from?* Molly had wild roses growing on the fence, but they were nothing like the plump, fragrant roses in the arrangement. There were lilacs on either side of the front porch, Marida's few herbs by the kitchen door, but no foxglove or daisies. Mentally, she scanned the few buildings that comprised the town, but she could not recall seeing anything like the flowers adorning her room.

A horse's whinny not far off forced Crissa's attention back to the present. She could hear the steady beat of trotting hooves coming closer. There was nowhere to hide, no sturdy stick with which to arm herself. She was out in the open, fully exposed, and completely vulnerable. Pulling the small gun from her pocket, she snapped the chamber open and anxiously peered in the barrel. Satisfied the pistol was loaded, she stuffed the gun back in her pocket, keeping her thumb firmly on the hammer. There would not be time to fumble around cocking the gun if she actually needed to use it.

Squaring her shoulders, Crissa strode ahead to meet the approaching rider. A sleek mare pulling a white buggy emerged from a veil of dust in the distance. As the rig drew near, Crissa recognized Rachel Hampton sitting regally behind the reins. The fringe on the buggy's hood swayed to the smart steps of the horse.

"Why, Crissa," Rachel exclaimed, drawing the horse alongside Crissa, "whatever brings you out alone this evening?"

Crissa's pent-up breath escaped in jagged gasps.

"Child?" Rachel bent over the side of the buggy to examine her. "Has something happened? You look positively affright!"

"Mrs. Hampton!" Crissa cried. "Please, help me! Garth . . ." Clinging to a spoke of the wheel, Crissa felt her knees buckle, and blackness overcame her.

★ ★ ★

Vaguely aware that someone was sitting her up, Crissa struggled to force her eyes open. This was a mistake at best. The foggy image beside her was still, but the world around that image spun crazily. Closing her eyes, she let her head drop back onto the arm holding her shoulders and struggled to keep what little dinner she'd had where it belonged.

"Come, now," the image scolded. "There's no time for this nonsense."

Crissa felt several smart taps on the side of her face. "I cannot—" she struggled to say. Again, someone was slapping her face.

"Come on. Open those eyes."

The image of Mrs. Hampton squatting next to her came into focus at last. Crissa managed to sit up despite her churning stomach.

"Well, then?" Mrs. Hampton demanded. "What's this all about?"

The urgency of her flight pervaded Crissa's confusion. "Garth—" How could she explain? "Gone to the mine. After Warren Adams. He took guns."

"What do you mean, gone after him? Speak up now!"

"Garth found a letter Mr. Adams wrote." *I must make Mrs. Hampton understand.* "It said something terrible. Now Garth has gone after him. Please! We must get to the mine!" Crissa labored to her feet

172

and crawled into the wagon. She thought better of telling Rachel that Drake was involved, as well.

"Tarnation!" Mrs. Hampton boosted Crissa up to the seat. "I told her this would happen!"

Ruth? Mrs. Hampton knew? Crissa pressed the heel of her hand to her throbbing forehead and tried to put her dislike of this woman out of her mind. "Please, Mrs. Hampton, we have to hurry. Garth took his guns. He means to kill him."

"Means to kill him," Rachel mimicked Crissa's words. "More likely Garth'll let off his bit of steam, then stomp off somewhere to pout."

"No!" Crissa cried. "You did not see the look on his face. I have never seen anyone so angry!"

"Once you've lived with Garth a while, you'll come to know his temper's quicker than a hair trigger. And you'll also come to know that Garth doesn't have the guts to take on anyone bigger or more powerful than himself. It's a common shortcoming of men in these parts."

"You are wrong this time." Struggling to control her own temper in the face of this frustrating woman, Crissa kept her voice measured and firm. "If you will not take me to the mine, I will walk to town and find someone who will."

"All right then!" Rachel barked. "I'll take you out there, though God knows as well as I do it's a waste of time." Rachel snapped the reins of the horse and the buggy lurched forward. "I should have known no good would come of you marrying Garth." The words were said through gritted teeth and not meant to be discreet.

"Me! But I did not do anything."

Rachel was driving the buggy eastward, in the opposite direction from the mines.

"Stop!" Crissa cried. "You are going the wrong way! The mines are back that way!"

"Humph," Rachel snorted, giving the reins another crack. "If there's going to be two fool men out there fighting, I'm surely not going in empty-handed. I planned on a nice, quiet day of shopping, not busting up a gunfight. Besides, it'll be dark before we get back. Be best for us both to have a rifle handy."

"But we will be too late!"

"Nonsense! Those two roosters'll spend half the night strutting and crowing before one of 'em gets up the nerve to finish it. Now quit your squawking before you spook my horse."

Closing her eyes, Crissa sat back on the seat and tried to breathe deep, relaxing breaths. Lulled by the swaying of the buggy, her mind again reflected on the enigmatic flowers left in her room. Images of roses swayed through her half dream, intermingled with fluffs of tiny daisies and graceful spires of foxglove . . . just as they had been carved on the grave markers.

Jolted from her dream, Crissa gripped the side of the buggy. *The grave markers! Garth! He must have brought the flowers when he heard I was coming back to Willow Springs.* Goose bumps prickled Crissa skin with an icy stroke. But how were the flowers connected to Molly's death?

Molly had been sitting on Crissa's bed, watching out her window, most likely. Surrounded by flowers and eating cookies. Crissa's breath quickened. *The cookies!* Molly never made cookies, only cakes or pies. Marida would not have made them. She thought cookies were a waste of precious time.

Crissa straightened, heart pounding in her chest as she realized her train of thought might reveal something more sinister. She struggled to recall the cause of Molly's death. Heart problems, Doc Robbins had said. Heart flutters. *Who else had had them? Signe's neighbor in Salt Lake City! The midwife gave that woman foxglove tea to slow her heart down!* The image of the plate of cookie crumbs on the nightstand flashed through Crissa's mind. *It must have been in the cookies! But who would want to poison Molly?*

Crissa's skin turned to ice as she realized the truth. *Not Molly, but me! The cookies were in my room. Molly ate the cookies someone left for me. Who else knew I was coming back that day? And why would they want to poison me?*

The image of the bottle of foxglove on Garth's shelf took focus in her mind. If enough were used, it might give someone a heart attack. But the foxglove was Ruth's, and Ruth had already been dead several years. It had to have been Garth. But why? Revenge?

For the attempted rape, maybe? Then why would he turn around two months later and blackmail her into marrying him? Would Garth even know how to make cookies? If Garth was in love with Crissa as he claimed, surely he would not have tried to poison her. But who else would know to put foxglove in the cookies? Who else would want to harm her? Crissa pressed her cool hands to either side of her face.

"Headache, dear?" Rachel was watching her.

"Yes," Crissa replied, rubbing her forehead between her brows. "A small one, I suppose."

"I wouldn't wonder." Rachel clucked to the horse, turning it onto a rutted lane. "I'll fix you a tonic when we get home. We're nearly there. I'd bet you haven't had a decent meal all day."

Scanning the landscape around her, Crissa saw nothing but flat land to the east. To the west, the land was also flat until it met with the foothills of the Deep Creek range. Ahead, to the north, the land rose almost imperceptibly. In fact, the only indication it was a hill was the top of a cedars just barely visible above the crest. The faint lane bowed around the hill, disappearing into the distance.

"Mrs. Hampton? Have you ever seen roses that are this big around?" Crissa held her fingers in a circle about the diameter of a coffee cup. "They smell wonderful, like fine perfume."

Rachel nodded her recognition. "You mean English roses. My grandmother carried starts with her when she came to America from Cardiff."

"Is that right?" Crissa wondered at a woman going to such great lengths to cart roses across the ocean.

"My grandmother adored roses, and roses adored my grandmother," Rachel boasted. "I'm sure they never would have survived for anyone else. When my parents married, Grandmother brought cuttings of all of her plants and helped my parents get their own garden started."

"Really?" Crissa's nausea was returning and she listened to Mrs. Hampton's recollections, trying to keep her mind from the dizzy hunger she was feeling.

"My father was one of the original Thomsonians, you know."

"Thomsonian?" Crissa shut her eyes against the swaying landscape.

"An herbalist! Why, Samuel Thomson is the leading homeopath of modern day! A devout student of Dr. Hahnemann, let me assure you."

Herbalist? Homeopath? Hahnemann? Just trying to keep track of Mrs. Hampton's lecture made Crissa want to lean over the side of the buggy.

"Naturally, I was interested in herbal medicine from the time I was big enough to hold a pestle in my hand," Rachel continued. "I studied midwifery in Philadelphia, don't you know."

"Really." If they did not stop soon, Crissa was sure she would keel over, tumble off the wagon, and die of starvation right there in the road.

As if in answer to Crissa's thoughts, Rachel reined the horse to the left, guiding it around the edge of the hill and down a steep embankment. What had looked like a gradual rise from the road dropped off sharply on the other side of the hill to form a sheltered valley, obscuring the Hampton ranch from the Overland Trail. Bypassing a run-down shack that evidently served as a stable, Rachel drew the rig directly to the yard.

The house faced southward, positioned atop a small knoll. "Oh my!" Crissa gasped as she viewed the landscape. Surrounded by a white picket fence was the most beautiful, luxuriant garden Crissa had ever seen. A sundial anchored the center position of the garden, which was separated into three areas by small boxwood hedges. Bushy tomatoes, carrots, potatoes, onions, tall spires of corn and brussels sprouts, and beans trellised into teepees occupied the southwestern wedge of the garden. A beehive surrounded by parsley, rosemary, basil, dill, and other herbs filled out the southeastern wedge. Strawflowers, bachelor buttons, marigolds, and lavender were among the myriad of flowers and small shrubs dominating the northern half of the display nearest the house. A river-stone path led to the porch and front door.

"Oh, my," Crissa murmured as she got out of the carriage.

"Yes, indeed," Rachel responded from beside her. "Quite a sight, wouldn't you say?"

Crissa touched a leaf of a vine with dark purple berries. "What is this vine climbing the fence?"

"Belladonna, dear. I call it nightshade."

Closing her eyes, Crissa smiled and breathed deeply the heavenly mixture of fragrances.

"Come along inside, then. I'll fix you something to eat."

"But, Mrs. Hampton," Crissa reminded her, "there is not time. We have to get to the mines."

"It won't take any time at all." Rachel took Crissa by the elbow and led her to the stone pathway. "You're not fit to go anywhere until you get some nourishment. Just some cheese and a bit of bread. You'll collapse if you don't eat something."

"I will be fine, really," Crissa pleaded. "If something should happen . . ."

"Nothing's going to happen, dear. We'll get there. I'll fix you a bundle to eat on the way. Now come inside. No sense you taking heat stroke out here."

Though the sun was beginning to slip behind the mountains, it was still mercilessly hot and humid. Crissa felt her dress sticking to the powder burns on her stomach each time she changed position. It would feel heavenly to slip out of the unbearable heat for just a few moments and enjoy a cool parlor.

"Your garden is lovely," Crissa said, aiming for polite conversation as she followed Rachel. "I am surprised you get it to grow here in the desert."

"My father taught me a thing or two about irrigation when he was alive. I found a spring at the base of the hillside by the cedars. It was only logical to divert the water up to the house by way of channels."

"What a lot of work you must have put into it."

"And quite worth the effort, wouldn't you say?" Rachel surveyed her domain proudly.

"What is this growing between the rocks?" Crissa wondered at the small round leaves growing between the paving stones. The mild, earthy fragrance reminded her of Marida's pasta sauce, and her stomach ached with the memory.

"Thyme." Rachel paused beside a towering hollyhock to pluck a few dead blossoms. "Are you interested in gardening?"

"My father mostly tended cattle in Sweden," Crissa replied, "but when we moved to Uppsala, we had a few acres in barley. My mother grew a few flowers near the house, but my father thought they were a worthless waste of space."

"Is that a fact?" Rachel said, sniffing.

Bending to examine a mound of pinks, Crissa smiled at Rachel, trying to soothe her absent father's affront. "Perhaps that is why I find your garden so appealing."

"Quite so." Rachel led the way up the walk toward the house.

Crissa's breath ceased when she viewed the array of flowers framing the porch railing. Creamy damask roses, their heady scent engulfing all who passed; tall spires of purple foxglove; and airy clouds of miniature daisies all intermingled just as they had been in the bouquet left in Crissa's room. As they had been, etched in the markers above the graves. As they had been painted on the demi-tasse cups Rachel gave as a wedding gift.

"Where did you find so many flowers?" Crissa sucked a deep gulp of the perfumed air engulfing her.

"I brought what I could when I moved out here. The rest I ordered through an herbalist's catalog."

"What made you settle in Willow Springs, Mrs. Hampton?" Garth had not painted a picture of a young woman so devoted to her sister that she would settle out in the middle of nowhere just to be near her.

"My first husband died in Philadelphia. He and Warren Adams had been friends since their youth, so naturally when Warren found out I was a widow and with child, he felt it his obligation to look after us." Rachel smiled at Crissa, a very smug, self-satisfied smile. "His wife was most kind and sympathetic toward me."

Something about her story didn't ring true in Crissa's mind, but she certainly was not in a position to cast any doubt. "And Suzanna was the child?" she urged.

Rachel's lips clamped in a hard line for the instant before she turned her back on Crissa. "No. That child died at birth. I married Suzanna's father a few years later."

"Oh," Crissa murmured. "I am sorry." Odd, but Crissa had never considered Suzanna's father. She had never heard him spoken of in town or seen any evidence of a Mr. Hampton. The widow of Warren Adams's boyhood friend—the same phrase she had read in Warren's letter only hours earlier. The same phrase Warren had told his wife regarding the woman who was carrying his child. Crissa stared at the back of Rachel's head. Could it be?

Crissa stifled a gasp as she realized the truth. Ruth was not Garth's mother—Rachel was! She ached for Garth. He worshipped Ruth and disrespected, if not despised, Rachel. First his father and now his mother. His entire family was a lie.

Mrs. Hampton quickly changed the subject. Pulling a leaf from a mound of miniature white daisies, she handed it to Crissa. "Here. Suck on this. It will help your headache."

The daisies from the bouquet! "What is it?" Crissa sniffed at the leaf, pinching it between her fingers, and grimaced at the pungent odor it released.

"Feverfew," Rachel answered. "It won't taste pleasant, but it will calm what ails you."

Crissa paused with the leaf suspended in front of her mouth. Garth had said: "My ma had to rely on Rachel's folk-medicine 'til she finally died." Rachel Hampton knew how to use foxglove; she had studied to become a midwife. She would certainly know how much to mix in cookies to ensure a person's death. Crissa stared at Rachel, who was absently picking wilted leaves from the bushy feverfew. And Rachel grew the precise flowers that had been such a mystery. And there was no doubt as to why Rachel would want to hurt Crissa: Suzanna. With Crissa out of the way for good, Drake would marry Rachel's precious Suzanna.

Crissa watched Rachel look at her, but she could not turn away, could not speak, could not breathe. Feeling faint, she watched as darkness collapsed in from the edges of her vision until only Rachel was visible. Was it the twitch of a smile Crissa saw reflected in Rachel's face as unconsciousness folded over her?

CHAPTER 19

Heavy, red velvet curtains cloaked Rachel's parlor in darkness, leaving only a narrow streak of light sneaking in between the overlap of the drawn draperies. Illuminated by this errant shaft, a trickle of dust fairies danced for Crissa. Richly furnished with a grand piano, two high-backed sofas, and several slipper chairs, the parlor seemed a shrine for some long-forgotten royalty.

The only air circulating was that which Crissa had disturbed when she sat up on the stiff couch. Suffocating, stale . . . not unlike the viewing room in her grandparents' house where dead relatives were laid out until their burial.

"Oh! You're awake, dear!" Rachel swept into the room, her voice sweet and congenial. Crissa jumped at Rachel's voice, as if one of her departed relatives had arisen.

"What? How did I—?"

"Why, you swooned from the heat, child. Looked for a moment like you'd seen a ghost! Gave me quite a fright, I can tell you. Don't know how I got you this far before you collapsed."

Rachel grasped Crissa's elbow and pulled her from the velvet chair. "Well, now, we can't let you stay in here. This is the company room," she scolded. "Just look at you! You're filthy! Why, you'll have dust all over everywhere." Leading Crissa across the hallway into the kitchen, Rachel clucked and cooed like a worried dove.

What has come over Mrs. Hampton? Crissa wondered, allowing herself to be shooed from the "company room." She was being so warm and caring—not at all the vinegary, high-handed woman who had made Crissa so uncomfortable since coming to Willow Springs. Crissa sat at an elegantly carved table more suited for a dining room than a kitchen and rested her forehead in her palm.

What would Suzanna think? Crissa wondered. *Here I am in her kitchen, being entertained by her mother.* "Where is Suzanna tonight, Mrs. Hampton?"

"She stayed in town awhile longer. Annabelle Taylor's going into the dressmaking business, it seems. Suzanna's over there having a new dress fitted."

Rachel swept around the room, lighting the oil lamps in each of the four corners and the fat brown candle on the table. She slid the pewter candleholder closer to Crissa and waved the refreshing fragrance toward her. "Lovely, isn't it? Breathe deeply, dear. It will help you relax."

Rachel's kitchen was certainly the most unusual kitchen Crissa had ever seen. One sink, placed where a person could view the front yard, was equipped with the expected array of pots, pans, knives, colanders, and such. A buffet and hutch, centered on the side wall, was filled with candlesticks and vases and a large collection of the foxglove-painted china that Rachel had shared with Crissa.

But it was the back wall that held Crissa's attention. Recessed in a wide counter, another sink was surrounded with shelves of glass bottles and jars, various-sized tins, and an assortment of baskets, all seemingly bursting with dried or fresh flowers, herbs, and powders. No water pump was attached to the sink, but there were several bottles of miscellaneous liquids within arms' reach. A tall stool was positioned in front of the counter, as well as a stepladder to reach the higher shelves. Clumps of red peppers, buttercups, nettle, basil, chamomile, dill, foxglove, the daisy-like feverfew, and a variety of other plants that Crissa did not recognize dangled from a board suspended from the ceiling. Each type of herb and flower had an open cheesecloth pouch suspended just below it to catch any dried material that happened to fall. Another board was suspended behind the first, this one displaying tied bunches of vines, bundles of willows, ropes of bark, and an array of flowers tied into bouquets.

"Quite a sight, wouldn't you say?" Mrs. Hampton interrupted Crissa's inspection.

"Yes," Crissa agreed. "I have never seen anything like this. What is it all?"

Rachel smiled again, obviously well pleased with the effect her display had on her visitor. Running her hand along one of the lower shelves, tapping a bottle with a black-rimmed label back into perfect alignment, Rachel was absorbed with her collection. "Medicine has been rather a hobby of mine for many, many years. My father and grandfather were doctors in the old country, and I grew up fascinated by their ministrations."

"Are these all from your garden?" Crissa asked, sweeping her arm at the massive expanse.

"I received a few boxes of treatments when my father passed on, but I cultivated the rest of them myself."

Following Rachel's gaze, Crissa remembered the discoveries she had made outside: that Rachel must be Garth's mother, and that it had to have been Rachel who poisoned Molly. "It was you!" she whispered before she could stop herself.

"Me what, dear?" Her voice was gentle, but a malevolence glinted in Rachel's eyes that unnerved Crissa.

"You must have worked . . . very hard," Crissa stammered, "on your . . . your garden."

"Yes, I did." The upper curve of Rachel's mouth lifted in a self-satisfied sneer. "Do you know much about herbs, child?"

"Not very much, really."

"Come, relax for a moment, then. Let me fix you a cup of tea. Perhaps you will find gardening suits you."

Tea? Has she forgotten about Garth? "Thank you, Mrs. Hampton, but really, we must be going. Perhaps I could eat a piece of cheese on the way."

"Nonsense, child. What is your hurry?"

"Garth!" Crissa wanted to shake the woman. "The letter! He means to kill his father!"

"The letter," Rachel said softly. "Yes, the letter." Rachel reached for the teakettle beside the front sink and absently pumped water into it. "Tell me about the letter, dear." She blew softly on the embers in the stove until they glowed red, then fed in a handful of kindling. "Where did he find the letter, Crissa?" The fire sprang to life, and Rachel turned to face Crissa.

Watching her minister to the stove, Crissa was mesmerized by Rachel's kind voice. Her heart thumped wildly in her chest, but her mind still clung to the hope that this woman would help her.

Rachel smiled at her. "I'm waiting, Crissa. Where was the letter hidden?"

"In the bonnet. The lining."

The corners of her smile faded for an instant before Rachel turned back to making tea. Taking a square of cheesecloth and a bottle from the shelf, Rachel spooned a small heap of dried leaves into the center of the cloth. The label on the bottle bore a picture of chamomile.

"Does your head still hurt, dear?"

Crissa nodded again.

Rachel placed a strip of bark in her mortar cup and began grinding it. "A bit of white willow bark will do the trick." Using her pestle, she guided the coarse powder onto the cloth.

"And did you read the letter?"

"Yes." Crissa's thoughts were becoming jumbled. Each breath was warm and comforting, laden with the candle's sweet scent.

Rachel grasped a pinch of something from another bottle and sprinkled it in the tea mixture, then washed her hands at the sink. "So you know that Warren Adams is Garth's father?"

"Yes."

She tied the tea bag, placed it in a china cup, and poured water from the kettle over it. Holding the bag between two spoons, Rachel gently massaged it, forcing water through the leaves. At last the water turned a mossy-brown color, and a spicy fragrance filled the room. Using one of the spoons, Rachel lifted the bag from the cup and squeezed it once more, careful not to touch the bag herself.

"Sip this, child," Rachel coaxed, placing the cup in front of Crissa. "It will help ever so much."

Crissa stared at the cup. Her hands felt so heavy. It was decorated with roses . . . and daisies . . . and foxglove.

"Go ahead now," Rachel urged. "Drink up."

Crissa watched little undissolved black flecks swirling slowly in the tea. Her hands were so heavy . . . so tired.

Standing at the counter, Rachel hummed softly, her back to Crissa. She pulled a square basket from the shelf and picked through its contents.

"So you read the letter." She didn't turn around, just paused for a moment before continuing. "And now you know our little secret . . . Too bad, really. I think Garth might have been quite happy with you."

Like distant rolling thunder, warnings tried to break through Crissa's clouded mind only to be enfolded by the fog and die.

Choosing a few long stems, Rachel laid roses on the counter, arranging them in a narrow fan. "Roses for a peaceful journey." She looked over her shoulder and smiled at Crissa. "All I ever wanted was his happiness, you understand—his and my Suzie's." She turned back to her work. "That's why I made Warren give Ruth the inn. A boy needs an inheritance, you see. I couldn't let him have the ranch, of course. Where would that leave me?"

Lifting one of her leaden hands, Crissa captured one of the stubborn flecks on her finger, then lifted it to her mouth. It felt gritty on her tongue, like sand. She pushed the grain between her teeth and bit through it. A sharp, bitter taste filled her mouth. She tried clumsily to wipe the taste from her tongue, then skimmed her finger along the top of the tea to capture the rest of the flecks and smeared them on the table.

Rachel slid the first basket to the side and removed another one from the shelf. "Let's see now. Some michaelmas to honor St. Michael." She placed a feathery spray of daisies among the roses.

"Ruth. Now, she's the one who tried to spoil everything, you understand—selling the inn like that. I tried to stop her before the deed could be transferred, but she held on through the winter.

Never was one to go quietly, I can tell you. It's a shame Garth had to lose her that way, but I really had no alternative." Rachel looked over at Crissa. "Enjoying your tea, dear?"

Rachel pushed the basket of daisies back in its place and took down another basket. "We certainly couldn't send you off without a dash of foxglove. Strengthens a frail heart, you know. A nice dose of courage to carry you home." Rachel laid a few spires of lavender bells on top of the bouquet and then tucked several more rosebuds among them.

"Garth's a good boy, Crissa. A bit high-spirited at times, but he means well. I'm glad I could give him a bit of happiness. He's been working himself so hard since I had Warren take him on at the mine. And now that he's married you . . . why, I've never seen a body want anything as much as he wanted you. Three hundred dollars was a small price to pay to see him so happy—if only for a day or two."

"Jen—" Crissa forced the word out. She was so drowsy she wasn't even sure the word had been audible. The face of Donald Jenkins floated in the back of her mind, and she clung to it—the face that was the only salient image she could summon. "You paid Jenkins?"

"I thought Garth would have told you."

Leaning forward on her forearms, Crissa struggled to keep her head from bobbing—struggled to form the questions that must be answered. "Drake . . . thinks his . . . father . . ."

Rachel's voice took on the familiar hard edge that Crissa had always associated with her. "Drake? Did Drake come to see you?"

"Yes."

"Curse that boy! I told him to stay away from you! I've planned it all so carefully, and now he's going to get in the way again!"

Get in the way? Crissa's mind slid back to the day Garth proposed. He had said the same thing—that she had gotten in the way.

Rachel was towering over Crissa, shaking her finger in Crissa's face. "The first time Drake met you, he started mooning over you. How is he supposed to want to marry my Suzanna when some cheap foreigner is throwing herself at him?"

Foreigner? Throwing myself?! Crissa desperately tried to shake the numbness from her mind. She had to defend herself!

Splotches of purple darkened Rachel's face. Her lips contorted with rage. "I've been planning their marriage since they were babies—struggling to keep Suzie in beautiful clothing, working day and night to make the ranch pay for itself!" She strode back to the counter and leaned on her hands. Her shoulders heaved with each breath.

Her voice was quieter now, and she kept her back turned to Crissa. "It's all I've got, you know. This ranch. All I can offer as Suzie's dowry." She drew a narrow white ribbon from a basket and tied it around the bouquet, letting the ends of the ribbon trail down the jumble of stems. She kept talking while she worked, and Crissa realized Rachel was no longer talking to her.

"Be nice to keep it in the family. Warren gave it to me when Garth was born—the ranch and the inn. The inn was to be Garth's one day. 'Til Ruth sold it, of course, and he was left with nothing. Did the best I could by that boy, but . . ." Rachel snipped a branch of cedar from overhead, then laid the spray of flowers on top of it. "There. A nice gift to welcome the spirit." She tied the bundle with a wide black ribbon and twined the ends up through the cedar.

"All I've got left is my sweet Suzie. Drake'll make a nice husband for her. Only fitting that Warren's blood should mingle with mine again. Got to do something about that foreigner woman, though." Rachel took a horehound drop from a tin and popped it in her mouth. Sucking contentedly, she continued to talk to herself while she fussed with the flowers.

Watching her work, Crissa pored over what to do. She still felt so tired—so relaxed. Her arms and legs felt lifeless, and her head kept bobbing, but her mind was beginning to clear. She knew she was in some kind of danger, but didn't want to make the effort to get away. Had Rachel already given her something? But how could she? Crissa hadn't eaten anything here, and after she bit into the grain in her tea, she had pushed that away as well. She tried to concentrate on Rachel, but Rachel's image, caught in waves rising from the flickering candle, was impossible to focus on. Crissa laid her head on her arms to rest . . . just for a moment.

★ ★ ★

The clippity-clop, clippity-clop was so faint at first that Crissa couldn't quite make out what they were—hoofbeats. A long way off . . . but coming this way. One horse? Many? Just one . . . coming very fast. Crissa felt Rachel brush past, but she couldn't open her eyes. Rest . . . a moment longer. The hoofbeats were very close now, but they were not slowing down. Who could it be? Should go out . . . The hoofbeats slowed abruptly and stopped. Then Crissa heard a man's voice.

"Evening, Rachel."

"Warren." Rachel's voice was syrupy sweet again. Warren? . . . Drake's . . . and Garth's father . . . still alive.

"May I come in?" His voice sounded so somber.

"Why don't we sit out here awhile?"

"I have some news, Rachel. We'd best go inside." Crissa forced her head upright and struggled to open her eyes. *Please . . . come . . . help me.*

She heard Rachel's slippered feet shuffle past the kitchen door, followed by a man's heavy boots. Spurs jingled lightly, skimming the floor. *No! . . . In here!* He was saying something. "Let's sit in the kitchen, Rachel. I could use a cup of coffee." The clomping boots returned and drew near. Crissa could barely make out a tall shadow standing beside her.

"Oh, I beg your pardon. I didn't realize Mrs. Hampton had company," he said. "Why, you must be Miss Engleson." He paused. "Rachel? What's wrong with the girl? What's that—Rachel! It smells like a medicine tent in here!"

"Leave 'er alone, Warren. This is none of your affair."

"You trying to drug the girl? What's the matter with you?"

Crissa watched his arm sweep in front of her, and the flickering light toppled to the floor. A boot stomped down hard. She felt herself being lifted in his arms. Rachel stood in the corner by the door with her arms folded across her chest, silent.

Suddenly Crissa was sitting on a bench in the garden. She welcomed the cool night air. A mild breeze stirred the air in advance of a line of swollen clouds. Someone was pressing a wet handkerchief to her brow, her neck, and her arms, Crissa felt her mind clearing and the overwhelming fatigue ebbing from her limbs.

Warren Adams hovered over her, wetting the handkerchief in a shallow irrigation ditch. What was it about him? The eyes. Those deep-set azure eyes, rimmed so thickly with black lashes they looked as if they had been lined with kohl. Soft, comforting eyes framed by black brows that lifted at the center edge in concern. So like Drake's—

"Feelin' any better, Miss Engleson? S'pose I should be callin' you Mrs. Wight."

Mrs. Wight. The sound of her new name brought a pang to Crissa's chest. It just didn't fit—not yet.

"I've just come from Gold Hill—from the mines. I'm afraid I have some bad news."

Crissa nodded. Drake? Garth? Whatever the news, she wasn't ready to hear it. Too much had happened already today. She needed some sleep—and a decent meal. She needed to hold Amy in her lap and sing lullabies or wake up and find this was all a bad dream. But it wasn't. The dusky sky lit briefly with a glimmer of lightning hiding behind the clouds.

Mr. Adams turned his back to Crissa and stared at the advancing clouds. He cleared his throat several times before continuing. "Garth came up to the number four—that's one of the mines—and he was powerful angry. I think if Drake hadn't been there—" He sat beside her on the bench, twisting his hat absently in his hands. "I wish there was some other way to tell you, Crissa. There was a fight, and the boy tripped on a pile of rocks. Hit his head." The last word caught in his throat, and Warren turned his head away. "He's dead."

Sitting there in stunned silence, Crissa willed the knot in her throat to swell up the rest of the way and suffocate her. What could she say? Drake—it couldn't be. She had never loved a man the way she loved Drake. He couldn't be taken from her. And here was his father, fighting his own grief, trying to be so kind—

"I am sorry," she whispered. "I am so, so sorry." The two sat in silence for several minutes while the night settled in around them.

"Thank you for coming, Mr. Adams," Crissa managed at last. "I know it must have been difficult for you."

"Yes, well," he said, clearing his voice. "I don't suppose it'll ever get easier." He looked off in the distance, shaking his head. "I should've done more for the boy. Encouraged him to make his own kind of life. Done less meddling in things that weren't none of my business."

Crissa wondered if he was referring to the Pony Express, to Drake's dream of ranching, or if he was referring to her. Warren looked toward the house, where Rachel stood waiting on the porch. "Guess I should break the news to Mrs. Hampton. You come along with me. I'll fix you a sherry. There's no call for you to go back home directly."

"Of course," Crissa agreed, wondering how Rachel would take the news after her recent tantrum.

"Rachel," Mr. Adams directed, "let's go into the back parlor. Pour some of that sherry you've been hoarding. You'll be needin' it."

Crissa glimpsed Rachel's hand gripping the porch rail. Mr. Adams's hand was firm on Crissa's elbow as he led her past Rachel and down the hall. A shudder swept over her as they passed the kitchen, which was still smelling faintly sweet from the candle.

They entered a large room at the back of the house. A billiards table dominated the space, leaving room only for a shallow cupboard and a few chairs on the far side of the room. Animal heads displayed on the wall surrounded an ornately carved fireplace on the side nearest the door. A rifle and a long-barreled pistol were mounted above the mantle. Warren led Crissa to one of the chairs and strode to the liquor cabinet.

"Warren?" Rachel asked, picking a piece of lint off a mounted buffalo head. There was a distinct tremor in her voice. "What has happened?"

He considered her for a moment before speaking. "There was a fight at the mine, Rachel." He poured sherry into a slender crystal glass. "Drake and Garth." He walked around the billiards table to where Rachel stood by the fireplace and handed the glass to her. "Rachel, Garth is dead." The glass slid from her hand, landing with a soft thud on the thick rug.

For a moment, there was no sound in the room. No movement, no breath.

Garth! The name thundered in Crissa's ears. *Garth, not Drake.* Tears flooded her eyes. *Not Drake!*

"My baby," Rachel whimpered. "My baby's dead." She turned toward Crissa, her trembling fists clutched side by side. As she spoke, her voice strengthened from sorrow to fury. "It was you. It's always you. You killed him the same as you killed Molly. Those cookies were meant for you! If you had only stayed away, they wouldn't have been necessary. It's your fault Molly died. And now you've killed my baby." A low, almost animal cry erupted from Rachel's throat as she lunged for the pistol propped on the mantle. "You've killed my baby!"

Crissa watched, paralyzed, as Rachel swung the pistol around, pulled back the hammer, and aimed it across the room at her. Falling to her knees, Crissa instinctively covered her head with her arms. A shot rang out, followed by another, and Crissa cringed before the impact. Nothing. She looked across the table to where Warren Adams stood, his own pistol gripped at arm's length, still in the motion of recoiling upward from the jolt of the shot. A wisp of smoke dangled in the air above the barrel. Rachel Hampton stood where the impact had thrown her against the fireplace, her mouth gaping open, blood quickly soaking the front of her dress. A feeble gasp, and she slid to the floor.

★ ★ ★

"Where is Drake now, Mr. Adams?" Crissa and Warren sat in front of the liquor cabinet. Warren poured a short gin and held it out to Crissa, but the smell of it made her queasy stomach nearly turn. She sat the glass to the side and watched Warren drawing his whiskey down in deep gulps.

"At Doc Robbins's, I expect." Warren rested one elbow on his knee, his head cradled in his palm. "Nothing serious, but he got knocked around pretty good before . . ." He took another pull of his drink and stared at the floor. "I guess we should head into town. Suzanna will have to be told." He finished his whiskey in one long gulp.

"Best clean her up some 'fore we go," he said, looking down at Rachel's body. "You go fetch some napkins."

Crissa shivered at the thought of walking through the house alone. Only the lamps in this room and the kitchen had been lit. The rest of the house was shrouded in darkness. Rachel had tried to kill her twice tonight. Was her spirit still lurking here, somewhere, waiting to try again?

"In the kitchen," Warren directed.

Walking as quickly as she could, Crissa focused on the light at the end of the hall—the kitchen. It wasn't a great distance, but she turned into the room out of breath, with goose bumps. Pieces of the tainted candle lay on the table.

No napkins were on the counters. Surely they would be kept in the buffet. Crissa crossed the room and knelt down in front of the cupboard. She located the basket of napkins easily enough. She was lifting it from the shelf when she heard a horse approaching. Crissa froze. Who could it be? The saddle creaked as the rider dismounted. Then she heard a patter of feet running up the porch steps. They were too soft to be a man . . . Suzanna!

"Mother?"

What will she think to find me here! Crissa stood up from behind the table into full view.

"Mother?"

Dashing to the doorway, Crissa tried to intercept Suzanna. She must not find her mother yet. "Suzanna!" Crissa called, trying to hold her voice steady. "Hello."

The puzzlement in Suzanna's eyes at seeing Crissa instantly turned to fury. "What are you doing here?"

"I . . . was just—"

Suzanna's eyes dropped to the basket of napkins Crissa still held. "Where's my mother?" She looked quickly in the dark front parlor before hurrying down the hall. "Mother?"

"Suzanna! Don't—" Warren tried to stop her from entering the back parlor.

"Mother!"

A heartrending scream pierced the house, and Crissa leaned against the doorway to gather her courage.

"You!" Suzanna screeched, seeing Crissa in the doorway.

"No, Suzanna, it was me." Warren tried to place himself between the two women. "Your mother had a gun."

Hatred glowed in Suzanna's eyes as she advanced on Crissa. "This had something to do with Drake, didn't it! Everything was fine until you showed up." Her voice was deep and choked with tears. "You've ruined things for Drake and me." She advanced toward Crissa, backing her into the hallway. "Drake loved me! He still loves me!" She shoved Crissa against the wall.

Without flinching, Crissa tried to reason with Suzanna. "I never meant to hurt you."

"You're a liar!" Tears spilled down Suzanna's cheeks. "All my mother ever wanted was for me to marry Drake. You've taken him, and now you've—" Suzanna lunged at Crissa, pinning her against the wall, fingers curled around her neck. "Killed my mother!"

"No, Suzanna!" Crissa gasped, trying to pry Suzanna's fingers from her neck. Crissa pushed her away, only to have her spring again. Crissa ducked, but Suzanna grabbed her hair. Crissa glanced at Mr. Adams, but he stayed where he was.

"Did he bed you, strumpet?" Suzanna forced Crissa to the ground and grabbed for her throat again. "That's the only way he would ever want you!"

Crissa's slap across the face set Suzanna off balance long enough for Crissa to roll away from her. "I never—" Crissa hissed, jumping to her feet. "He loves me!" she said. She backhanded Suzanna aside her head, sending her sprawling. Years of indignation and injustice erupted in Crissa's rage. "He could never love you!" Gripping Suzanna by the front of her dress, Crissa heaved Suzanna against the wall. The gilt-framed mirror beside them tumbled from its place, shattering as it glanced off Suzanna's left shoulder. Suzanna clutched her gashed shoulder and stared for a moment at the blood seeping up between her fingers.

"He was going to marry me," Suzanna sobbed. She swung her right fist feebly at Crissa, then grabbed the console as she stumbled. In one clumsy motion, Suzanna fell, pulling the heavy table on top of her.

Warren sprung forward to help Crissa lift the table from Suzanna's legs.

"Everyone *thought* Drake would marry you, Suzanna," Crissa whispered. "Everyone but Drake."

CHAPTER 20

Wind whipping her hair made it nearly impossible for Crissa to look ahead of the buggy as they raced to town. Cradling Suzanna's head in her lap, Crissa tried to cushion her from the worst of the bumpy ride. Mr. Adams had thought it best for Suzanna to stay at home with Crissa while he went into town to fetch the doctor, but Suzanna refused to stay in the house with her dead mother or with Crissa. Mr. Adams had insisted on driving—he knew the road and the lay of the land—leaving Crissa in the back of Mrs. Hampton's buggy. Suzanna lay in front of Crissa, moaning occasionally. Crissa pressed a cloth to Suzanna's shoulder, trying to curtail the bleeding gash the broken mirror had made. Suzanna's exposed knee was rapidly swelling around the swath of cloth Mr. Adams had used to hold the bone in place.

Crissa felt the rig tilting as they rounded the curve where the Overland and Gold Hill roads merged. The road was like a washboard from the rain's uneven runoff, and the buggy shuddered, nearly on two wheels for twenty-five or thirty yards. Crissa braced a foot against the side of the wagon to try and cushion some of the vibrations.

"You all right?" Mr. Adams called back to her. Though he was no more than three feet in front of her, the wind snatched his voice, making him barely audible.

"Fine!" Crissa shouted in return.

"Passed the halfway point! Won't be much longer! It's a good road from here on!"

Crissa nodded again, struggling to keep her balance when Mr. Adams hit another rut. *Is this his idea of a good road?* Crissa wondered. A sliver of moon tried to break through the clouds now and again, but it offered barely enough illumination for Crissa to see the road. Squinting her eyes against the wind rushing at her, she peered ahead, searching for a glimpse of lights from the few houses leading to town.

It wasn't long before the road did smooth out and Mr. Adams pulled up in front of Dr. Robbins's place.

Thank goodness, Crissa thought. Her feet had gone completely asleep—one stuck out to brace herself, the other folded underneath her to provide Suzanna a little extra cushioning.

Mr. Adams leaped from the buggy to the porch and pounded on the doctor's door before bounding to the back of the wagon. He lifted Suzanna in his arms and carried her into the building just as the doctor was opening the door. The door slammed behind them, and Crissa was left alone in the buggy.

Gingerly testing her weight against the pins and needles stabbing her feet, Crissa climbed from the wagon. A faint light glowed from the downstairs window of the inn—someone must still be awake. She desperately wanted to see Marida, but she should at least look in on Suzanna first.

Crissa tiptoed up the steps and listened at the doctor's door. Would it be improper for her to peek inside to see how Suzanna was doing? Was the doctor still working on Drake as well? She knocked softly on the door.

"No visitors!" Doc Robbins yelled in response. Crissa fled the porch and leaned against the buggy until her heart stopped hammering. She reached out her hand to stroke the horse's neck.

"What a pretty thing you are," Crissa whispered, trying to divert her thoughts for a while. "We'll have to make sure you get some nice, sweet hay at the livery." The mare nuzzled Crissa, sniffing at her hair, and snorted her approval.

Several minutes passed before Mrs. Robbins emerged from the doctor's office. Drying her hands on the skirt of her white apron, she shook her head with pity and made a clicking noise with her tongue. "Nasty business, what?" she said to Crissa. "Mr. Adams tells me you've been through quite the ordeal this evening."

Crissa nodded. "Yes, ma'am."

"Such a shame." Mrs. Robbins looked Crissa over quickly, turning her this way and that for her superficial inspection. "You're uninjured?"

"Yes." Crissa felt almost guilty that she was the center of the trouble, yet she had not been seriously injured.

"This is good." Mrs. Robbins's crisp English accent gave her an air of efficiency, quite in keeping with a doctor's assistant. "Well. I suppose you'll want to see your young man, then."

Crissa bowed her head and followed Mrs. Robbins to a door on the side of the building.

"He's in here." Mrs. Robbins turned the doorknob for Crissa. "I'll leave you alone a minute. I left the lamp on. Don't let him frighten you."

Frighten me? She stepped into the room. He must be hurt more than Mr. Adams had said. Mrs. Robbins softly closed the door, and Crissa stood for a moment, letting her eyes adjust to the dim light. As her eyes adjusted, she peered around the bare room. There was no furniture save for a single, waist-high table against the far wall. "Drake?" Crissa tiptoed toward the sheet-draped form on the table. "Are you awake? It is Crissa. Drake?"

Crissa felt the blood draining from her face. The sheet had been pulled up over his head. Feeling the tears pool in her eyes, she lifted the sheet back. Garth's peaceful face lay beneath. Gasping, Crissa let the sheet fall from her hand, then spun to escape the room.

Why would that horrible woman send me in here?

But of course she would.

"To all the world he is my husband," Crissa whispered.

Turning back, she gazed sadly on Garth's face. An ugly bruise had risen around his eye, and his bottom lip was split. Crissa's tears splashed on the cold table—tears for the little boy who had borne so much hurt, for the son deprived of his natural mother and father, for the man who had promised to be a good husband. And he had tried, as much as a man who had never had a loving home could be expected to try.

"*Dyr Gud*," Crissa whispered, "*ropa hans spöke hem, och bevilja honom fred*." Dear God, call his spirit home, and grant him peace.

Smoothing the hair from his forehead, Crissa passed her hand over the sticky wound at the top of Garth's head. Shuddering, she wiped her hand on her skirt. "I am sorry, Garth. I did grow to care for you." The similarities between Garth and Warren Adams were more evident now—the deep-set eyes lost in shadows, the strong nose curved slightly like a beak. "Your father cared for you also, in his way. I'm certain of it."

Crissa pulled the sheet down to reveal Garth's shirt. His leather vest had been buttoned over his shirt, and someone had tied a string-tie under his collar, obviously preparing him for burial. Gingerly placing her hand on his chest, Crissa pressed several different places before slipping her hand in a pocket on the inside of his vest. She withdrew the letter, the one Mr. Adams had written, and slipped it into her skirt's pocket. "It no longer matters, does it? Enough people have already been hurt trying to hide the truth." Replacing the sheet, Crissa turned and stepped away.

Emerging from the little room, Crissa was caught in Marida's tight bear hug. The breath was nearly snatched from her lungs, so tight was the embrace. A worried voice was chattering in her ear in words Crissa could not make out. Now cooing, now scolding, now dismayed—Marida didn't pause long enough to take a breath. Crissa caught Vic's eye and managed to mouth, "Help!"

"Marida," Vic said softly, prying his wife's arms from around Crissa. "That's enough, *il mio amore*."

Tears streaked down Marida's face as she patted Crissa's cheeks. "Oh, *mia* Crissa, *mia* Crissa, how you worried me."

With Crissa in the middle, the three friends made their way to Henders Inn. Vic held one of the swinging doors wide for Crissa and Marida to pass through. Only the lamps at the head and foot of the stairs and one lamp in the corner of the dining room had been lit. "Someone wait for you," Marida whispered in Crissa's ear. "We leave you alone." Marida kept watching over her shoulder as Vic steered her toward the kitchen.

Drake was there, sitting in the corner where they had first met, the glow of the lamp highlighting his hair a blue black, his face hidden in the shadows. But he was there.

Before the notion had become a complete thought, Crissa knelt at his side, pressing his hand to her lips, feeling safe, at last, with Drake, who caressed her hair and wiped the steady stream of tears from her cheek.

"I thought," Crissa said, gulping through the tears, "you were—" A shudder went through her body, and she buried her head in his chest.

Sucking a breath through his teeth, Drake held her head from him and smiled weakly. "I reckon Garth did his bit of damage."

"You are hurt!" Gingerly lifting the edge of Drake's partially buttoned shirt, Crissa surveyed the bandages binding his chest. The left front of his collar was torn loose. Turning his head gently to the light, Crissa discovered several fresh stitches just under the left side of Drake's jaw. Crissa bit her lips, trying to stem the new tears.

Hooking a chair with his boot, he slid it closer for Crissa to sit in. "Hey, now," Drake murmured. "I broke a couple of ribs is all. I'll be fine in a few days' time."

"Everything that has happened, it is all because of me."

"You can't be blamed for anything that's happened here. It's not your fault."

Wiping the tears from her face, Crissa took a deep breath and exhaled. Drake would never let her assume the blame for Garth's death. She tried to smile and shifted the conversation. "You did not have to ride here from the mine, I hope."

"Sheriff Hawkes brought me in on a wagon."

"Sheriff Hawkes!" Crissa's eyes widened with fright.

"Don't worry," Drake reassured her. "He was just making his rounds up there. I don't think he'll be asking you any questions. For all he knows, Garth came up to the mine, corned almighty, and picked the wrong man to whup."

Crissa remembered the wrenching premonition she had had when Garth pulled his flask out as he rode off that last time. He was so full of hurt and liquor. "He was out of his mind with one thing and another." She looked at Drake, hoping he could understand some of the pain Garth had borne.

"I never should have taken up the fight," Drake said softly, "seein' how drunk he was. He just came busting into the office, cussing at my father and me. He was throwing chairs and books all over, and when he started calling you . . ." Drake took Crissa's hands in his, squeezing them tight. "I just lost control. I didn't want for him to—I didn't mean to kill him."

Lifting Drake's hands to her cheek, she closed her eyes. How was it possible she could care so much for two men who hated each other so greatly? Yet even with such a history of hatred, Drake was grieving for his enemy's death.

"Did my father come into town with you?"

No one in town, besides the doctor, knew about the events at the Hampton ranch, Crissa realized. Surely there would be no love lost between Drake and Mrs. Hampton, but Suzanna had said he loved her. Would he blame Crissa for the latest trouble?

"Crissa?" Drake called her from her thoughts. "My father?"

"He came into town," Crissa answered.

"I wonder where he is? I would've thought he'd—"

"He is at the doctor's."

Drake sat up straighter, craning his neck to see out the window. "Is he hurt? What happened?"

"No," Crissa stammered, "he was not hurt."

"Then why—"

"It is Suzanna." Crissa had Drake's full attention. "I think I may have broken her leg."

Drake's mouth fell open, and a smile played at the corner of it before he snapped it shut again and took a couple of breaths to ensure a serious demeanor. "You . . . broke her leg?"

"It is not a laughing matter!" Crissa scolded him. "There has been much sadness, and I think I may be in very serious trouble now."

Drake's face was instantly sober. "What's happened? Tell me everything."

Trying to remember all that had happened, Crissa related the events of the evening: Garth vowing to kill Drake and Mr. Adams; Crissa running to get help and meeting Mrs. Hampton on the way; the discovery of Mrs. Hampton's herbs and flowers; the tainted candle and the bitter granules in her tea; Mr. Adams's rescue, and the news he bore.

"I wonder what made him think of looking for you at the Hamptons'?" Drake mused.

"He said he had gone out to Garth's cabin first, but when he found I was not there, he went to tell Mrs. Hampton. She was his . . . aunt, I believe."

"Yeah, she was," Drake agreed.

"When Mrs. Hampton learned that Garth was dead, she became *sinnessjuk* . . . like her mind was not right. She tried to shoot me with her gun, but your father shot her."

"And you drove her all this way with her wounded?" Drake interrupted.

"No." Crissa filled her lungs, trying to find the courage to continue. "Mrs. Hampton is dead."

Drake's eyes widened markedly. "Dead?"

Crissa heard the faint squeak of the kitchen door and knew that Marida had heard the news as well.

"Then how did Suzanna come into this?"

It was difficult to remember exactly how they had fought; it had happened so quickly. But the vision of those last terrifying moments played with slowed-motion clarity in Crissa's memory. "When the mirror fell, I feared Suzanna would be crushed, but then she tried to hit me and lost her balance, and she pulled that heavy table over. If your father had not been there, I know I could not have moved it off her legs."

Drake's brows hooded his eyes as he listened to Crissa. He rubbed his face, then pulled his fingers back through his hair, leaving black tufts in their wake. "What I can't figure is why Garth would want to kill my father? And why would Rachel go to pieces over Garth?"

They had good reasons, Crissa thought to herself. *But what good would it do for me to tell their secrets now?* She shrugged, shook her head, and felt in her pocket to make sure the letter was still well hidden.

"Well, I don't see how anyone could hold you responsible for Mrs. Hampton's death," Drake continued, "and you were just defending yourself against Suzanna. I don't think you have anything to worry about."

For the moment, Crissa reminded herself.

Marida bustled from the kitchen, balancing a large tray on one hand, a pottage table on the other. She deftly set the small table down next to Drake and Crissa, and then unloaded her tray onto it. "I fix you soup and biscuits," she said, squeezing Crissa's thin arm. "You look like vulture bait."

Crissa had to smile at Marida's good-natured jab. "It has been so long since I last ate." Closing her eyes, she inhaled the delicious aroma. "It smells wonderful."

"I saw the sheriff and Mr. Adams come this way," Marida said, ladling the soup into two bowls. "You want me hold them off while you eat?"

Drake looked at Crissa, letting her decide.

"No. I will have to speak to them sooner or later. I may as well do it now."

Marida held her ladle in the air like a sword. "They upset you, I make them sorry they ever come." And she marched off toward the kitchen.

Crissa watched the front doors, waiting for the two men to enter. She wished she knew more about the sheriff, knew if he would be eager to turn her in for the bounty or if he would try to help her. Did Drake know him any better? "Why would the sheriff's rounds take him all the way to Gold Hill?"

"It's really not that far from here. Besides my father's house, Gold Hill is just a mining camp. There wasn't much use for a full-time sheriff. But with all the comings and goings between Gold Hill and Willow Springs, it soon became necessary to have a lawman handy."

"So Mr. Hawkes was elected sheriff." Just saying the word *sheriff* made Crissa's heart thump a little unsteadily.

"Well, not exactly elected. My father hired Hawkes for the job."
Crissa raised her eyebrows.

"We've—my father—has a lot at stake here. Not only the mines, but several ranches as well. The livelihoods of many people are in my father's care, including the sheriff's."

"So the sheriff has an added interest in your father." Becoming more and more aware of the influence Warren Adams held over this town—this whole area—Crissa felt herself more in awe of him. It was little wonder Drake had tried to break free of his father's shadow and make his own name. "When we first met and went on the picnic together, you sounded as if you did not like your father very much."

"My father tends to get caught up in his own importance. Forgets he started out just like any other man in this town. I don't want that to become me. But this is one problem I think he can help us with." Drake nodded his head toward the door. "Here they are."

"Mrs. Wight." Mr. Adams held out his hand to Crissa. "I see you've found a bite to eat. How are you feeling now?"

"Much better, thank you," Crissa replied.

"You know the sheriff, I believe?"

"Yes, we have met." It was here, in this dining room, that the sheriff had interrogated Crissa while the doctor was upstairs examining Molly. Was it her imagination, or had the sheriff looked at her suspiciously even when the doctor pronounced Molly's death a result of natural causes? Did he look at her the same way now? Crissa nodded toward the two other chairs at the table. "Will you sit down?"

"Glad to see you weren't hurt, ma'am." Sheriff Hawkes tipped his hat to her but left it on his head. He wasn't smiling.

"Mr. Adams, how is Suzanna?" Crissa rushed before the sheriff could begin his questions,

"She's in a lot of pain, for sure, but she'll pull through. Doc says she's a lucky gal. The mirror cut her right near a big artery. Says she could have bled to death. He's set her leg, and she'll be up and around in a month or so."

Crissa sighed. "Thank goodness she will be all right. I was so worried. I truly did not mean to—"

"There now, ma'am." Sheriff Hawkes sat forward, his voice sympathetic, but his brow was furrowed as if something else was bothering him. "Mr. Adams told me what all went on over there. Mrs. Hampton had tried to drug you, and Mr. Adams shot her. Then the daughter came at you?"

"Yes." Crissa shuddered, remembering the strength with which Suzanna had held her by the throat.

"I told him about Rachel confessing to poisoning Molly Henderson too," Mr. Adams added.

Hawkes nodded, stroking an unlit cheroot, just as he had back then. "I figured Molly was too healthy to just up and die like that. But without a suspicious cause of death, there weren't much more I could do."

"I understand."

"Do you, ma'am?" the sheriff asked, peering at her. "Do you understand? I sure don't. What would make a respectable woman like Mrs. Hampton put poison in cookies? Fine, upstanding member of this here community, trying to drug *you*?" Leaning on his forearms, Hawkes continued rolling the cheroot on his fingertips. His eyes, not more than twelve inches from Crissa's face, pierced her. "You seem to be the only one strong enough to talk to me that might be able to shed some light here. Just what was it that had her dander up?"

After all she had learned tonight about the intricately woven lives of Willow Springs' leading citizens, what could she say now? That Rachel was trying to get even with Mr. Adams for jilting her and refusing to claim his unborn child? That Rachel had given the child to her sister and then had turned around and poisoned her? That she had paid a hired killer for information about Crissa's past? Was Mrs. Hampton so desperate for Suzanna to marry Drake that she would murder someone? How much could Crissa expect the sheriff to believe? And how much of it mattered? Crissa pressed the pads of her fingers to her temples.

"That's enough, Oscar," Mr. Adams broke in. "Rachel was

clearly out of her right mind. This young lady just happened to be in the wrong place when she snapped."

Glaring at Mr. Adams, the sheriff was obviously struggling to stay calm. "With all due respect, sir, I have two dead bodies, and a gal over at the doc's who's been battered up pretty good. I can't let Mrs. Wight just waltz outta here."

Two bodies. *But there were two more bodies the sheriff does not know about,* Crissa thought. Jenkins and Carter. With Garth dead, no one knew what had happened to them. If she did not tell the sheriff, no one would ever know—but if they were found, would not someone suspect her?

"She won't be waltzing off on you!" Turning to Crissa, Drake took both her hands in his. "As soon as we can get this mess cleared up, me and Crissa are going to be married! That's if she'll have me."

Crissa felt her mouth drop open, her cheeks flush, and her stomach twist into a nervous knot, but she was powerless to do anything besides sit there, thrilled and mortified, at Drake's public declaration.

"Well, I'll be hanged." Mr. Adams grinned from ear to ear before assuming his serious demeanor once more. "Don't get me wrong, Drake. I think she'd make a fine wife for you. But, son, it was just yesterday she was wed to another man. And only a couple of hours ago she was widowed. You gotta know people are going to talk."

Recovering from the shock, Sheriff Hawkes frowned with disapproval. "And her new husband not even buried yet."

Ruddy color flushed Drake's cheeks. "Now don't get your britches twisted, Hawkes. I've been in love with Crissa pretty much since the first time I laid eyes on her. It was purely my dang-fool pride that kept me from poppin' the question right up front. She only married Garth 'cause she was forced into it."

What? Drake, no! Not like this! Crissa urgently kicked him under the table, trying to get his attention. She did not want her past to come out like this.

Smiling, Drake looked at Crissa and squeezed her hand again. "It's all right."

It's all right? Is that supposed to comfort me? "Drake, please—"

"What d'ya mean, forced into it?" the sheriff demanded.

"Blackmail," Drake blurted.

"By who?" Mr. Adams was quiet, ominous. His brows were pulled down, hooding those cold steel eyes—so like Drake's.

"Garth," Crissa whispered.

"And a fellow named Jenkins," Drake added.

Mr. Adams's eyes narrowed to angry shards. "Figured as much."

"You knew him?" Crissa exclaimed. "What did he tell—"

Mr. Adams put up his hand. "Nothing at all. I don't go in for them charlatans, and I booted him outta my office faster'n the devil at church."

Leaning an elbow on the table, Sheriff Hawkes rubbed a hand over his unshaven beard. "Now back up a minute," he directed. "This fellow, Jenkins, he came to your office?"

"Said he had some information on a lady Drake was sweet on. Implied she weren't the sort of woman I'd like the family name to be tied to." Mr. Adams looked at Crissa. "I didn't wait for him to tell me any more. I threw him out on his ear."

"Then when this Mr. Jenkins didn't make any ground with Mr. Adams," the sheriff continued, "Garth bought his information?" He was leaning across the table, ignoring the two men, waiting for Crissa to answer.

"No."

Hawkes slapped his hand on the table. "Then who in the name of—" A frustrated sigh slipped from his lips, and he tempered his voice. "Who bought the information, Mrs. Wight?"

"Rachel Hampton."

"What?" Drake and the sheriff chorused.

"I'll be hanged." It was Mr. Adams's turn to be stunned.

"She paid Jenkins three hundred dollars, then told Garth about it. Garth said if I did not marry him, he would make the information public. I did not know until this evening that it was she who paid him. When Drake came to see me this morning, he found out about the blackmail, and he thought it was his father who had made the arrangement."

"Drake!" Mr. Adams exclaimed. "Is that why you came slamming into the office?"

Drake fiddled with a scratch on the table, avoiding his father's stare. "Well, yeah—"

"Tarnation, boy! What would cause you to think a thing like that about your own father! Tarnation! I'm the one who tried to protect you from that con man!"

"Why would Mrs. Hampton get involved in something like this?" the sheriff demanded of Crissa, interrupting the quarrel between Drake and his father.

Crissa shook her head. "I do not know. Unless she was worried that Drake would marry me instead of Suzanna." Her eyes filled with tears as she remembered the agonizing decision to marry Garth. "Please, you must understand. I promised Molly's children I would never leave them. If I am sent to jail—"

"Hey, now," Drake murmured, wrapping his arm around Crissa's shoulders. "We're not going to let anyone put you in jail."

Sheriff Hawkes eyes narrowed. "You didn't kill anyone. Why would you worry about going to jail? Unless there was something to Jenkins's information?"

Crissa's mind reeled. What had she said? She dropped her gaze, careful to avoid the sheriff's stare. If she could just rest a while before answering any more questions.

Removing a small flask from his pocket, Mr. Adams added a splash to Crissa's water glass and pushed it toward her. The three men sat in silence while Crissa sipped the water and dried her eyes.

She was so tired. She had been through so much since the wedding. She was just . . . so tired. "Yesterday," she whispered to the men. "The wedding was just yesterday."

Warren Adams nodded and patted her hand. "We'll go now."

"What?" blurted the sheriff.

Mr. Adams fixed his steely eyes on the sheriff and repeated his words slowly. "I said, we'll go now. The lady's plum wore out, and it won't do anyone no good for us to stay here any longer." He turned back to Crissa. "You go get a good night's sleep. Nothing's going to change overnight. We'll get this sorted out in the morning, when you're up to it."

"But you can't—" Sheriff Hawkes's face had turned red.

"I just did. Drake," Warren said, nodding toward the kitchen, "see if Mrs. Danello can put Crissa in a room next to hers. She can keep an ear open in case she needs anything." He stood up, indicating the meeting was over, and replaced his hat on his head. "You sleep tight now, ma'am. And send Drake to fetch us when you feel up to talking. I'll be over to the doc's." With that, he turned and strode from the inn.

The sheriff followed, red-faced and muttering angrily to himself. Pausing at the door, he turned and pointed a finger at Crissa. "Don't you even think about leaving, ma'am."

★ ★ ★

Crissa woke to the sound of muffled whispers and giggles. "Shh, you're gonna wake her up!"

"Lookit! Her eyeballs are moving!"

"Quiet, she's dreamin'!"

"I told you kids to stay out of there!" a gruff voice whispered, drawing closer.

"Lookit, Drake, lookit! She's wakin' up!"

Crissa recognized Amy's voice and opened her eyes. Will and Amy both jumped on her at once, laughing and squealing, kissing and hugging. *This is the way a day should begin*, Crissa thought, returning their affection.

"'Bout time you woke up, sleepyhead," Drake teased, standing in the doorway.

Crissa smiled at him, thinking that, yes, this was *definitely* the way to begin a new day. Stifling a yawn, she hugged the children again. The sun was streaming fully in the window. "I did sleep awhile, it seems. It must be ten o'clock already."

"Ten thirty, to be exact," Drake said, "and then some."

"What do you mean?"

Will bounced up and down on the bed, laughing. "You slept clean through yesterday!"

"Yeah!" Amy chorused. "We wanted to wake you up, but Marida said she'd whup us if we did!"

Crissa had vague recollections of stumbling out of bed a few times to use the chamber pot, then settling back into blissful slumber. "Well, thank you for letting me have such a lovely rest. Will you two please tell Marida I am awake?"

"Aw, do we have to?"

Placing her hands on her stomach, Crissa looked at Will and Amy wistfully. "I am awfully hungry."

"All right!" the children chorused, bounding from the room.

"I guess I should get up now." Raising her eyebrows at Drake, Crissa hoped he would insist she stay in bed a while longer. "Your father and the sheriff must think I am quite the lazy bones."

Sitting on the bed beside her, Drake wrapped his arms around her and snuggled her up close. "My father thinks you've been through more'n your share of heartache lately."

"And he does not know the half of it."

"I had a talk with him and the sheriff yesterday."

Crissa stiffened in Drake's arms. She knew the two men must have been anxious to hear about her trouble in Boston, but surely they could have waited for her. "I should have been there!"

"I know, I know." Drake tightened his arms around her. "But all I could think of yesterday was letting you rest. Please don't be upset. It turned out all right."

"How could it turn out all right? I am wanted for murder! Sheriff Hawkes will send me back to Boston!"

"No, he won't. Not yet, anyway. My father insisted that you stay here in Willow Springs until we can verify the status of any warrant."

"But that might take months!" Pulling away from Drake, Crissa drew her blanketed knees up under her chin.

Drake shook his head. "The telegraph line's completed into Colorado. We'll send a letter with a rider until he meets up with a telegraph office. He can wire Boston from there. It might take a week or two to get an answer back, but I doubt it will take much longer."

Staring out the window, Crissa tried to imagine what would happen in two weeks' time. If the warrant was still active, would a marshal come to take her back to Boston? If the warrant was not active—or if it never existed—what then? She was still married to Eric Lundstrom.

"Don't cry, darling," Drake whispered.

She hadn't realized she was.

"It'll be good news. I'm sure of it."

"But I still will not be free to marry."

"Shh. I told you I'd take care of that, and I will. I don't know if we can get your marriage annulled or if you'll have to file divorce papers—though you do have grounds. You will be my wife, Cristalina Engleson, even if we have to move to Mexico."

Crissa's eyes flew open. "Drake!"

"See there? I knew you still had some fire left in you."

"You are a—a—"

Drake smiled. "And you are beautiful." He leaned down and kissed her fully on the lips. "You'd better get dressed now. I'll wait for you downstairs." He kissed her once more before leaving her room.

★ ★ ★

The three men—Drake, Mr. Adams, and Sheriff Hawkes—were waiting at a table when Crissa descended the stairs. Marida came in with a plate of hotcakes and eggs and set it in front of Crissa with a warning to the men not to bother Crissa until she was finished eating. Despite her audience, Crissa ate ravenously. Then she felt ready to face their questions.

"Drake told us about your trouble in Boston, Crissa," Mr. Adams began. "A fellow should be locked up himself for treating his wife that way."

Murmuring her agreement, Crissa hid her smile behind her napkin. *A fellow is only allowed to treat a woman that way if they are not married?* She wondered if Mr. Adams had really treated Rachel Hampton any differently when she was carrying his child. Or Mrs. Adams, for that matter. Crissa watched him trying to appear benevolent, and her respect for him slipped further away.

"I'll send word to Boston," the sheriff said, "and see what this warrant is all about. In the meantime, I'd like you to answer a few questions about Mrs. Hampton." Sheriff Hawkes looked hesitantly at Warren Adams, as if seeking permission to continue. Mr. Adams dipped his head once and folded his arms across his chest.

"I will tell you what I can," Crissa agreed.

"Tell me how you met up with Mrs. Hampton yesterday."

"After Garth left for the mine, I started running to town. I met her on the road, and she offered to drive me out to Gold Hill."

The sheriff sipped his coffee. "But she took you out to her place instead?"

"She said it would be dark before long, and that she wanted to get a rifle."

"Wish you women would just leave the sheriffin' to me," Hawkes grumbled. "Then maybe we wouldn't have this kind of trouble."

Crissa watched Drake and his father exchange uncertain glances. Either there was more "sheriffin'" to do than she had imagined, or maybe Sheriff Hawkes didn't have the Adamses' complete confidence.

"So," the sheriff continued, "what happened once you got to her ranch?"

"Well, she persuaded me to come inside for something to eat. I had not eaten much since the day before. Sheriff, as I walked through her garden, I recognized each of the flowers that were left in my room the night Molly Henderson died. And I know at least one of the flowers, foxglove, can be used as a medication—or a poison." Crissa paused, waiting for the sheriff to respond to this information, but he sat impassively, waiting for Crissa to continue. "I think Mrs. Hampton knew I suspected her of killing Molly Henderson." Step by step, question after question, Crissa detailed the events of that night with Mr. Adams's help. The pieces of Mrs. Hampton's evil designs seemed to fit so naturally in place, Crissa had to wonder if Sheriff Hawkes was indeed inept not to have suspected Mrs. Hampton long ago.

"You're trying to tell me," the sheriff balked, "that Rachel Hampton killed her own sister just to preserve an inheritance for her nephew?"

"She told me," Crissa explained again, "that if Ruth died before the deed was transferred, the sale would not be valid, and Garth would inherit the inn."

"Why would she care whether Garth inherited it or not?"

Crissa knew that without knowing the entire truth, the story did indeed sound farfetched. She looked at Mr. Adams, for some sign, some acknowledgment of the truth, but he sat there, arms still folded, staring coolly at the sheriff. "Perhaps she was concerned that Garth had no father. She did not tell me her thoughts, so I can only guess."

Hawkes stuck a toothpick in his mouth, sucking noisily. "What could'a been going on in that woman's mind?"

"That's the point, Hawkes!" Mr. Adams snatched the toothpick out of the sheriff's mouth and flung it across the room. "She was plum out of her gourd! She killed her sister, she killed the Widow Henderson, and she would'a killed Crissa too! How sane could a woman be to carry on like'n that?"

Hawkes shook his head slowly. "She seemed like such a fine, respectable lady. And she was set on killing you just so Drake would marry her daughter?"

Crissa nodded.

"D'ya figure Suzanna was an accomplice to all this?"

"No," Crissa said. "I think she honestly believed Drake was in love with her and would one day marry her."

"She'd have no call thinking that way," Drake said, frowning at his father, "if you and Rachel hadn't kept throwin' us together all the time."

You did not look like you minded being with her, Crissa thought resentfully. *You are a grown man, old enough to say "no, thank you" if you did not want to escort her.*

"I said," Sheriff Hawkes interrupted her thoughts with his rising voice, "is there anything else we should know about?"

"Like what?" Crissa demanded, startled. "I mean—no, of course not." She felt the eyes of all three men upon her, and she dabbed at her mouth with a napkin, keeping her eyes lowered.

"Well, then," the sheriff continued, scooting his chair back from the table and standing up. "I'll get that letter ready to send to Boston."

Mr. Adams stood to leave as well. "And I should send word to Jake Hampton. Rachel's husband," he explained in answer to

Crissa's questioning look. "Suzanna was no more'n four or five when he left. Last I heard, he was prospecting in Peru. Little place called Callao, I believe."

"And what about that Donald Jenkins fellow?" Drake asked his father.

"I'll get a couple of men to roust him out. Figure he's got some explaining to do."

"No!" gasped Crissa.

Each man stopped where he was and turned to face Crissa. She looked from face to face. Her thoughts were a jumble, the only constant being the image of Jenkins advancing toward her through the woods. Mr. Adams stared at her blankly, the sheriff's eyes were filled with suspicion, and Drake—the color had drained from his face.

"There was a shivaree," Crissa whispered, "after the wedding." She paused for Mr. Adams and Hawkes to sit down and to summon her courage to continue. "Garth took me to his house, and . . . a bunch of men broke into the cabin. They were drunk. They grabbed me and carried me on a horse. We were in the mountains. They left me alone with Mr. Jenkins and Mr. Carter."

"Boyd Carter?" Mr. Adams interrupted.

Crissa nodded.

"He hasn't shown up for work in two days."

Crissa's eyes filled with tears as she remembered the hapless Carter, and the way she had stumbled upon him. "Mr. Jenkins killed him. Cut his throat."

"And where's this Jenkins now?" Hawkes demanded.

"I do not know, exactly. He is dead. I shot him."

Mr. Adams sat back in his chair, running his hand through his hair. "You what?"

"He tried to . . . force himself on me. I ran through the woods, and that is when I found Carter. I grabbed Carter's gun, and Jenkins kept coming. I shot him. He just kept coming."

Sobs burst from Crissa's throat, but not a man offered her comfort. Each sat, absorbed by his own thought. Still pale, Drake stared at the table. Tears brimmed his eyes.

It was the sheriff who broke the silence. He cleared his throat and rubbed his hand up and down his face. "Mrs. Wight, does anyone else know about this?"

"I told Garth. He found me . . . after."

"And with him dead, there really isn't anyone who can back up your story."

Crissa realized what the sheriff was implying at about the same time Drake and Mr. Adams did.

"Now you hold on there!" Mr. Adams exclaimed.

"Filthy son of a—" Drake was halfway across the table before his father could reach out and press him back into his chair.

The sheriff eyed them calmly before continuing. "And where are the two bodies now?"

"I do not know. Garth buried them before he—" Sobs welled up in her throat again as she relived those last moments with Garth. "Before he went to the mine."

The sheriff sat picking at a scab on his hand. He looked at Crissa occasionally before digging at the scab again. "You certainly seem to have a knack for leaving dead bodies scattered behind you."

"Hawkes!" Warren Adams had clearly grown impatient with the sheriff. "Surely even you can see this was a matter of self-defense!"

"As much as you might want to believe that, I've got one person, and only one person's story. I can't just let her go until I've got some way of verifying her claims." Glowering at Mr. Adams, the sheriff asked one more question. "Mrs. Wight, did you recognize any of the other men who spirited you off?"

At last! Crissa thought. At last she could give him the name of someone who was still living. "Wakelin!" she declared. "A friend of Garth's named Wakelin was with those ruffians when they came to the house. I heard his name mentioned several times."

The sheriff nodded. "Now we're getting somewhere. I'll question Ted Wakelin, then. Let's just hope he doesn't have anything contrary to say. I do reckon it could've been a case of self-defense, Mrs. Wight, 'less Wakelin comes up with something you've forgotten."

"Then I am free to come and go as I please?"

"Well, not quite. There's still the matter of that woman in Boston.

I don't see any need to confine you, though. I trust you'll stay in town 'til we get the word from the marshal?"

Drake rose and stood behind Crissa, his hands possessively cupping her shoulders. "Like I said, Sheriff, she won't be going anywhere."

CHAPTER 21

A small group clustered on the hillside to bury Garth the next evening. He had few friends, and not many townsfolk were inclined to postpone their evening chores to shed a tear for his passing.

Arrangements were made quickly and quietly. Crissa insisted that Garth be buried beside Ruth in the ragtag garden by the house. Declining the bishop's offer to recite a eulogy, Crissa stood by her mother's dictum: If you can find nothing kind to say to my face, do not bother when I am dead. Only Crissa seemed to care about the person Garth had vowed to become. Only she had seen his desire to be a suitable husband. Only she knew the secret of Garth's parentage and of what he had been deprived. If Garth could watch from heaven, he would know the kindness Crissa felt toward him. Bishop Belnap repeated the Lord's Prayer, Crissa placed a branch of Ruth's wild rose hedge atop the plain casket, and thus Garth Warren Wight was laid to rest on the evening of Tuesday, September 2, 1861.

Mr. Adams took Crissa's arm and led her a little ways from the group. After a moment of small talk and condolences, he explained his purpose. "Mrs. Wight, Crissa, yesterday at the inn, I seemed to sense . . . you seemed to be . . . uneasy. Preoccupied, perhaps. Is there something, some unfinished business, between us?"

What would become of our relationship if I told him I know he was Garth's father? Crissa wondered. But how could she marry Drake without confronting Mr. Adams with the truth? She withdrew the letter from her pocket as if it were a fragile flower that would crumble and be swept away by the wind.

Warren Adams took the letter, blanching a bit as he realized what it was, then slowly opened it and read the contents written so long ago. "So you know," he said at last. "And Garth knew?"

"Not until the day he died."

"And this is why he threatened to kill me. Does Drake know?"

"No," Crissa said softly. "After Garth died, and then Rachel, I felt enough people had been hurt by your secret. If you want Drake to know, I will leave it up to you to tell him."

Folding the letter once more, Mr. Adams looked downhill to where the little group was lingering by Garth's grave, then northwestward toward Gold Hill. "You're right, Crissa. Enough people have already been hurt. I was a foolish young man when this happened. I tried to make it right the best I knew how, but I never could correct the wrong I had done. Drake was scarce more than a baby, and my wife, Claire, was pregnant with Oliver. She never did fully recover from that birth. I couldn't leave her, didn't want to, and I just never had the heart to tell her. I hated seeing Garth grow up the way he did, but the more I gave, the more Rachel took. I couldn't think what more I could do."

Taking a match out of his shirt pocket, Mr. Adams struck it against his thumbnail and held it to the corner of the letter. "Garth, Rachel, and Ruth are all gone now. I will carry the memory of my sins with me forever. There's no sense letting this hurt anyone else." He glanced up at Crissa, as if remembering she was there, and then dropped the burning letter and ground the embers out with his heel. "Thank you for, well, for your consideration. You will make a fine wife for Drake, Crissa. I'm right pleased to have you join the family."

Warren Adams is a manipulative man, Crissa realized, *whether he means to be or not.* He had made mistakes that had seriously affected many people. But that was twenty-three years ago. It was not up to her to judge his past mistakes; she would leave that up to a higher power. For now, she was grateful for his kindness and acceptance.

★ ★ ★

The days crept along, one after another, while Drake and Crissa awaited word from Boston regarding her fate. Crissa saw Drake only in the very early mornings and in the very late hours after dinner. Most of his time was spent fervently completing the house. Crissa spent her time at the inn, dusting, mopping, and trying to stay busy. Though she played with Will and Amy and helped care for the few guests who took meals at the inn, Crissa was intensely lonely without Drake. If she left the inn at all, someone was continuously watching her; she presumed the sheriff had assigned men to make sure she did not leave town. The threat of being summoned back to Boston hung over her, weighing her spirits with darkness and allowing her little joy in being with her beloved charges.

On the Tuesday following Garth's funeral, Marida persuaded Crissa to go up to Garth's house with her to gather anything Crissa might want to keep. The house felt like a tomb to Crissa. Every memory held the specter of sadness.

Marida set Will and Amy to work pulling weeds from around Ruth's grave and marker. The newly turned earth of Garth's grave was still fresh and soft. Crissa could not look at it without remembering the traces of newfound sensitivity she had uncovered in Garth.

Inside the sweltering cabin, Crissa set to work sifting through the few furnishings and belongings. "Marida," Crissa suggested, "do you think Bishop Belnap could find someone who could use any of these things?"

"You make wonderful idea!" Marida exclaimed. "So many families come to Willow Springs with nothing. Some still sleep on straw mat on floor!"

Crissa plumped the fat mattress on the bed and smoothed the quilt. "Then someone will appreciate this all the more. I will send word to the bishop that he may have anything that might be useful."

"Don't you want keep anything?" Marida asked, inspecting the finely crafted gun cabinet. "This too nice."

"Then I give it to you," Crissa declared. "You take it. Maybe Vic will enjoy the gun collection."

Standing back a ways, Marida narrowed her eyes a bit, as if pondering Crissa's decision. "No, no, no," she said finally. "Vic can take guns out. Can build his own box. I use this for dishes and pretty things. Vic can build shelves. Here, and here." She demonstrated with her hands where she would like shelves to be.

So the two women set about dusting and straightening and arranging items to be claimed. Crissa took the bottle of dried fox-glove from its hiding place on the shelf and dumped it out behind the cabin, then used her foot to mix it in with the dirt so it could harm no one else. "If Garth held the deed on this land," Crissa declared, coming back inside, "I will turn it over to Bishop Belnap and the Church as well." The last item to be attended to was Ruth's carpetbag under the bed.

Crissa laid the dress, the bonnet, and the fan out on the bed. A few of the nearby women were young enough that one might appreciate having a fancy frock. Pulling the daguerreotype from the bag, Crissa dusted a bit of lint from the glass. Marida sat down on the bed beside her to inspect the photo. "Ruth Wight and Rachel Hampton were sisters," Crissa explained. "I will give this to Suzanna."

It was Tuesday when word finally came, eight days after the sheriff's letter had been sent on its race to Boston. Crissa, Will, and Amy were returning from a picnic by the stream when Marida stood on the back porch, banging on a cast-iron pot with her big wooden spoon to summon them back. "A rider coming!" Marida yelled. "Might be news!"

The group arrived just as the rider dismounted in front of the inn. "Do you have it?" Crissa begged, recognizing the rider as the boy sent to Colorado. "Do you have the letter?"

"Yes'm!" Gasping for air, the young man looked at the throng of eager faces. "Is Sheriff Hawkes here?"

"Why, no. No, he is not here. Please, give me the letter!"

"Sorry, ma'am, my orders are to report to Sheriff Hawkes directly."

"But it is my letter! It is about me!"

"I'm sorry, ma'am, but I jist can't—"

"Boy!" Stepping to the front of the group, Marida took over. "The sheriff is up at mine. You get on that horse and you fly to him. You hear me, boy? You fly! And you get him back here, pronto!" Marida clapped her hands loudly while the rider scurried to remount and fetch the sheriff.

"Now, you, Will." Marida took the boy by the shoulders and led him to a harnessed horse at the livery. "You ride good, no?"

"Yes'm."

"You go find Drake and Vic. They at the house. You tell them letter come. You bring them back. You do that?"

Will nodded.

"That's good boy." Marida hoisted Will up into the saddle and gave the horse a solid swat on the rump. "You hold on, Will!" she called after him. "Don'a you fall off!"

She turned back to the inn, where Crissa and the rest of the ladies were watching her with amusement. "What'sa matter? You no wanna see letter?"

For a good half hour, Crissa waited for Will to return with Drake and for the sheriff to arrive from Gold Hill. Every scuffle from the street sent her running to the porch, expecting it to be them. *Where can they be?* she wondered. Why did they not come? Had something happened to Will? To the other rider? What could be taking so long?

Marida brought sandwiches and lemonade out from the kitchen. "You eat now," she ordered. "You wasting away."

"I could not possibly," Crissa objected. "We have just come from the picnic. Save these for when the men come in."

Crissa pulled a chair out onto the porch so she could watch for the men coming—and to spend a few minutes alone. What if the warrant for her arrest was still active? Would she have to return to Boston? Or would a judge come out to Willow Springs to try her? What if she were unable to prove herself innocent? Was there a place where they locked women away? Or would they hang her? Drake would never allow that, but what could he do? Once more, the overwhelming urge to just get on a horse and ride away enveloped her. And what would happen to little Will and Amy? If there was to be a trial, Crissa decided, she wanted it to be in Boston, where her precious children would not have to witness it.

And if the warrant were no longer in effect? *Perhaps they have found the real murderer,* Crissa thought. Would she be allowed to divorce Eric? Would he agree to a divorce? How could she prove he had been unfaithful to her?

Pain drilled at her temples. With every possible answer, there seemed to be another problem to surmount.

"Crissa," Marida spoke close to her ear. "Listen. They're coming."

Crissa heard pounding hoofbeats approach the town. A curl of dust hung in the distance to mark their passing. The women were waiting on the porch as Drake and Vic rode in.

Leaping off his horse, Drake grabbed Crissa. "Where is it? What did it say? It's good news, isn't it?"

"Wait," Crissa said pressing her hand to his mouth. "The rider, he would not leave it. He said he could give it only to the sheriff."

"Hellfire!"

"Drake!"

"Sorry. Well, what are we waiting for? Let's get out there!"

"Marida sent the rider to Gold Hill," Crissa told him. "He will bring the sheriff back here."

"That could take an hour or more!" Drake fumed. "When did he leave?"

"It has been more than half of that already. See? It will not be long now."

"And what'm I supposed to do in the meanwhile?"

Marida pushed the tray in front of him. "You have sandwich."

"I'm not hungry," Drake replied, stuffing half a sandwich in his mouth.

★ ★ ★

At last, Sheriff Hawkes arrived, riding full-bore, with the telegram still sealed and Warren Adams galloping just behind. With all assembled in the dining room, the sheriff gravely opened the telegraph. He read it through once silently before clearing his throat to announce the verdict.

Sheriff Robert Hawkes Stop Willow Springs Utah Territory Stop
Regarding matter of warrants for Cristalina Engleson Lundstrom
Stop Mr Eric Lundstrom shot and killed during robbery attempt Stop
Confessed prior murders Stop All charges against Mrs Lundstrom
dropped Stop Detail arriving with mail Stop Superintendent Evon
Delany Boston Stop.

Several moments of stunned silence passed while the telegram
sank in. Shot and killed. All charges have been dropped. *Can it be
possible? Eric has been shot and killed, and there are no charges against me.*
Tears welled in Crissa's eyes as she contemplated the news.

A wild whoop rang through the hushed inn, and Drake grabbed
Crissa around the waist, twirling with her through the room.

The official letter arrived the next Monday. Crissa shut herself
in her room before daring to read the short letter. She could share
the details with Drake later. The superintendent's handwriting was
large and sprawling. What he lacked in spelling ability he also lacked
in grammar.

Crissa struggled to understand what he had written. Eric had
been befriending prostitutes, then robbing them to pay his gambling
debts. He then slit their throats and slipped away. In the process of
one such robbery, he was shot by his victim's manager and died.

Shuddering at the thought of the man she had been living with,
Crissa dropped the letter. Despite the mid-August heat, she felt an
icy chill. She knew Eric had been gambling. Had he also been mur-
dering women even before Crissa left? How long before he would
have killed her as well?

Crissa stuffed the letter in her bureau drawer, then washed her
hands in the basin. She splashed water in her face, wishing she could
wash away the sickening knot in her stomach.

★ ★ ★

It didn't take long for word to spread through Willow Springs
that there would soon be another wedding. The biddies who normally would have delighted in haranguing Crissa about remarrying
so soon were politely silent when they learned Drake Adams would
be the groom.

Drake didn't press Crissa to set a date for the wedding, but she knew he had sent to Salt Lake for a ring. He wound a length of string around the ring finger of her left hand while supposedly "just fidgeting." As eager as she was to be Drake's wife, it didn't seem proper to announce a wedding date so soon after being widowed.

Even with all the time he spent working on their new house, he still wouldn't let Crissa come see it—he wanted it to be her wedding present. So Crissa relegated her days to playing with Will and Amy, scrubbing the inn until it sparkled, and taking long walks to tend Molly's grave.

Crissa was descending the hill from the cemetery at Dutchman's Pass when she spotted a distant plume of dust signaling an approaching stagecoach. Hoping there would not be unexpected boarders for dinner tonight, Crissa quickened her pace nonetheless. Marida joined Crissa on the porch of the inn while they waited to see if any passengers would be staying over. The coach, a simple, undecorated model, wasn't painted with the typical bright lettering of the Overland Stage. After pulling up at the station platform, the driver jumped down and pulled open the door for his passengers.

Why did this driver look so familiar? Crissa wondered.

Marida clapped her hands over her mouth, trying to suppress giggles. She put a hand on Crissa's back and pushed her out into the road. "Go! You go see!"

Shading her eyes against the afternoon sun, she began walking forward. "Charlie?" No, it could not be. "Charlie Callahan?" She was running now. "Charlie?"

He turned around in time to catch her as she bounded toward him. "It is you!"

"That it is, me darlin'!" He laughed, holding her clear off the ground in his bear hug.

"Do not waste it all on old Charlie!" a man boomed behind her. Crissa turned in time to see him leap from the coach.

"Lars!" Tears sprung to her eyes to see her friends again. "And Signe? Did you bring Signe?"

"Of course!" Signe stepped from the coach to join the embrace.

"And the children!" Crissa exclaimed, catching David in her arms while Britta and Aigner danced around her. Marida, Will, and

Amy waited anxiously while introductions were made. Then the happy group made their way back to the inn. Crissa held her arm linked through Charlie's the entire way.

"Tell me, Signe, what brings you here now?"

"Your young man, Mr. Adams, sent a letter by Pony Express to Lars," she said. "The letter said a telegram came from Boston and that there is no longer a warrant for your arrest. We came to share your happiness."

"You came all this way just for me?"

"And to see you married!"

"Married!" Crissa gasped.

"Your Drake, he must love you very much to send for us. He hired a coach just for us, and Charlie to drive it!"

They had arrived at the inn and made way for Lars and Vic to come through with the luggage. "My parents," Crissa said to Signe. "Why did they not come? Is someone ill?"

"Pish," Signe replied through pursed lips. "No one is ill. Your father, he is an old fool. He said he has seen you get married once, there is no need to see you get married again. We begged your mother to come whether he would come or not. He got that stubborn look on his face and folded his arms like this, and she said she could not go without him."

Laying her hand on the side of her face, Crissa shook her head and sighed. "And to think I sometimes miss him."

"He always miss you, Cristalina. I think maybe he blames himself for your troubles—because he made you marry that man."

Crissa lowered her eyes. Her father did force her to marry Eric Lundstrom, and if it had not been for that, perhaps she would still be back East, married to someone else. *But then I would not have come to Willow Springs*, she reminded herself. *So without Eric, I would not have met Drake.* "Herrens vägar äro förunderliga," she murmured.

"Indeed he does," Signe agreed. "God works in mysterious ways indeed."

★ ★ ★

It was nearly suppertime before Drake returned to the inn. Crissa was slicing apples into a pie crust when he tiptoed behind her and kissed her on the back of the neck. "You had better not let my beau see you doing that," Crissa teased.

"He's the one gave me the go ahead," Drake murmured, kissing her neck again.

Crissa laid her knife on the table and turned to wrap her arms around his neck. "Thank you."

"So you like that, do you?" He kissed the front of her neck.

"No! Well, yes, but that is not what I am thanking you for."

"What else've I done that pleases you so?"

Crissa tipped her head toward the dining room. "They are here. Lars and Signe and Charlie."

"So soon!" Drake stepped back, disentangling himself from Crissa's arms. "I've been working all day. I should clean up before I meet them!"

"I will hear nothing of it!" Signe said from the doorway. She strode toward him with her hand extended. "You must be the Mr. Adams."

"No, ma'am," Drake stammered, wiping his hands on his pants. "That's my father."

"Signe," Crissa interjected, "I would like you to meet Drake Adams, my fiancé. He insists we never call him Mr. Adams," she whispered with a wink. "Drake, this is my good friend, Signelill Bjorkson."

Drake took her hand in his. "It's my pleasure, Zinal—Mrs. Bjorkson."

Signe and Crissa both giggled at his butchered pronunciation attempt.

"Please, you will call me Signe." She looked at Crissa. "I got so tired of having to explain my name every time I met someone after I got to America. Here you must do everything American way, I suppose."

"And now that you are here, Signe," Drake said, wrapping his arm around Crissa's shoulders, "we can be married right away."

Church services were held early that Sunday, two days after the stage came, to give the women of Willow Springs time to decorate the church for Drake and Crissa's wedding. Great boughs of cedar woven with ribbon were hung around the doorway and above the church altar. Nosegays flowing with fragrant flowers from the Hampton garden decorated the pews. No one had thought it necessary to bother the recuperating Suzanna by asking permission first.

Lars and Charlie were kept busy helping at the church and keeping Drake from going up to see Crissa. Every now and then, Crissa recognized Lars's hearty laughter or a snatch of one of Charlie's Irish songs. Crissa could only guess at the wiles it had taken to get Lars to participate in such physical activity on the Sabbath.

Crissa stood in her bedroom at the inn, once more plagued with trying to assemble an outfit suitable to be married in. She had ripped the dress she had worn to marry Garth into rags the morning after she returned to the inn. The gray mourning dress also held too many painful memories. The only dress remaining was her brown calico work dress. Marida and Signe dashed about trying to find accessories that would transform the plain dress into a beautiful wedding gown. A shawl, a satin ribbon—but still, underneath, it was a drab brown dress.

"You wear my wedding dress!" Marida exclaimed.

"It would never fit!" Crissa stood there, wringing her hands, eyeing Marida's frame. "You are at least three inches taller than I am. And you have much wider shoulders than I. It would fall right off me."

Marida eyed Crissa in return, walking a slow circle around her. A smile curled the corners of her lips. "You try it on."

Crissa and Signe looked at each other doubtfully. "There are people waiting for us," Crissa huffed in frustration.

"I said you try it on!" Marida bounded from the room, leaving Crissa no alternative but to sit and wait.

"Now," Marida ordered as she strode back into Crissa's room with yards of white satin flying behind her. "Get out of ugly dress and put this on."

Crissa unbuttoned her simple dress and let it fall to the floor.

"Now hold arms up," Marida directed as she held the gown

above Crissa's head and helped it slide into place. "Hold still while I fasten buttons."

The dress hung loosely as Marida began fastening the buttons below the small of Crissa's back and working up past her waistline. As the fastening proceeded toward her shoulder blades, Crissa felt the bodice tightening with each new button. At last, Marida finished with the uppermost button at Crissa's neck.

"Now, turn and let me see you," Marida commanded.

Crissa turned, and her reflection stared back at her from the mirror. She could not find the words to describe how she felt. The square neckline that had been cut modestly for Marida's measurements lay wide across Crissa's white shoulders. The gathered sleeves fell just enough off her shoulders to accentuate her swanlike neck. Her bustline took up any slack that might have been expected and rose fully above the lacy edge of the bodice. Marida tucked the flowing skirt into scallops, leaving just enough length to brush the floor, lending an ethereal effect to the picture.

Crissa turned toward Signe. "Well?" There was no sense trying to hide her smile—Crissa felt beautiful. And that feeling was reflected in the faces of Marida and Signe.

"One more thing," Signe whispered, wiping the tears from her eyes. "Your mother sent this for you to wear. It is your grandmother Gerda's brooch." Threading white ribbon through the closed hasp of the brooch, she tied it around Crissa's neck so the filigreed heart hung just at the hollow of her throat.

Lifting the sides and crown of Crissa's hair, Signe wound them into a knot and secured it with two pearl-headed picks. Then she slicked locks of hair with pomade and wound them around her finger into ringlets. "I ordered this through a magazine." Signe giggled, showing the bottle of hair lotion. "But where would one wear such a fancy hairstyle in Salt Lake?"

Marida kissed Crissa and then went next door to the church, leaving Crissa and her friend alone.

"Thank you for being here, Signe." Crissa stared at the reflection of the two women in the mirror and thought of her mother. How could a mother and daughter look so different from one another?

Her mother, tall, sturdily built, with chestnut hair and brown eyes; Crissa, short, thin, with the expected blonde hair and blue eyes of a Swede.

"You are not so different, you and your mother," Signe mused, as if in response to Crissa's thoughts. "It seems such a short while ago that she wore that brooch on her wedding day. She had that sparkle in her eyes then, the one you have now, when she prepared to marry your father."

"I wish she were here."

"I wish it also, *min älskling*. She would be so proud to look at you—and your father also."

"I find that too hard to believe."

Signe shook her head. "He does love you, Cristalina. He chose your name when you were born—did you know that? He loved you from the first moment he saw you. And you must believe that he always will. The way he is now, it is just his way."

Smiling, Crissa nodded and then rose on her toes to receive Signe's parting kiss.

★ ★ ★

Molly's piano had been rolled into the church for services this morning. Now Crissa listened to the flowing music being played as she crossed the short expanse separating the inn from the church. She could see Suzanna watching out an upstairs window at Dr. Robbins's, where she was still convalescing. Lars and Charlie waited for Crissa at the entrance of the church, and Charlie gave a nod inside the door when Crissa arrived. The pianist ended the song in a fumble of mismatched chords.

Feeling just a bit light-headed, Crissa took the arms of Lars and Charlie as strains of the familiar wedding march wafted through the open doors. How could she choose just one of these men to give her away? They had both become so dear, had both offered her such comfort when she needed it most. And now, standing at the head of the aisle, was the man who had become more important to her than any man on earth. Dressed in a finely cut black suit, Drake stood tall and relaxed, patiently waiting for her to join him at the altar. *How can he be so calm?* Crissa wondered. Each step nearer to him made her heart pound in her chest.

Lars and Charlie led her to stand beside him, then stepped back. A peaceful calm descended on Crissa as Drake took her hand in his. The bishop spoke briefly before leading Drake and Crissa through their vows. As if in a dream, Crissa declared her love and fidelity, then lifted her face to Drake's sealing kiss.

"Will the congregation please arise to receive Mr. and Mrs. Drake Adams," Bishop Belnap directed.

It is no dream, Crissa thought. *We are married!* The congregation erupted into applause as the newlyweds made their way outside.

Drake pulled her around the corner of the building and swung her high in his arms. Holding her close, he whispered, "You're mine, my darling. You're finally, finally mine!"

★ ★ ★

It was early evening before Drake and Crissa could break away from the dinner in their honor at the inn. Drake urged the horses pulling their gaily-festooned phaeton into an easy canter. They continued northward when the road forked to the Overland route, and still northward past the trail that led off to Garth's house. None of this mattered to Crissa this evening—no sad memories could invade her happiness tonight. She was with Drake, her husband, and they were going home.

Drake turned the horses onto a cleared pathway that led through the meadow where they had first picnicked. The grasses and buttercups were dry weeds now, but it did not matter; it was their meadow. A few moments later, the horses and phaeton clattered over an arched bridge that Drake had built across the stream, and Crissa viewed her new home.

Surrounded by young saplings, the home rose two stories and had an additional gabled attic. A railed porch surrounded the ground level, and there was even a swing suspended in front. Areas of the yard had been set apart by rows of rocks. Everything was just as Drake had described it when he first brought Crissa here, only she had never imagined he could accomplish so much in one short summer.

Drake sat beside her, eagerly watching her every reaction. Crissa nearly laughed when she looked at his expectant face. He was chewing his lower lip.

"Well?" he prompted her. "Do you like it?"

"We shall have to have many children to fill such a grand home," she answered. "Come show me where we shall begin." She took his hand shyly, expecting him to lead her inside.

Instead, he hesitated. "Wait. Listen."

She heard them in the distance, drawing closer—loud and raucous laughter coming from what sounded like a large crowd of people. Turning to him, her eyes wide with fright, she begged, "Please, do not let them take me again." When he made no effort to flee, she pleaded again, "We must leave here! I—I cannot go through that again!"

"Shh," he said, leading her to the porch swing. "Don't be frightened."

The crowd burst into the clearing, led by Vic, Marida, Will, and Amy. Crissa's friends from Salt Lake came next, followed by what looked like the entire population of Willow Springs. Blankets were spread on the ground, food laid out, and a group of men began playing the instruments they had carried with them.

"This, my darling," Drake shouted over the confusion, "is a real shivaree!" They looked out over the happy gathering. "They've come to welcome us to our new home, and you can bet they'll be here most of the night!" Taking Crissa by the hand, Drake led his bride into the house and shut the door behind them. Kissing her softly, he lifted her in his arms. "And you can bet they'll never miss us."

DISCUSSION QUESTIONS

1. How did you feel about the opening of the book? Were you immediately engaged with the characters, or did it take you a while?

2. Did you find Drake's tale of how the Ely strike was found believable?

3. Did you find the characters interesting? What did or didn't you like about the main characters?

4. How do you feel about Crissa leaving Boston as she did? Was she right to flee? Should she have stayed there to clear her name from the beginning?

5. Did you find Crissa's stay in Salt Lake believable? Did you learn anything new about the history of the period?

6. How do you feel about Drake's reaction to Crissa's marriage to Garth? Did your feelings for him change during this period?

7. Did the events at Mrs. Hampton's house surprise you? Why or why not?

8. Did your feelings about Garth change by the end of the book?

9. What were your favorite passages or portions of the book?

10. Were you satisfied with how the book ended? What would you have changed?

ABOUT THE AUTHOR

Born and raised in Utah, Carolyn Steele was introduced to western novels at a very young age by her grandfather, the son of a gold miner. She has been writing technical and marketing communications for most of her adult life. Her nonfiction articles have appeared in numerous national magazines. She earned her undergraduate degree in communications from the University of Utah.

Married and living in Salt Lake City, Utah, Carolyn loves researching obscure history and then weaving it into stories. She also enjoys family dinners with her children and grandchildren, photography, travel, golf, reading, and all forms of needlework.

0 26575 14573 1